Berkley Sensation titles by Kelly Moran

RETURN TO ME
ALL OF ME

Slowly, like a predator, he strode toward her and cupped her cheeks. This time the kiss stole her sanity. The precision with which he slid his hands down to cup her breasts through the bra, the deliberate and meticulous way his fingers grazed her nipples, spoke of his familiarity with the female form. He knew how to touch, to taste, to drive her out of herself and back with crushing velocity.

She never knew being touched, being kissed, could be like this. Potent. Insistent.

Breaking the connection, he grazed his lips over her jaw, down her throat, and licked her collarbone. "I want you so badly I can't think."

His voice alone could make her damp and dreamy. A coarse murmur with need raking it raw. Hadn't he said something similar, before the party? Yes. "You promised you'd make me forget to think."

He groaned into her neck, a purely male sound of pleasured frustration. "Consider it done."

all OF
me

KELLY MORAN

BERKLEY SENSATION, NEW YORK

BERKLEY
SENSATION

An imprint of Penguin Random House LLC
375 Hudson Street, New York, New York 10014

ALL OF ME

A Berkley Sensation Book / published by arrangement with the author

BERKLEY SENSATION® and the "B" design are registered trademarks
of Penguin Random House LLC.
For more information, visit penguin.com.

ISBN: 978-0-425-27688-4

PUBLISHING HISTORY
Berkley Sensation mass-market edition / September 2015

PRINTED IN THE UNITED STATES OF AMERICA

10 9 8 7 6 5 4 3 2 1

Cover photo of "Couple" by Uwe Krejci / Getty Images.
Cover design by Lesley Worrell.

Penguin
Random
House

Writing is often called a solo profession, and sometimes it is. But the characters in my head keep me company, much as they do for the hero, Alec. I'm blessed to have a great group of author friends who are supportive, and so this book is dedicated to them. Carly Phillips, Carla Neggers, Brenda Novak, Sharon Sala, Caridad Pineiro, AJ Nuest, Vonnie Davis, Mackenzie Crowne, and JM Stewart . . . Thank you!

Acknowledgments

An author doesn't get from manuscript to book alone. I have so many people to thank. To my agent, Dawn, thanks for believing in me. My editor, Julie, and everyone at Berkley for making this the best story possible, you guys are awesome. And to a few exceptional people on my street team, a special shout out to: Hannah Duckett, Tracey Parker, Kay Megonnell, Charlotte McFall, Casey Lalkas, Elizabeth Dent, Joy Whiteside, Lesa Goodwin, Tracy Comerford, and Sally Wagoner.

chapter
one

It was a dark and stormy night.

Alec Winston cursed and shoved back from his desk. He swiveled his chair away from the computer and the one line he'd managed to write in almost a year. Pathetic. He'd typed it as a joke, something to propel him out of this writer's block, or whatever it was, but the joke was on him. He'd fired his agent because the guy had demanded new material, and now he was seriously close to breaching his contract with the publisher. Deadline one passed two months ago.

Twenty-five bestsellers, twenty of them number one on the lists, three book-to-movie options, foreign language rights in fifty countries, and he'd been reduced to *it was a* fucking *dark and stormy night*.

He ran his hand down his face and rubbed his jaw. The three-day-old growth scratching against his palm was the only sound in his otherwise quiet home office. Before him, New York City bustled on outside the window, completely unaware of the pile of shit thirty floors up. Night had fallen while he'd stared at the monitor, but the city was never dark. Skyscrapers and streetlights and headlights cut through the inky blackness. So different from back home, where he could spend all evening counting stars and never catch them all.

Surprised by the tinge of homesickness, he made his way out of the room and into the kitchen to start a pot of coffee. Coffee cured everything.

While salvation brewed, he leaned against the counter and thought about the trilogy proposal which had landed him a seven-figure advance. The readers liked his prophecy-themed dark cult series so much that Hollywood was filming the second book. Working off the interest from that, he'd roughly sketched out a timeline for the next series and passed it off to his editor.

Except that's where the inspiration had ended. Died a slow, agonizing death like his characters. Oh, the irony. No matter how hard he tried to grasp a tangible thread of his former brilliance and put words to paper, it flittered away.

He shook his head and poured himself a cup of coffee. Turning toward the living room, he sipped from his favorite mug and stared at the room that had cost him more to redecorate than his first royalty check. The ostentatious interior designer had read all his books and raved on and on about ideas, until he'd agreed to something just to shut her up. The result was the nightmare before him.

Christ, he wrote about nightmares. He didn't want to live in one.

Slate-gray walls, so dark they made the two thousand square feet look like two hundred. A red leather sectional and creepy as fuck sculptures were supposed to bring a "splash of color." To top off the monstrosity, framed copies of his book covers lined one wall and movie posters based off his books scaled the other.

He hadn't had guests over in six months. Not that he'd ever had many parties. Or friends. He was a writer, and writers would rather write about people than talk to them. His own head was much more interesting. But still, it would've been nice to have the option of company, should he want it. He used to get a kick out of watching people, imagining their worst fears, plotting their fictional demise.

Maybe if he headed over to Central Park tomorrow, sat on a bench and observed, he'd get some ideas flowing.

The house line wailed from his desk in the other room, the ringing insistent. Just like his agent and editor and adoring fans. He almost didn't answer, but hell, it's not like he was getting any work done. Coffee in hand, he strode into his office and picked up the phone.

"How goes it, big brother?"

Despite the fact that his muscles were unfamiliar with the gesture, Alec smiled. "Hello, Jake. You're calling rather late." He leaned back in his chair, his gaze automatically falling to the shelf across the room where a picture of them in their youth grinned back at him. Two skinny, pale boys with their arms around each other on the beach.

"Am I interrupting?"

Jake was the only one who knew about his writer's block, and the knowledge made Alec's face heat in shame. "No. Still a blank page."

"Maybe a change of scenery will help."

Jake had suggested it before, but Alec was hell-bent on doing this alone. He would get through this somehow. It was just a blip in his career was all. Except it was going on a year now, and this blip had quickly become an epidemic.

"I'm fine. Just need to work through it."

Jake grunted. "How's that going for ya?"

Alec frowned but said nothing.

"I can hear you pouting from here." His brother laughed, and the sound immediately jarred him back to childhood. Not an unpleasant feeling. "Come on," Jake continued. "What can it hurt? A little sun, a little breather. It'll do you some good to come home."

Alec didn't have an aversion to going home. He did, however, have an aversion to his father's inability to display any tact whenever Alec was within a ten-mile radius. Whatever. Family was family, and his could be worse. "I need to get this book done, not go on vacation."

"You can work from anywhere. There's this little thing called technology—"

"Har, har." He sighed. "I'll think about it, okay? Happy now?"

He glanced once more at their picture, taken one hot summer day at the beach near Covington Cove. Not the actual name for the private area of Wilmington Beach, but more an unofficial nickname given by the Covington staff through the years. Alec and Jake's father worked as a gardener for the Covingtons, back before they sold the seasonal property. Their son, Cole, owned it now. Being the good son, Jake took over the family landscaping business instead of making shit up for a living, and still worked for Cole.

Which reminded him . . . "How are things between you and Lacey?"

"That's the other reason I called." Jake cleared his throat. "I asked her to marry me."

Alec stilled. Jake had had a crush on little Lacey Covington since he'd first laid eyes on her. Dad had brought them to work with him on the Covington estate when Alec was eight and Jake was six. After reconnecting recently, Lacey and Jake had been dating for about eight months.

The Covington kids were nothing like their self-righteous parents, but Alec had read Cole's memoir, just like every other person in America, so he knew what Cole and his wife, Mia, had gone through to get their happy ending. It had taken them ten years, thanks to Cole's mother and her threats.

The whole thing made Alec nervous. If Kathryn Covington decided to meddle in her daughter Lacey's life the way she had in her son, Cole's, Jake would wind up on the losing end. Jake was a hard worker and made a decent living. But the Covingtons had more money than God.

"Aren't you going to say anything?"

Alec swiped a hand down his face. "I'm sorry. You just surprised me. Can I assume she said yes, since you're telling me?"

"She did. She said yes."

Alec could hear the smile in Jake's tone, which caused his own lips to curve. His little brother, getting married. "Congratulations, man. I'm really happy for you." And he was. Lacey was a lovely girl. But . . . "Don't you think it's kind of soon? You've only been together a few months." His own haunting experiences rose up to choke him.

"You know when you know."

He'd have to take his brother's word for it. Love had never slapped him upside the head. He preferred to keep it that way. He'd come close to love once, and he was still paying for it. "Well, I am happy for you. Did you tell Mom and Dad yet?"

"Yep." Jake laughed. His brother was always laughing, it seemed. Jake was light where Alec was dark. Amazing they got along at all, really. "They're excited. Lacey wants to do it at the end of summer."

"*This* summer? As in three months from now?"

"Yeah. She wants the ceremony right here on the beach. Something small."

Alec propped his feet up on his desk and crossed his ankles. "Correct me if I'm wrong, but she is a woman *and* a Covington. Is small even an option?"

Jake's silence was lengthy. "Things have changed since you were home last. Lacey and Cole aren't in contact with their mother, and their dad is trying to be more a part of their lives. He's not the arrogant prick he used to be."

John and Kathryn Covington's divorce had been splashed all over the society pages and newspapers alike. John had bowed out of politics, claiming he wanted to spend more time with his family. Meanwhile, Kathryn turned into America's most hated bitch, both from her reaction to the divorce and how Cole had described her in his memoir.

"Come home," Jake implored again. "Get to know Lacey a little better, spend some time with the folks. Heck, sit on the beach and drink piña coladas. Stay for the summer. You can leave after the wedding. Maybe it'll help get your head back into the book."

It did sound good. His life was in New York now, but nothing imminent tied him here at the moment. What he'd been doing to write his next book sure wasn't working. Alec reached over and swiped the nose of his Derek Jeter bobblehead, thinking as he watched the toy swivel.

"You can stay in our guesthouse, so you don't have to worry about Dad. You'd have it all to yourself."

"Is the house finished?" Alec could've sworn they'd just broken ground on Lacey's McMansion not long ago. She'd designed it herself, according to Jake, and planned to build on an unused area of the original Covington property.

"Yep. They finished it last month. I'm just touching up some landscaping." He paused to clear his throat. "I moved in with her when she asked."

Alec tipped his head back and stared at the ceiling. Perhaps a trip down the coast was in order just to ensure Jake knew what he was getting into. To guarantee his little brother wasn't making a mistake, like he had. "I'll drive down this weekend."

Jake paused. "Really? You can make it work?"

He looked at his computer monitor. *It was a dark and stormy night.* "Yeah, I can make it work."

When he hung up with Jake, Alec transferred his files to a flash drive and shut down his PC.

The weekly call to Laura's group home went as always: polite to the point of sterile, and it took him three attempts to dial. The night manager didn't seem concerned he was leaving town for a few months. Out of respect, Alec never visited, but he did check in to see how she was doing. Laura's father would raise hell tomorrow when he heard Alec was gone.

His anger couldn't be helped any more than Alec's attempts to right things. Both futile.

Alec made arrangements for someone to come in once a week to keep an eye on the apartment and then shot off a text to his editor. He packed up his laptop and shoved some clothes into a suitcase, setting them by the front door. After checking that all the lights were off, he went to stand by the window and take in the skyline view of New York.

It was a beautiful and ugly place down below. Filled with crime, poverty, and desperation. It also held sprawling parks, generous people, and easy access to anything the heart desired. Before his first book hit the bestseller list, he had moved to this city, known as the center of the publishing world, to immerse himself in it. To keep his edge and his finger on the pulse of the industry.

He had to admit, people recognized him wherever he went. He brushed elbows with producers and screenwriters. Booksellers and editors and marketing people, all willing to bend over backward to accommodate him. Adoring fans with blogs and websites and Facebook pages. But there was no one he could call at two a.m. just because. No one to argue with over a bad call in the Yankees game or grab a beer to discuss their day.

A city full of eight million people. It was all rather lonely sometimes.

He shook his head. It was only Thursday, but he didn't have anything else to do. He could take his time driving down to Wilmington, unwind a bit. Besides, now that he had a plan of action and an objective set forth, he wouldn't be able to focus on much else. Why delay his departure?

He turned his back on New York, gathered his luggage, and locked the door on his way out.

* * *

"Ginny is so excited you're coming," Mia said. "She's beside herself. When do you get in?"

Faith held the phone to her ear and traced a lazy pattern over her comforter with her finger, calculating the distance between Charlotte and Wilmington. "I should get there in a few hours." Her head whipped up with a thought. "I hope that's okay. I know it's a day earlier than we discussed."

Mia Galdon—no, make that Mia Covington—had contacted Faith a couple months ago, asking if she'd be interested in the opportunity to be Ginny's private tutor. Faith had been one of the people who had worked with Mia's sister at St. Ambrose before Mia pulled her out of the private school. Faith was the first person Mia called for the job, but Faith had had to finish out the school year and tender her resignation, thus the delay. The decision had been eating away at her ever since, until she was pretty certain she'd developed an ulcer.

Faith had missed working with Ginny when they'd moved to the coast. The teenager was a sweet, chipper girl who'd struggled with her disability in the public school system. At St. Ambrose, she'd flourished, learning to read and write and do the simple activities of daily living.

But that wasn't the only reason Faith had agreed to take the position and move hours away from everything she knew. It was also because Mia genuinely loved Ginny, was an active part of her life, and had once given up everything she'd had for her sister. Faith could relate.

"Of course that's okay," Mia assured. "Like I told you, the guesthouse is ready for you." She paused to say something to someone in the room and then came back on the line. "It'll be nice having someone work one-on-one with her again. The Down syndrome groups and programs here just aren't cutting it for her. You were always her favorite teacher."

Faith, never really comfortable with compliments, didn't say anything and knew all this, as Mia had told her more than once. Mia seemed to need the reassurance of the repetition, though.

"I'm looking forward to it. See you soon."

They disconnected and Faith looked around her bedroom. The walls were the same white they'd been as a child. A functional desk, dresser, and bed were the only furniture pieces. There were no pictures on the wall, no little trinkets or baubles. No life, because she'd never had one.

Nerves swam in her belly at this new venture. She'd never left Charlotte before. She'd never left her parents' house and lived on her own. At twenty-seven years old, if she didn't do it now, she never would. The opportunity was perfect. The Covingtons were matching her old salary at St. Ambrose, and accommodations were included. She wondered what it would be like, living alone. Probably no different than home.

She sighed and stood. It was time to let go, and in doing so, maybe her parents would, too. She'd been stuck in this rut for too long, not moving forward because she feared her parents needed her presence. But that was her own wishful thinking.

Faith doubted they'd notice she was gone.

She closed her bedroom door behind her, as her parents preferred it, and stopped outside Hope's room. Her bedroom door was always open, as if their parents expected her to one day return. But Hope was never coming back. If not for the silence and disappointment etched in her parents' eyes, Faith would assume she was the only one who knew that.

She didn't know why she did it, but she stepped just inside the doorway of her sister's room. Unlike her own, splashes of color were everywhere. The walls were a fading rose, the bedspread a deep lavender, the curtains navy blue and homemade. It would seem like a mismatch to anyone who hadn't known Hope. The wood of the dresser, shelves, and bed was painted a moss green. Pictures of Hope adorned every nook and cranny. Stuffed animals were neatly lined up on the bed.

The room hadn't changed in years. A thin layer of dust coated the dresser to her right. For a fleeting moment, Faith considered writing her name in the dust, but shook away the impulse.

Descending the stairs, she moved past her luggage stacked by the front door and made her way into the living room. It resembled any other family room in small-town America: powder-blue walls, country-style plaid couches in cream and navy, plush beige carpet, and a white mantel with family portraits.

The pictures drew her eye. She inspected the photos in their mismatched frames, feeling like a spectator in her own house. Her parents after they brought Hope home from the hospital. Hope, cheerleading at a homecoming game. Hope, posing in her senior prom dress, her many friends gathered at her side. They'd all shaved their heads, too, to match Hope's. The last picture was Hope and Faith sharing a hospital bed after a treatment.

That was the only photo Faith was in. If she didn't know better, she'd swear it was a shrine to Hope's memory, but the mantel had always held these reminiscences, or ones like it, since Faith was a toddler. If Faith wasn't next to Hope in a picture, she wasn't displayed.

She tried to draw bitterness from deep inside, allow herself to grow angry, but neither emotion would come. Because she knew her place in this family, always had. Knew why she was conceived. And it wasn't for a photo on the mantel.

From the other room, the murmurs of her parents' conversation rose. A quick glance at the clock told her they were sitting down to dinner. Five-thirty on the button, every evening. They'd started without her. Not the first time.

Faith's plan was to eat with them and then hit the road, but her stomach clenched and she didn't think she'd be able to keep anything down. Still, she should try. Their last remaining child was leaving home. Surely they'd want some time together first, to talk about her new adventure and wish her luck. They must be giving her time to finish packing.

When she stepped into the kitchen, her parents were standing by the small oak table, their backs to her. Faith glanced at the stove. The casserole dish, which had been used to bake chicken and vegetables, was empty.

Mom had only made enough for two.

Her chest grew tight, and she tried to inhale a deep breath, yet tears burned her eyes anyway. Tears. She hadn't cried in ages. Such a useless action.

Mortified, she took in the familiar kitchen to level her emotions. White pine cupboards, green tile counters, checkered laminate floor, fruit bowl next to the wine rack. Faith never drank wine. Maybe she should start.

When she felt more in control, she cleared her throat and walked over to the table. The years had been kind to her mother. Her wavy brown hair, which once trailed down her back, was cut in a bob and interlaced with gray, giving her a distinguished look. Because she'd been a stickler for healthy eating, her lean, lithe frame resembled that of someone much younger. Until you looked in her eyes.

Her dad turned to look at her, by all accounts seeming confused. He had stormy hazel eyes, just like Hope's, and thick white hair that had once been chestnut, like Faith's. He, too, had remained in fit shape, though his shoulders sagged as often as his smile.

"I didn't mean to disturb you. I . . . just wanted to say good-bye."

It dawned on her, too late, that he'd thought she left already. Without a good-bye? Without a hug and kiss and *I'll miss you*? If she'd been more rational, she would have remembered they didn't hug or kiss in her family. Not anymore.

"Should I make you a sandwich for the road?" Her mother didn't meet her gaze, but her tone was as formal and polite as always. Like she was speaking to a member of the choir instead of her daughter. "I got a pound of that shaved turkey you like."

Faith didn't care for turkey. That had been Hope's favorite. "Thank you, but I'll be okay. I had a late lunch."

"Well, drive safely," Dad said. He opened his arms to offer her an awkward hug and wound up patting her on the back instead. "Bye for now. Call us when you get there. Don't forget to wear sunscreen. UV rays on the beach can be brutal."

She wouldn't know. She'd never been to the beach.

"Yes, do drive safely." Mom's focus returned to her meal as they both sat down. "Good-bye, Faith."

She opened her mouth to say . . . something, but the words wedged in her throat when she realized that's all she'd get. But what had she expected? A total personality change?

Slowly, she nodded her head.

A hot ball of pain burned in her stomach. She had walked through each room of the house before entering the kitchen, as if her brain knew this was a semipermanent good-bye, even if her heart held out hope. She'd wanted to take in the details of home so she could remember it, store away the visual in her mind's memory box. It was a silly, fruitless notion. There was no imprint of her here.

"I love you," she whispered, because she did. She'd loved them with the same childish heart that had dreamed of a way out. Or a way in.

"Back atcha," Dad called.

Mom hummed her response, a cross between agreement and dismissal.

Without further ado, she walked down the hall and gathered her luggage by the front door. One suitcase held her books, a lovely escape she thoroughly enjoyed, and the other her clothes. There were two boxes of therapy materials in her car, and another box with cosmetics. Still, after twenty-seven years, there should be more to pack. More to a life than this.

Anxiety clawed at her throat. She could still tell Mia she

couldn't accept the offer. She hadn't signed a contract. Maybe she could get her old job back at St. Ambrose. A comfortable, albeit lonely, existence here had to be better than what was out there. What did she know about being out in the world? Failure loomed. Humiliation at every turn.

She surprised herself by opening the door, then paused. She strode over to the mantel, grabbed the picture of her and Hope, and left.

chapter
two

After dinner, Lacey and Jake had taken Alec on a tour of their new home. He was impressed. The original Covington beach house, just next door, where Mia and Cole resided, was right up there with the homes of crowned royalty. Lacey's home was slightly more subdued, but still demonstrated the wealth she'd been born into. Because Lacey and Cole had broken up the estate, the lot she built on wasn't overly wide, so she'd designed up.

Three floors of magazine-quality interior design. There were pale hardwood floors throughout. Each room was painted in a different shade of coastal pastels. The greens, browns, blues, and grays served as both masculine and feminine accents. Much more inviting than Alec's gruesome apartment.

The main level had a living room with deep-cushioned corduroy couches, a floor-to-ceiling white brick fireplace, and black stained tables. The kitchen appliances were stainless steel, the counters white marble, and the cabinets mahogany. A long, polished kitchen table along the wall held a small stack of newspapers and a bowl of keys. He pictured Lacey and Jake drinking coffee together there in the mornings. A small library and half bath finished things off.

The second level held four bedrooms, all with an accompanying bath, but the third floor rocked him back on his heels. There were wall-to-wall windows facing east, with a wondrous view of the ocean. Lacey had clearly set it up as her studio. Acrylic paint tubes, canvases, and brushes lay scattered over several tables. More than ten easels dotted the space. A small sink occupied a corner, along with a recliner that had seen much better days.

Alec raised his brows at the chair. "You still have that thing?"

Lacey wrapped her arms around Jake's waist, her soft blond hair long enough to brush Jake's hand as he held her arm in place. Her blue eyes lit with mischief. "He watches me paint from that chair."

"Can't get rid of Black Beard," Jake said unapologetically. "It's a staple."

"It's probably held together by staples." Alec grinned. Jake had bought the recliner for his first apartment eight years ago. It should've been junked eight years ago. The fact that Lacey let him keep it said a lot about her.

They made their way back downstairs and onto the front porch, where Lacey and Jake sat side by side. The only thing not picture perfect was Lacey's yard. There were several large holes in the lawn and various pieces of equipment lying around.

"What's your plan for the landscape?"

Lacey settled into the crook of his brother's arm and set the swing in motion. "Jake's going to line the driveway with palms and Myrica. The base of the porch here will have mountain laurels. Since the mimosa grove separates Cole and Mia's property from ours, we decided on dogwood trees where the holes are dug. We'll line the side of the house and path around to the beach with wild oats and sea grass."

Growing up with a father who owned a landscaping business, he knew what each of those plants was and could picture how the estate would look when finished. He approved. Alec also noted how Lacey always used the term "we" when referring to anything regarding the house. She'd already accounted for and accepted his brother in her life and home. It wasn't *hers*, but *theirs*.

Some of his tension eased. They really did seem happy. Lacey was always touching Jake's arm or shoulder or hand, and Jake never went more than thirty seconds without a smile or a glance at her. The princess and the gardener. Huh.

A car door closed in the distance. Between the neat rows of mimosa trees, a woman exited a white compact car and stared at Cole's house. From this distance he couldn't make out much more than shoulder-length reddish-brown hair and blue jeans.

He jerked his chin in her direction. "Who's that?"

"Must be Faith Armstrong." Jake shrugged." Ginny's private tutor. She's supposed to be getting in from Charlotte today."

Ginny being Mia's sister. He hadn't seen them since his teen years. He was pretty sure Ginny was still in diapers then. "I remember Ginny being quite a handful."

Jake nodded. "She's mellowed a lot. Mia's great with her."

He remembered that, too.

A teenage girl came bounding off the porch next door and jumped into the woman's embrace, nearly toppling them both to the ground. His lips curved listening to Ginny's laugher. Kid had a great laugh. Cole and Mia watched from the doorway. Their voices mingled with the roar of the tide, and he couldn't make out what they were saying.

"You'll get to see them tomorrow," Lacey said. "We're going over there for lunch, if you're up to it."

"I'm up to it."

She nodded. "We should get you settled into the guesthouse so you can write your next masterpiece."

Alec kept his sarcastic comment to himself and grabbed his bags from the trunk. The guesthouse was on the south side of the property, nestled between several pine and palm trees. Close enough to the big house for access, but far enough to offer privacy. Inside, the kitchen and living room were separated by an island. White wainscoting lined the walls below a chair rail, and the space above was painted navy. Several seascape paintings and white leather furniture served as accents.

"The bedroom and bath are through there." Jake pointed down a short hall. "There's a desk in the bedroom. You can move it wherever you want."

Alec nodded and glanced out the sliding glass door off the kitchen. The private beach was devoid of people. The waves left a white foam as they pounded the sand and retreated, and the sky began to darken with dusk, taking with it some of the heavy humidity. He had forgotten how beautiful Wilmington was at sunset.

If he couldn't write here, he may as well find a new vocation.

"Is everything okay?" Lacey's voice held a worried note. "Do you need anything?"

He forced a smile and turned from the view. "Nope. This is perfect. Thanks for the invitation."

Her shoulders relaxed. "You just come up to the house if you need something. We stocked the fridge and cabinets. Well, Jake did. He knew what food you preferred—"

Alec grinned. "Thank you, Lacey. I'm good. I'm pretty easy to please, actually."

Jake snorted. "Come on, honey. Let's leave my brother to his brilliance."

After they'd gone, Alec stepped out onto the back deck and braced his forearms on the railing. He breathed in salty air as some of the stress left his body. A soft, humid breeze blew in off the ocean, cooling his skin. He closed his eyes to listen to the surf and the gulls squawking as they skimmed the water, searching for fish.

It had been a long, long time since he'd felt this relaxed.

Now all he needed to do was channel that semblance of peace and get a story down.

When he opened his eyes, the newcomer from next door was standing in the surf on the other side of Cole's property. Dark had descended at a leisurely pace, just like everything else on the southern coast, but there was enough moonlight to make out her profile. She stood motionless, facing the ocean with her arms crossed in front of her, so still she could've been made of marble.

Curious, he descended the deck stairs to the beach and hiked in her direction. If she heard him coming, she gave no indication. Not wanting to startle her, he cleared his throat when he got close enough for her to hear him over the waves.

She turned abruptly and must've forgotten her feet were buried in the sand because she had to throw out her arms to steady herself. "I'm sorry, I was just . . ." She pointed to the vast expanse of ocean as she righted herself.

It was too dim to make out much of her features, but from what Alec could gather, he never would've noticed her in a crowd had they met anywhere else. Plain wasn't the best term to describe her, but it was adequate. Something about her voice knocked him back a step, though. It barely rose above the tide and had a musical quality.

She must've taken his silence for something dire, because she wouldn't look him in the eye. "I didn't mean to disturb you. I'll just head back—"

"You're not. Disturbing me, I mean." He took a half step forward to see her better, but he wound up disappointed because it was too dark. "Besides, the ocean belongs to no one. You're free to walk here regardless of who finds you disturbing."

She didn't seem to locate the humor in his remark as he'd intended. She rubbed her arms, despite the late evening heat, and turned toward the house as if undecided as to what to do next.

"I'm Alec, by the way. Jake's brother."

"Oh. Yes, of course. Mia said you were coming."

God, that voice. Like a mermaid call, a singsong lilt from underwater. Fascinating.

Her frame was slender to the point of breakable. The hem of her jeans was rolled to her calves, baring a flash of pale skin. No polish on the toes. Pity. He had a thing for that. A plain white tee covered most of her torso and was too baggy to determine if she had any curves. His gaze traveled up. Her neck was long, regal almost, adorned with a thin chain that disappeared underneath her shirt. Best he could tell, she had a triangular-shaped face and pointed chin. Her eye color remained a mystery.

"And you're Faith, correct? The therapist."

"Er, yes. I'm a special needs teacher, but I have a degree in occupational therapy, too."

He nodded, hoping she'd keep talking. He was getting all kinds of ideas flitting through his mind about a character for his book just from her voice alone. Each time she stopped talking, the ideas drifted away. Which was interesting, because didn't all women talk? A lot? Not her. Maybe she was nervous, given his celebrity. How he hated that.

Just as he was about to encourage more, she pointed to the house. "I should get back inside. It's getting late."

It was barely nine.

She walked away, and Alec watched until she disappeared behind the dunes. Not even a *good-bye*, or *see you later*, or *nice to meet you*. He shook his head and walked back the way he'd come.

Faith closed the back door to the Covington guesthouse and leaned against it. Exhaustion and nerves warred through her body and she fought to rein them in. She wasn't used to all this attention, and today she'd received a lot. Well, since arriving in Wilmington, anyway.

She thought she'd be uncomfortable meeting Cole Covington for the first time, but he was an unusual mix of genuine and nice. Faith allowed herself to relax in his company after a few minutes. Not so with Alec. Perhaps because he'd snuck up on her in the dark. She'd picked a time without anyone else on the beach to go out and take in her first real glimpse of the ocean. Even the air was different. Lighter, and scented with an odd mix of fresh fish and brine. The water lapping at her feet was cool and hypnotizing. She'd been so wrapped up in a mix of emotions, she hadn't realized she wasn't alone.

What he must think of her. Then again, he probably wasn't thinking of her at all. Why would he?

His fame didn't faze her and hadn't been what had brought on a sudden flare of nerves. Authors, even ones as big as Alec Winston, were just people like the rest of them. Flesh and blood and souls in want of something. No, it was the way he'd stared at her, like he was picking apart her brain. A puzzle to fit together. In all her years, no one had ever wanted to know what made her tick, and in two minutes he gave her the impression he desired nothing more.

Maybe it was a writer thing.

She focused on why she was here, bringing Ginny to mind and smiling. Ginny had been happy to see her. She couldn't remember the last time that had happened either.

Shaking the thoughts away, she shoved off the door and made her way to the living room to get her luggage. Her internal clock was declaring bedtime. She hadn't even really had the chance to settle in, but there would be time for that. Time was something she had in plenty.

Taking her cell phone out of her pocket, she checked the screen. No messages. Same as the last hundred times she'd looked. A pang of disappointment hit her right in the stomach. She didn't know why she expected her parents to call. And it was after nine. Too late for her to try them. They'd be in bed by now.

She fished her pajamas and toothbrush out of her suitcase and came across the photo of her and Hope that she'd hastily shoved there before getting on the road. She sat back on her heels and stared at the two of them, her chest growing tight.

Ten years and it still seemed like yesterday that they'd buried her sister. Faith hadn't felt whole since. In fact, the hole in her chest seemed to grow with each passing year. One day it would consume her until nothing remained but a black void.

"We finally made it to the beach," she whispered, tears blurring her eyes.

She hadn't cried in years, and now twice in one day she'd had to bite them back. She sighed and rose to her feet, setting the picture on the small fireplace mantel next to a conch shell. Hope would've loved it here.

Faith turned, doing a quick survey of her new place. The sea-foam-green walls and white wicker furniture echoed the simple fashion of every beach house—at least the ones in movies. For her, it seemed the perfect escape. She had no expectations, but was satisfied with the amount of room offered. Yet it wasn't her home any more than her parents' house had been. She got the strange sensation she didn't belong anywhere.

In a few months, she'd go apartment hunting. Once she knew the job was secure and Wilmington was where she'd stay, anyway. No sense in rushing things. She'd built up a lot in savings from not paying rent. Even though the Covingtons compensated her well, she couldn't afford a beach-front location, but perhaps something within walking distance so she could stare at the ocean. There was something almost . . . healing about it.

Pulling her mind out of the pity party, she slipped into her pajamas and brushed her teeth. Before turning in, she walked to the bedroom window and looked outside. She wondered if she'd ever get used to the sight. Her imagination didn't do the ocean justice. A full moon illuminated the black ripples, the vastness of water stretching on forever.

Alec wasn't standing in the sand any longer, but she could all but feel him still in front of her. There was a quiet, humming presence about him that his novels' back-cover photos didn't portray. His thick, longish black hair curled just above his ears, and though she couldn't see them on the beach earlier, she knew his eyes were bluish gray. The square jaw and a shadow of a beard barely growing in gave him a hint of danger. His wide shoulders and taut muscles were a thing of beauty, if not a little intimidating. He was taller than she expected, too—at five foot five, she'd had to crane her neck to look at him. And handsome, especially when he smiled at his own self-deprecating humor.

Turning from the window, she climbed into bed and stared at the ceiling. Her first trip to the beach, something she'd always dreamed about but never accomplished before now, and Alec Winston left an imprint tied within her memory.

Faith hadn't yet decided if that was a bad thing.

chapter
three

"We're not leaving for a couple weeks."

Faith watched Ginny closely, looking for any signs the sixteen-year-old was upset with what Mia had just told her. She didn't find any. Ginny continued to color her picture of flowers, concentrating on what was in front of her.

Mia exchanged a look with Faith from across the kitchen table, her eyes concerned.

Faith gently stilled Ginny's hand with her own. "How do you feel about Cole and Mia going on a little trip?"

Instead of answering, Ginny asked a question of her own. "What's a honeymoon?"

Mia smiled and ran her fingers through her short black hair before answering. "When two people get married, they take a vacation together afterward, so they can get closer. That's called a honeymoon."

Ginny mulled that over and tapped her chin with a finger. "But you're already married."

"Yes," Mia hedged. "There was a lot going on after the wedding six months ago, though. We had just moved here, remember? Things are settled down now, so we'd like to take that trip."

"I can't come?" The question was asked matter-of-factly and without sadness, apparently a distracted thought, because she'd already gone back to coloring.

"Not this time, pretty girl. But I won't go if you're scared or worried. Talk to me."

Faith rested her chin in her palm. Mia used that phrase a lot with Ginny. *Talk to me.* It allowed for open communication between them and worked very well in getting Ginny to relay her feelings.

"How long will you move away?"

Mia reached for Ginny's hands. "I'm not moving away. Never. I'll be back in just under two weeks. We can talk by phone every day."

"No." Ginny slapped the table. "How long will you move away?" Her voice rose in frustration and Faith realized what Ginny was trying to say.

"Do you mean how far are they traveling?"

Ginny nodded, anger deflating.

"They're going to Cozumel, which is in Mexico. To fly there by plane, it takes about two hours. So she won't be very far away at all."

"And," Mia added quickly, "you get to stay at Lacey and Jake's house. Won't that be fun?"

"I want to stay here." Her voice had an edge of hysteria that Faith knew preceded a tantrum.

"That's okay, Ginny." Faith kept her voice cool and calm. "You can stay here with me. Or maybe Jake and Lacey could stay here for those two weeks. We can ask them at lunch today. Would you like that?"

Ginny nodded and picked up her crayon again, clearly done with this conversation.

Mia blew out a silent breath and tilted her head toward the dining room.

Faith nodded and followed her out of the room.

The Covingtons' maid, Bea, was busy setting the table for guests when they walked in. Chicken salad, croissants, and fresh fruit were laid out, along with a pitcher of sweet tea. White china and crystal glasses of water reflected the sunlight streaming through the window.

"This is ready, Miss Mia." Bea wiped her hands on an apron.

Mia nodded. "It looks delicious, Bea. Have you eaten?"

"No, ma'am. I'll wait until your company leaves."

Mia waved her hand. "Don't be silly. Everything's set out. You go relax for a while."

Bea hesitated, a wrinkle creasing the dark cocoa skin of her forehead. After a few moments, she swiped a hand over her tight bun, nodded, and stepped out.

"She's still a little frightened of Cole," Mia said. "He tries so hard to put her at ease, too."

That was the odd thing about the Covingtons. They didn't treat their staff like staff. They never barked orders or pretended they were invisible. At St. Ambrose, the students came from affluent backgrounds and knew it. As a teacher, Faith had often been demeaned and dismissed as if not important. In the two days since she'd arrived, Mia and Cole had insisted she eat with them and spoken to her as if she were their friend, not an employee. It made it hard to understand the boundaries.

"Maybe we should put off the trip," Mia mused, interrupting Faith's thoughts.

"What's this?" Cole strode in the room wearing faded jeans and a white button-down shirt. He still had a trace of a limp from the injuries he'd endured overseas, but one had to look closely to notice. The long, purplish scar on his neck, however, was blatant. He wrapped his arm around Mia's waist and kissed her briefly on the mouth. "You want to postpone the honeymoon again?"

There was no animosity in his tone, just humor. They were a cute couple. Affection shone in their eyes, and whenever Cole looked at Mia, it was like he was seeing her for the first time. Faith wondered if it had anything to do with how long it took them to get back together. She'd read Cole's memoir, every captivating, painful word, and she felt like she knew these two on a level too personal for comfort.

Mia brushed a strand of Cole's blond hair from his forehead. "Ginny's upset about us leaving."

"I'd rather have you alone, but we can take her with us. Family vacation?"

Mia looked unsure, her gaze traveling over Cole's shoulder and around the room. "We haven't had any time to ourselves, but I also don't want to leave if she's worried. There hasn't been any stability in her life—"

"Stop it. She had you." Cole turned his brown eyes to Faith. "What do you think?"

They also asked her opinion a lot, which was both humbling and flattering. "You don't leave for two more weeks. It'll give her some time to get used to the idea. I would just keep reminding her that you'll be back. Perhaps have Jake and Lacey spend a little more time with her to get her used to the transition."

Cole nodded. "If that doesn't work, we'll take Ginny with us."

Faith opened and closed her mouth, hoping she hid her surprise. It took a special kind of person to be willing to take his wife's disabled sister with them on a honeymoon. For the first time since accepting the job offer, Faith knew it was the right choice.

Alec followed Lacey and Jake into Cole's house and whistled through his teeth. "Nice digs, Cole." He hadn't been inside the house in years, not since John and Kathryn Covington owned the place, but it looked different now. Instead of expensive paintings by famous artists and deco wallpaper, there were rich blue-gray walls and family portraits.

"Alec Winston." Cole shook his hand. "Been a long time. How's the new book coming?"

"It's coming." Not at all, but it would. Hopefully before his publisher threatened to sue.

Jake snorted. "He has writer's block."

Cole's eyebrows shot up. "For how long?"

Alec narrowed his eyes on his brother before turning back to Cole. "A while. I'll work through it."

"It's been a year." Jake shrugged when Alec shot him another glare. "Cole's an agent. He'd understand. Maybe he can help."

Further awkward conversation was avoided when Mia strolled in. Jesus, her blue eyes were still one of the most intense things Alec ever had the pleasure of seeing. Last he'd seen her, her black hair had trailed down her back. She'd cropped it all off since then.

"Look at you, all grown up." She smiled and drew him in for a hug. "And you finally grew into your shoes."

"Har, har." Yeah, he wasn't so gangly anymore. He released her and stepped back. "You are as lovely as ever."

"Aw. Still know all the right words."

They'd never had a romantic history. Mia had only ever had eyes for Cole, and Alec had only ever wanted to live in the fantasy inside his make-believe stories, but they'd had some good summers long ago.

Jake snorted again at Mia's comment, insinuating he didn't, in fact, currently have the right words due to his writer's block.

Alec pinned his brother with a shut-up-or-die glare.

"Let's have some lunch and you can tell me about your problem." Cole gestured deeper into the house.

Alec glanced heavenward and followed them into the dining room. Faith was standing next to the table where Ginny was seated. In daylight, her reddish-brown hair was lighter than he'd first estimated. The thick waves brushed her delicate shoulders. Today she wore khaki capris and a fitted green blouse of some kind with little ruffles on the capped sleeves. Why he noticed that, he didn't know. A scattering of pale freckles dusted her nose and cheeks, indiscernible had she not been standing in the sunlight.

"Faith, this is Alec, Lacey, and Jake." Mia smiled and directed her gaze from Faith to her sister. "Ginny, do you remember Alec?"

He didn't see how she could. She must've been in kindergarten last they'd crossed paths. Yet the girl nodded and grinned from ear to ear. Her droopy eyes and low ears, the typical characteristics of Down syndrome, were a telltale sign of her disability, but she had sparks of Mia in her, too. Dark hair and a pretty smile.

"Ginny has an excellent memory," Mia informed, pride resonating in her tone.

"You write scary stories." Ginny's speech slurred slightly and was louder than necessary.

"And how would you know that?" he teased. It was safe to assume horror fiction wasn't something Mia let her dabble in, even if she could comprehend the story.

"Mia has all your books. She reads with the lights on because they're scary and it's not so scary with the lights on but I don't think the dark is scary." Compound sentence complete, Ginny nodded. She was an adorable charmer.

He grinned. "Well, I guess I'm doing my job if she needs to leave the lights on, but good for you for not being afraid of the dark. Everything's still the same, even with the lights out. Right?"

"Right."

"I'll let you get on with your lunch." Faith smiled at Ginny. "We'll do your paint by numbers after you're through."

It didn't escape Alec's attention that Faith had yet to look him in the eye. He still didn't know her eye color, and for some unforeseeable reason, that bugged him. As she turned to leave, he had the oddest urge to grab her arm to stop her, probably because that voice still had his interest piqued. In the end, he didn't have to.

Mia took a step forward. "Where are you going?"

Clearly confused, Faith pointed vaguely toward the kitchen. "You have company . . ."

Her words hung in the air until Mia and Lacey shared a brief look. Mia turned back toward Faith. "Please stay. You're our guest, too."

Faith flinched. Literally flinched. As if the concept of being wanted was foreign. She obviously thought she was intruding. Her mannerisms made him think of a wallflower desperate to blend into the background. He'd bet, if she had one, she even apologized to her personal journal.

Dear Diary, I'm sorry to bother you . . .

"If you're sure," she said.

Uncomfortable topic out of the way, they sat down and passed the platters around. Once they had a few bites down, Jake leaned around Lacey to address Faith.

"Where are you from, Faith?"

She paused mid chew, her gaze never leaving her plate. Slowly, she swallowed and darted a glance in his brother's direction. "I'm from the Charlotte area."

"Do you have a big family?"

Alec knew his brother was just trying to break the ice, but he was only making the room arctic in the process.

Faith squirmed in her seat. "It's just me and my parents. They're retired."

"So, Mia. You've read all my books?" Alec wasn't trying to be an egotistical ass, but Faith needed saving. He'd wonder why later.

"Guilty. They scare the bejesus out of me, but I can't put them down."

Lacey laughed. "Have you seen the movies? I about died watching that last one. What was it called?" She turned to Jake for assistance.

"*Thread of Fear*," Jake supplied. "I still have the claw marks on my arms from her fingernails. Mia can go to the theater with her next time. I'm out."

"Oh no." Mia shook her head. "The books are enough for me, thank you."

Alec could feel his head expanding with the praise. Adoring public aside, it mattered what these people thought because they were connected to his roots. His beginnings. "What about you, Faith?"

"I've never seen your movies."

Head successfully deflated.

Ginny bounced in her seat. "Can I watch one?"

Cole laughed. "Not a good idea, darlin'." He tossed his napkin on the table. "So, Alec. Writer's block?"

Alec groaned. "Yeah, it's been an issue."

"Oh no." Mia turned in her seat. "You're not writing?"

He could kill Jake with his bare hands. Maybe he'd off him in his next book. If he wrote a next book. "All authors get it from time to time. Nothing to worry about."

Cole braced his elbows on the table. "What's your agent say?"

"I fired him two months ago." Alec didn't know why he was telling them this, but it wasn't as if they wouldn't hear about it.

Jake waved his hand. "There you go, Cole. Another client. My brother here needs an agent."

Cole shook his head. "I don't really handle horror. Mostly mysteries and memoirs, but if you have something, I can take a look."

That would be the problem, wouldn't it? He didn't have a damn thing. "I'll let you know."

"Can I excuse Faith?" Ginny asked.

For the first time since he'd walked in the door, Faith

grinned. It transformed her whole face from soft and frail to approachable. Sweet. "I think you mean may Faith and I be excused."

Ginny nodded. "Yes." She turned to Mia. "Can we?"

"Sure, pretty girl. I'll come check on you in a while."

Ginny pushed back from the table and rushed into the kitchen.

Faith stood. "She's excited. Art's her favorite subject." Hesitantly, she turned toward Alec but didn't meet his eye. "It was nice to meet all of you."

Lacey stood. "I'll come with you. I'm an . . . artist," she added. "I'd like to hang out with you two, if that's okay?"

Faith looked at Mia, who nodded.

"Lacey's very good. She painted those acrylics of the ocean in the guesthouse."

Alec wondered if she did the ones in his guesthouse, too. If so, she did have serious talent. Jake wasn't kidding.

"Really?" Faith's eyes widened, but damn it, he still couldn't see their color while she was only offering her profile. "They're beautiful. I'm a terrible artist. I have Ginny doing paint by numbers because it helps her recognize numbers, too, but I'm really bad with art projects. It would be great if you could offer ideas."

"Good plan," Cole confirmed. "I have to get back to work, but you guys carry on. Alec, great to see you again. How long are you in town?"

"At least until the wedding. End of August, maybe."

Cole nodded. "We'll be seeing plenty of you. Don't be a stranger."

Jake followed Lacey, Faith, and Ginny into the kitchen, leaving Mia and Alec alone. He offered to clear the table, but Mia refused.

"Listen, Alec, when Cole got back from Iraq, he was a mess. It took a long time for him to get back to where he is now. Writing helped him process the stuff in his head."

Alec didn't see her point.

"What I mean is, maybe you have the opposite problem. Maybe there's too much going on in your head for you to write."

A slow grin spread over his face. Mia had always been too kind and wise beyond her years. She'd picked the perfect profession, going into nursing. She was a natural. He didn't have anything going on in his head, though. Nothing he hadn't been living with for nine years, anyway. Thus, that couldn't be his problem.

He pushed the image of Laura from his mind and rose. "I'll think about it. Thanks for lunch."

Alec stepped off the front porch and made his way to the mimosa grove, half expecting to see a younger Mia chasing baby Ginny through the rows. Or Cole watching from an upstairs window. Lacey would be sitting somewhere, looking coiffed and perfect, while Jake thought up countless ways to ruffle her feathers.

Alec was older than them by a few years, much closer to Cole and Lacey's brother, Dean's, age than theirs. At least before Dean died, anyway. The summer of the accident, the Covingtons had packed up and never returned to Wilmington, and Mia had gone off to college. Strange how vivid the memories remained, despite the passage of so much time. They weren't close friends, any of them. Mia, Jake, and Alec were the help's children. To be seen and not heard.

The sun beat down hard as he passed the grove and arrived at the black wrought-iron fence separating the properties. Hot, humid air made sweat trickle down his back from the mild -exertion. Swinging the gate open, he bypassed the big house and walked to the guesthouse, thinking over Mia's words.

A year ago, he'd finished final edits for the last book in his series and sat at his computer to start the new one. His fingers had frozen over the keys and his brain had shut down. Just like that. One minute he had characters screaming inside his skull and plot upon twisting plot to hammer out, the next there was nothing. Worse than nothing—the silence in his head had become its own entity.

The only time in twelve months something had started to stir was last night on the beach, with Faith. Awkward, plain Faith Armstrong.

The air-conditioning soothed his heated skin as he made his way to the bedroom. Sitting at the desk, he booted up his laptop and opened a document.

An hour later, he was still staring at it.

chapter
four

Faith walked the length of the beach, toes squishing in the sand. The sun felt good, warming her clear to her bones. Before arriving in Wilmington, a cold had resonated from within her body, something she wasn't even aware of until she was standing in what she thought was the most beautiful location on earth. Granted, she hadn't traveled anywhere else, but nothing could touch this place. It was peaceful but never quiet. Between the seagulls and the waves, there was a constant hypnotic lull.

She checked on Ginny, who was down the beach away, collecting shells for tomorrow's art project. Lacey had given Faith some great ideas. She'd even offered to give Ginny an official art class at her home two days a week. Ginny was very excited at this prospect.

Faith closed her eyes and breathed deep, letting her body relax. Maybe if she and Hope had been able to make the drive to the beach, things could've gone differently. The fresh air and warm sunshine wouldn't have cured her sister's disease, but it would've lifted her spirits. Faith firmly believed that healing wasn't just medicinal. It involved diet and exercise and, most of all, peace of mind. Hope would've found peace here.

Longing and memory tightened her throat, and she wished desperately Hope were there. Even while she was sick, Hope had been a steady stream of support and love. More than sisters, they'd been friends. Faith hadn't had a friend since her sister died. Sure, she'd been friendly with coworkers and neighbors, but it wasn't the same.

"Alec!"

At Ginny's excited call, Faith startled and turned. Alec slowly made his way over, barefoot and wearing board shorts. Nothing else. The skin on his chest, sun-kissed and taut over lean, lithe muscle, was lightly dusted with black hair. He moved with the grace of a predator. His body wasn't bulging like a bodybuilder, but his abs, shoulders, and biceps were defined. She swallowed hard and forced herself to take her gaze off his chest before he noticed.

"Whatcha doing?" He crouched down next to Ginny and peeked in her bag.

"Collecting shells. We're going to do art."

"Fun. You have a lot there." He looked at Faith, a slow, lazy grin quirking one side of his mouth as he stood and closed the distance between them. Definitely predatory.

She forced her gaze to focus on his face so she wouldn't be tempted to do something else, like touch him. She hadn't been touched in so long. "Good morning."

"It's afternoon, actually."

"Right. Yes."

He dipped his head, leveling his gray-blue eyes on her as if probing for something he couldn't grasp. After a few moments, he straightened and nodded. "Amber," he announced.

"What?"

"Your eyes. They're amber. Not quite like a good whiskey, but more like organic honey. Around the edges they darken to a golden brown."

Stunned stupid, Faith opened and closed her mouth.

"You had me in fits over that. You never quite look me in the eye and it was too dark last night to see. As someone whose vocation depends on details, madness loomed if I didn't get an answer soon."

She tilted her head, not quite sure if he was making fun of her or deadly serious. "You would've gone crazy if you didn't know my eye color? Is that what you're saying?"

"Something like that. Problem averted."

She grabbed the pendant hanging from her neck and slid it back and forth on the chain. "You're a strange man."

He smiled openly, showing a row of straight white teeth and crinkling the skin near his eyes. Holy cow, the transformation was hypnotic.

He shrugged. "Writers are a strange lot. I've been called worse."

He turned toward the water and she used the momentum of him looking away to peek at Ginny. She was sitting in the sand, lining up her shells into neat rows.

"I've startled you out here twice now, while you stared at the ocean. You looked lost in thought."

She answered without her usual filter. "I've never seen the ocean before."

He abruptly faced her. "You lived in Charlotte, a few hours away, but have never seen the ocean?"

As if she needed him to point out her boring life. "I never found the time, I guess."

"Huh." He turned to the water. "What do you think, now that you've seen it?"

There were no words. Besides, he was the writer. "It's . . . vast and serene. I love the immeasurability of it."

"'Immeasurability,'" he repeated. "I like that word. Multiple meanings."

"How's the writing coming along?"

"It's not." He winced, and she felt for him. "I don't know what's wrong with me."

She thought about his ability to transport readers into his world. A genuine gift. He was obviously struggling without the talent. "Maybe you're trying too hard."

He laughed without mirth.

Her face heated. She shouldn't have said anything.

Ginny rose and bounded over to them. "Can we make brownies now?"

Alec groaned. "Brownies. My favorite food group."

As Ginny laughed at him, an idea floated to Faith's mind and a desperate urge to help him rose in her heart. "Why don't you join us?" Cole was in his home office and Mia was doing a shift at the VA hospital, so they wouldn't disturb anyone.

"Join you in making brownies?" He crossed his arms and looked down as if realizing his lack of clothes. "I'd need to change. And I'm a terrible cook."

"I'm teaching Ginny safety in the kitchen and the importance of following steps. You'd be supervised at all times."

He stared at her for a beat and barked out a laugh. "How can I refuse? Let me run up to the house and change. I'll meet you in a few."

She watched him walk away, admiring his body and trying to come up with ways to make him laugh again. She liked the feeling it gave her, warm and full. Drawing in a breath, she looked at Ginny. "Ready?"

They made their way past the dunes and to the back porch, where they rinsed off their feet with the exterior shower before going inside.

"What do we do first?" Faith asked.

"Wash our hands."

"Good girl. So smart."

Ginny washed her hands in the kitchen sink and Faith did the same. She had Ginny read her the ingredients needed, helping when she had trouble, and together they gathered what was required. They'd just preheated the oven when Alec strode in the back door.

"Are they done yet?"

Ginny laughed. "No."

Alec took a seat at the kitchen island.

Faith held out the box to Ginny. "What do we do next?"

Ginny read the instructions out loud, stumbling a bit, but eventually getting through. Faith helped her crack the eggs and measure out the oil and water. She let Ginny whisk until her arm got tired and then Faith took over. Batter in the pan, she waited to see what Ginny would do. Faith smiled when she remembered to put on oven mitts.

"Good job, Ginny."

While they moved around the kitchen cleaning up, she sensed Alec's gaze on her. When the mess was put to rights, she had Ginny head to her room to read for a bit. With the teenager out of listening range, Faith pulled a notebook and pen off the table and set it in front of Alec.

"You make me nervous when you watch me like that," she said.

He crossed his arms over the island and leaned into them. "Not my intention. I like to watch people, their mannerisms. Gives me ideas for characters."

The last thing she wanted was to end up as one of his characters. She shivered at the thought of how he'd translate her to paper. Yet, she wondered enough to pry. "And what did you conclude by watching me?"

A trace of a smile graced his lips as his eyes looked into hers. "You're not as shy as I thought, but I do make you nervous. I'm curious as to why. At first I thought it was that star-struck thing people always get around me, but I don't think that's it. And you're very good with Ginny."

She blinked. Her stomach fluttered at his observations and their accuracy. She focused on the Ginny comment—that was a safe topic. "It's my job to be good with her."

He was shaking his head before she even finished. "It's more than that." He pointed to the notepad in front of him and raised his brows quizzically. The light in the kitchen had made his eyes more gray than blue. A daunting shade of storm cloud.

Faith turned and grabbed the empty brownie box and set it on the island. "The notebook is for you to write down the ingredients, instructions, and nutritional content."

His amusement turned to skepticism. "Not a lot of faith in my future as a writer? Think I need to become a baker, Faith?"

Her face flamed. "It's transference. You're copying something already printed to get your mind back on the act of writing itself." Shame washed over her. What was she doing? "Will it hurt to try?"

Scratching the scruff on his jaw, he twisted his face in thought. He was so handsome it stole her breath, but he was so out of her league that she mentally slapped herself for even thinking of him that way.

After a few moments, he picked up the pen and began scribbling, gaze darting between the box and the notebook.

While he was busy, she peeked into the oven to check the brownies and hunted up some powdered sugar from the pantry. The scent of cocoa filled the kitchen and her mouth watered. She never really gave in to her sweet tooth. Her parents had instilled insanely healthy eating habits in her from birth, mostly due to Hope's illness. Even after she'd died, the routine continued. Faith never questioned it, never tempted herself.

Suddenly, a sound she couldn't decipher erupted from Alec, making her jump. He stood, tipping the stool backward. With rapid, jerking movements, he set the stool upright, put the pen down, and strode quickly out the door.

Faith stood, staring for several minutes after he left before picking up the notebook.

He had terrible penmanship. She scanned the page, reading

the copied instructions from the box until she arrived at the last line.

Eggs fell from the carton she held with her long, elegant fingers, landing in a splatter on the Mojave-tiled floor.

Well, well. That wasn't in the directions.

It was a dark and stormy night. Her golden eyes reflected off the flash of lightning, and he knew he had to have her. Alive as his slave or dead so no one else could claim her. Didn't matter. She'd be his. Tonight. She'd eluded him for too many years, trying not to dream or self-medicating in an attempt to numb her mind. Foolish. Her thin, weak frame hid beneath a black peacoat, but he knew every inch of that body. The wind caught her wavy brown hair, plastering the strands to her unremarkable pale face as she crossed the street. Closer to him.

Alec reread the paragraph for the four hundred and sixty-seventh time, but it was no use. Nothing came. That was all he'd gotten out.

Faith had done something to him earlier by making him write down those ingredients. Out of politeness, he'd complied, more amused by her tactics to help than thinking they actually would. Except they did.

For a time.

Now it was hours later, night had fallen, and all he'd jotted down was a lousy paragraph. He wondered if his editor would consider this book complete.

Scrubbing his hands over his face, he set the laptop aside and stretched his legs out in front of him. In the process, he knocked his handwritten timeline off the couch and to the floor. He bent to retrieve the pages and skimmed his notes.

The plot was to have the woman kidnapped and held throughout book one by the demon of nightmares. Her brother unearths all kinds of dark crazy while searching for her. In the rest of the trilogy, two more women are taken, one in book two and the other in book three, and the brother begins to find the childhood connection between them. Of course, he's tortured by his own nightmares. Yada, yada.

His notes on book one's female character didn't match the paragraph he punched out. Not the first time, wouldn't be the last. But he'd really veered this time around. Instead of blond locks and blue eyes with a killer figure, meant to embody innocence and desire intertwined, he'd gone and made her look just like . . .

Faith Armstrong.

He tossed the papers on the couch and laid his head back, staring at the ceiling. He'd been so intent on getting more written that he hadn't even bothered with a lamp. The illumination from his laptop cast a bluish glow. Reaching over, he wiggled the laptop so the reflective pattern moved on the ceiling. Shifted.

Like the way his Nightmare demon was supposed to.

Sitting upright, he grabbed the computer and set it on his thighs, fingers hovering over the keys. Hovering, but not typing. Hovering.

Come on, come on . . .

Fuck. He considered throwing the laptop across the room. At least he'd have an excuse for the lack of productivity.

Writer's block. How weak. He used to laugh when he heard the term from others in his circle. Alec never had a problem shutting his brain down, focusing on the story, even if it took three straight days and no sleep. Caffeine and sugar. Characters screaming in his ear. The only true escape from his guilt.

A quiet knock came from the front door. So quiet he chalked it up to nothing until it came again. A glance at his watch told him it was nine-twenty. Kind of late for a social call from Jake. Rising, he opened the door to . . .

"Faith?"

She held a plate in her hand and a wary expression. "Am I disturbing you?"

"No."

Her gaze darted behind him to the laptop on the coffee table. "I interrupted. I'm sorry." She looked at the plate in her hand and thrust it toward him. "Ginny felt bad that you didn't get any of the brownies we made."

He took the plate, grabbed her wrist, and tugged her inside before all the heat could crawl in. The brownies smelled good. Or was that her? "Yum." He shoved one in his mouth and spoke around the chocolate. "Sugar. Mmm."

"Yes, well . . ." Those golden-brown eyes of hers stared at his mouth, transfixed, before she shook her head. She glanced around, then peeked at the floor. "I should go."

He swallowed. "Why?"

"You're working." She pointed to the table.

Not wanting to corner her—because she looked cornered— he walked to the couch and sat. As an afterthought, he switched on the lamp. "I'm not working."

"But . . ."

"I was writing, thanks to you, but I seem to have stopped." He leaned forward and turned the laptop around for her to see. That got her to move deeper into the room.

She didn't look long enough to read the whole paragraph, which was just as well. She'd have to be an idiot not to see the similarities between her and his character. Most people would've chopped off an appendage to read his work before publication. Not her.

"That's good. You're writing again."

"You missed the part where I said I stopped."

"I'll go."

"I didn't stop because of you." He'd *started* because of her. "Have a brownie." He held the plate out, wiggling it like a taunt.

"I shouldn't. I'm not supposed to."

Huh. "You a diabetic?"

"Er, no."

"Allergic?"

She sighed. "No."

"Then have a brownie." She was so damn thin. Angular bones and soft skin. At least it looked soft.

She hesitated a moment and then took one off the plate, cupping her hand under it to catch the crumbs. It felt like a small victory when she took a bite.

"So, you don't usually eat brownies, don't stay awake past ten, and you've never seen the ocean until recently. What is it you *do* like to do, Faith?"

She stilled, swallowed the last bite, and avoided his gaze. "Why did you stop writing?"

"Answer my question."

"Answer mine first."

Ooh. A spark of challenge. "I guess because I can't."

"I can't either. Do those things." Her gaze lifted to his.

His question was what she liked to do, not what she couldn't, but now he was interested. "Why can't you?"

She took a page from his book and avoided answering. "Maybe you should try meditating."

Alec set the plate aside. "You mean like chanting 'ohm' while closing my eyes and going to a happy place?" He hadn't had a happy place in nine years.

This earned him a smile. "Something like that."

"You're one of those people." He fixed his expression to one of mock horror.

"What people?"

"The tree-hugging, holistic, all-natural types." He looked at her calves just below her capris. "At least you shave."

She sighed, but the smile remained. "You're very tense. Meditating might help you relax and clear your head."

He was tense? "*I'm* tense?"

Hello, pot, meet kettle.

Her smile widened, and there was something close to a

twinkle in her eye. She didn't wear any makeup, not even a swipe of lip gloss, but he found himself liking her face. It was fresh. Clean. He didn't know any women who didn't hide behind cosmetics. Or seduction. And yet Faith did neither. In fact, she always had one foot out of the room.

She stood. "Enjoy the brownies. Have a good night."

Like that. One foot out the door.

And just like she had the other night on the beach, she just up and walked away.

chapter
five

Faith was sitting on the couch in the guesthouse, staring at her cell for what had to be at least the past twenty minutes. It was Saturday, thus she was off for the weekend and left to her own devices.

It was also late morning, which meant her mother would be back from her garden club and her father would be done working in the yard. Right about now they'd be discussing what to make for lunch and if they should plan any activities for the afternoon.

A week and neither had called.

Her hands shook. She pinched her eyes closed and breathed deep, centering herself. It was just a phone call. She could do this. They were probably giving her space to settle in, not wanting to hover over her. She'd convinced herself what had happened when she'd left was just them having a hard time parting, and not wanting to be emotional in front of her. They were likely just waiting for her to reach out first.

Finding the number in her short list of contacts, she pressed Call before she could chicken out again. It rang and rang. Faith counted until eight rings went unanswered before she debated leaving a message. The answering machine kicked in and she froze. An automated greeting directed her to leave a message after the beep.

Her stomach rolled. Her hands grew clammy. Closing her eyes, she cleared her throat.

"Hi, Mom, Dad. It's . . . me. I just wanted to say hello. Nothing important. My accommodations are really nice and the ocean is beautiful." She shook her head. "I hope everything there is well. Please call if you get a chance. Thanks." She hesitated. "I love you."

She stared at the screen after disconnecting as it rang in her hand. It was them.

Dad's voice sounded distracted as usual. "So, the job is good?"

"Yes. I worked with Ginny before at St. Ambrose, so it was a smooth transition."

"Oh. Didn't know that."

She had told them before, after she accepted the position, but the knowledge obviously hadn't stuck. A lengthy, awkward silence followed and Faith hated it. Hope had been the conversationalist in the family. She'd brought out all the natural parental instincts in them. They never ran out of things to say with Hope around. But, wow. She'd been gone ten years now. Had it been that long since they had a real conversation? It was one thing to sit in the same room with them and not talk, but to sit on the phone . . .

"So, uh . . . how's the weather?"

Faith shook her head, her heart hurting. "Warm. Humid. There always seems to be a breeze off the ocean, though, so that's nice."

"Right. Right," he mumbled again after a second. "Well, don't go swimming alone. We'll talk again soon."

She dropped the phone on the couch after disconnecting.

The picture of her and Hope stared at her from the mantel, but she couldn't bring herself to look. Tears were already clogging her throat, dampening her eyes. Wrapping her arms around her middle, she bent over and forced herself to breathe through the looming panic attack. Why did her father even bother calling her back? Had he no interest in her life beyond the weather?

A knock sounded on her front door, making her jump.

Staring at the door, she wondered who it could possibly be. She was off for the weekend and had no friends in town. Not that she had friends in Charlotte either. Swallowing hard, she blinked rapidly to clear the signs of distress and went to get the door.

Lacey stood on her doorstep, looking bright and fresh in a blue sundress. Her long blond hair was down around her shoulders, half clipped up on one side. She smiled. "Hey, do you have a few minutes?"

"Sure." Faith waved her inside. "Is everything okay?"

"Oh, yes." Lacey sat on the edge of the wicker sofa and folded her hands in her lap. "We just didn't get to know each other very well the other day at lunch, so I thought I'd come by."

Well, how . . . unexpected. Nice. "Can I get you something to drink?" Except she didn't have much because she hadn't gone shopping yet. That was on the agenda for later.

"No, thank you. Sit with me?" She patted the cushion beside her. "I thought we could talk about Ginny's art class."

Relaxing a bit, Faith sat on the other side of the sofa and waited.

"I was thinking Ginny could come to my studio on Tuesdays and Fridays for a couple hours. I'd go over techniques and colors and so on. Maybe work with her on a few mediums until I figure out what she's best at."

Faith didn't want to deter Lacey, but it was entirely possible Ginny might not excel past basic fundamentals. Ginny loved art and was excited about working with Lacey, though. "If that schedule is okay with Mia, it's okay with me."

"I already talked with Mia, but wanted to run it by you. I don't want to mess with your lesson plans."

The nerves in her belly quieted. "That's very thoughtful. I can work around that."

She was actually thinking of dropping Wednesday afternoon lesson plans altogether and incorporating something like home economics. Teach Ginny laundry, cooking, cleaning. Ginny was very open to learning new things and Faith hoped to encourage more independence.

"Great." Lacey beamed. "Now, for the other reason I dropped by. Mia and I are checking out a new spa tomorrow and we wanted to invite you to come along."

"Why?" Dang it. She hadn't meant for that to come out so fast, but Lacey had surprised her. People didn't just invite her to things like that. Or to anything, really.

"It'll be fun. With the wedding coming up, I'm trying out a few salons to see who I like best. And while we're at it, we can get a mani-pedi."

Oh boy. This was so far out of her league it might as well be Saturn. "I'm not really good at that sort of thing."

"What thing?" Lacey tilted her head. Realization dawned in her eyes. "You mean the girly stuff? Don't worry about that. All you have to do is relax and have fun. They do all the work." Lacey straightened. "Do you ever wear makeup?"

"Only on special occasions. I never learned how to apply cosmetics."

"Your mom never showed you?"

She shook her head. Mom would be the last person to do such a thing, and by the time Faith was old enough for Hope to teach her, she'd been too sick. Faith's gym teacher had been the one to educate her on menstruation and sex ed.

"Well, you're pretty just as you are. I could show you a few things to bring out your natural beauty, stuff that wouldn't take a long time. And we could get our hair done, too. Maybe shape yours up a bit. You have such beautiful, thick waves."

Stunned into silence, Faith just stared. Compliments

weren't tossed her way very often, so she never knew what to do with them. She cleared her throat. "Thank you. That would be nice." And before she knew what she was saying, out came, "I'm used to being in the background. You'll have to forgive me. I'm not comfortable with a lot of attention."

Her face flamed. She turned away to stare at her hands, hoping Lacey didn't notice.

"Noted," Lacey said with a nod. She rose as if ready to leave. "I'd like us to be friends."

Friends. Another foreign concept. Perhaps this *was* Saturn. Or maybe Neptune? "Okay."

"I have a confession," Lacey said. "I don't have many friends."

Faith may have no life, she may be a plain homebody, but she didn't deserve to be made fun of. Irritation surged, until she looked into Lacey's eyes and realized she was genuine. Forget another planet. She'd entered an alternate reality.

Lacey walked over to the fireplace and fiddled with the seashells. "I spent most of my life in my mother's social circles being the belle of the ball and striving for perfection. Cole gave me the courage to break away from that and be myself. I'm still learning. Mia and I just grew close again these last few months. I'd like to get to know you better, too."

Faith had somehow found the courage to leave home and accept this job offer when everything inside her screamed for the holding pattern she was used to. Why not embrace the choice and take a chance? Otherwise she'd just *exist* here, like she did in Charlotte.

"Friends." Not a question, a statement. Something swelled in her chest as she said the word. Not altogether unpleasant.

"I'm looking forward to it." Lacey's fingers found the photo of her and Hope. "Who's this?"

A pang flicked her chest. Friends talk, right? "That's my sister, Hope."

"I thought you were an only child."

"She died just before my seventeenth birthday." Actually,

it was late into the eve of the night before that Hope's body finally gave out. Twelve-thirty-three a.m.

"Oh, how terrible. So young. Was it cancer?"

In the picture Lacey held, Hope didn't have any hair. It wasn't a far leap to assume. Faith nodded.

"I lost my oldest brother in a car accident years ago. It still hurts." Her voice was barely a whisper, and in her tone Faith heard every ache she herself had been living with.

"I'm sorry for your loss."

Lacey replaced the picture on the mantel. "I'm sorry for yours, too. She was very pretty."

Yes, she was. Everything, in fact, Faith could never be. "I spent a lot of time with her between treatments and other things. She was my whole life, so when she died, I didn't know how to make friends or be around people. I guess you and I are a lot alike in that regard." She glanced away from the avid interest in Lacey's eyes. "What time should I be ready tomorrow?"

Lacey smiled, picked up her purse off the table, and headed to the door. "Our appointment is at ten. We'll pick you up at nine-thirty."

Grateful Lacey didn't press the conversation, Faith nodded. "I'll be ready."

Alec climbed the few steps to Faith's guesthouse and lifted his hand to knock. But before he could make contact, the door swung wide and Faith stepped out. She startled and placed a hand over her heart.

"You scared me. I wasn't expecting you." Obviously. She was holding a small purse in one hand and car keys in the other. "What are you doing here?"

That question from any other person would sound accusatory. "Brought back your plate. The brownies were good."

She stared at the plate and then him. "That's a paper plate."

"Yes."

"Implying you don't need to return it."

He shrugged.

A wisp of a smile graced her lips. Her golden eyes were bright in the natural light and quite fascinating. "Still not writing?"

Busted. "It would seem so. You going somewhere?"

"Er, yes. Grocery shopping. I need a few things."

"Perfect. I'll come, too." Her brows lifted, so he elaborated. "I need to get out. I'm going crazy staring at my computer monitor."

"And you want to go shopping with me?"

Just take his Man Card now. At least it wasn't clothes shopping. "I'll drive."

She peered over his shoulder. "But my car is right there."

"Mine's more fun."

Her bow-shaped mouth opened and closed. Pouted. "Well, okay." She shut the door behind her and they stepped off the porch. "Define 'fun.'"

Alec grinned. "You'll see."

They headed through the grove in silence and crossed Lacey's yard to where he'd parked his car, in front of the guesthouse.

Faith drew up short. "You have a convertible?"

"It's a—"

"Mustang. I know." She stared at the car like she stared at the brownies—with longing. "I always wanted one."

A girl after his own heart. Most women wondered why he didn't drive a Ferrari with the money he made. He liked the American classic better, even though this was last year's remake. "Get in."

Once they were settled, he pulled the car through the security gate and onto the road. Out of the corner of his eye, he watched her tip her head back and smile. Her carefree expression made him grin. Her reddish-brown hair swirled around her face, but she made no attempt to bind it. No whining about how she'd have to fix it. She was such a contradiction from the rest of the female species.

On their way out of the subdivision, they passed a few of the other mansions nestled in the cove. The houses sat on a lot of land and were spaced pretty far apart, offering a great deal of privacy. The one closest to Lacey's property was in foreclosure. Alec remembered that house. His dad had tended the gardens there for an eccentric old broad who used to model back in the forties.

He pulled out and onto the main road, reorienting himself with where things were. Most of the shops around here were for tourists, complete with inflated prices, and not the full-on grocery store Faith was seeking. He quickly got off the main drag and weaved his way through traffic until he hit the northwestern edge of the city.

Faith didn't say a word on the drive. Just kept her head tipped toward the sun and eyes either closed or wide open and scanning her surroundings. She'd never been to the beach, he remembered. He'd have to take her around, show her some of the hot spots and happenings. Except he hadn't been in Wilmington long term in years. Perhaps he'd get Jake and Lacey, along with Cole and Mia, and they'd go out as a group.

He parked the car at a chain grocery and turned to face her, expecting a comment on his driving. She didn't offer one. Ever since Laura's accident, people—the ones who knew about Laura, anyhow—found it necessary to point out his recklessness when he got behind the wheel. He wasn't driving the car Laura crashed any more than he was an inattentive driver. Alec just craved the speed.

Faith's hair was all crazy around her head, her cheeks flushed. Without thinking, he pushed the strands off her face and smoothed them down. Then he got a whiff of her sweet scent and instead of pulling back, he let his hand settle into the softness.

Apparently it wasn't the brownies that he'd smelled the other night. It was her. Like a sugar cookie, or vanilla, or something wholesome to that effect. It made him want to bury his face in her hair and nibble his way up her neck.

"You okay?"

He blinked and dropped his hand. Cleared his throat. "Sure. You just . . . had your hair in your face. Ready?"

If possible, her cheeks grew even more pink. "Yes. Ready."

Hands shoved deep in his pockets, he followed her around the store as she added items to her cart. Wheat bread. Skim milk. Greek yogurt. Skinless chicken breasts. Broccoli, carrots, apples . . . Christ. Didn't she eat?

She bypassed the junk food aisle altogether.

"Okay, Faith. Hold up." He grabbed the end of her cart and pulled it down the aisle. Snagging a bag of potato chips, he tossed them in her cart. "Better. Let's find you some Twinkies."

"No. I'm fine."

"You're not fine. You need to eat."

She straightened. "I eat."

His lip curled as he looked in her cart. "Real food. Live a little. Buy the chips. Embrace the chips."

"I can't."

This gave him pause. "Why?"

Fumbling with the chain around her neck, she grasped the pendant and dragged it back and forth. Her gaze drifted away, light-years away, as if she was battling with herself over whether she should talk. He waited her out. He'd wait all day. Finally, she took a deep breath and leveled him with a stare.

"I only have one kidney. I watch what I eat, monitor salt intake, and avoid caffeine so I don't do any long-term damage."

Three things happened in the span of two seconds flat. He suddenly had the urge to punch his own face, draw her to his chest until he wasn't shaking anymore, and do whatever it took to wipe that expression from her features. Instead, his brain disconnected from his mouth. "Why do you only have one kidney?"

Her teeth went to work on her lower lip as she focused on his shirt. "Someone else needed it."

An elderly gentleman made his way toward them, lifted a bag of pretzels from the rack, and kept going. Alec kept his eyes on her face. This wasn't the time for this, nor was it any of his business, but hell if he was letting this drop. Call it writer's curiosity. When they were alone, he'd ask the rest.

He took the bag out of her cart and replaced the chips on the shelf. "You about done?"

"We can check out."

She spoke so softly that if he hadn't been watching her mouth, he might not have heard her. That mermaid voice that was doing funny things to him.

While she checked out, he bagged her groceries. They walked to his car, where he put the bags in the trunk. Once they were seated inside, he turned over the ignition, put the car in drive, changed his mind, and shoved the gear back into park.

"Are you dying? Is that it?"

"No." Just that. *No.* And an expression that was carefully blank.

He turned, his fingers tightening on the wheel as he stared straight ahead.

"People can live with only one kidney. I just don't take any unnecessary risks."

He had no clue why this sickening dread tore at his gut, or why her words made him want to break something. He barely knew her. He shouldn't be invested in whether she was sick or not. In honesty, she could have four hearts and six lungs, and it shouldn't matter.

"You're angry."

He put the car in drive. "I'm not."

"You are. I don't . . ." She reached out for him but quickly drew her hand away.

He pulled into traffic. "You don't what?" he asked, keeping his voice calm.

Instead of answering, she turned her head away and watched the scenery pass.

chapter
SIX

Alec strode into Jake and Lacey's house and called out for Lacey. Jake was working, but Lacey's car was in the drive. Their housekeeper came into the living room, wiping her hands on a towel.

"She's upstairs in her studio, sir."

He nodded his thanks and climbed the stairs to the third floor. Classical music droned from the speakers in the corner and Lacey, her back to him, was standing in front of a canvas.

"Knock, knock."

She turned but her usual smile was slow in coming. She walked to the iPod station and turned the music down. "Hey. Everything okay?"

No, but it wasn't her problem he couldn't shake the shit Faith had said from his mind. "I'm good. I was wondering if you'd be up for getting everyone together for a night out. Dinner, a club, something. Tonight's probably too late, but next Friday?"

"Do you mean with Cole and Mia?"

"And Faith."

Now she smiled like she meant it. "Sure. I'll talk to everyone. It'll be fun."

He nodded and turned to go, but her canvas caught his attention. Or rather, what she was painting on the canvas. "What's that?"

"Oh, come look." She wiped her hands on a cloth and handed him a printout. "I went over to Faith's earlier to invite her to join me and Mia at the spa tomorrow. She had this picture on the mantel of her and her sister. I snapped a picture with my phone."

"I thought it was just her and her folks." Wasn't that what she'd said at lunch this week? The photo was obviously taken years ago. Both girls wore big grins and hospital gowns. The other one, Faith's sister, had no hair.

"Her sister died from cancer. It must've been a while ago because that's the only photo she had out."

Cancer. That . . . sucked.

They looked like sisters. The facial shape and pouty mouth bore similarities. But where Faith's eyes were golden brown, her sister's were hazel. She also seemed to have a good four or five years on Faith,

Faith who ate only insanely healthy food, went to bed at a decent hour, and only had one kidney.

Someone else needed it.

Her sister? Alec didn't know a lot of the medical aspects of cancer treatment, but would a new kidney be a requirement? Maybe the sister had renal cancer? He shook his head.

"I thought I'd paint the two of them, but I don't know what her sister's hair looked like before she lost it all. Do you think she'll be upset I'm doing this?"

Hell if he knew, but it was a nice thing Lacey was doing. In the painting she'd started, she'd replaced the hospital gowns with regular T-shirts. Also gone was the hospital bed and the tubes and wires protruding from them both. Lacey had painted the ocean behind them instead.

Alec examined the picture more closely, wondering why Faith was connected to the equipment if she was healthy. Maybe this photo was taken when she donated the kidney. It was obviously a hard topic for Faith to discuss, as she'd changed the subject when he'd asked about her habits.

No wonder. He felt like an ass for teasing her.

He handed the printout back to Lacey. "I'm sure she'll love it. You can always ask her about the hair when you see her." If Lacey was attempting to replace the negative images by removing the hospital setting, then leaving her sister's head bald wouldn't be wise.

"I hope you're right. I don't want to upset her. I painted Cole, Dean, and I like this for Cole's living room. He loved it."

Dean being their brother who had died ten-plus years ago. It had hit Cole and Lacey very hard. Had hit everyone hard.

Lacey's painting captured Faith's smile and eyes in vivid detail. Guess her skills went beyond landscapes. "You're very good."

"You think?" She beamed a smile with all the innocence of youth, clearly not seeking compliments. Guess everyone had their insecurities. Even rich princesses.

"I do." He walked to the door. "Back to the writing cave for me."

Except when he returned to the guesthouse, intent on pounding out some words if it killed him, images of Faith with IVs and hospital gowns swam before his eyes, blending with images of Laura from years ago. The look on Faith's face when she'd explained her diet was just as haunting. He forced himself to think of the sweet smile Faith had when he drove with the top down, but that only caused more chaos in his head.

Fuck it. He scrubbed his hands over his face and retrieved

a beer from the fridge to sit out on the back deck. But he couldn't sit either. So he paced.

Eventually, the restlessness eased and he leaned against the railing. Dusk was starting its descent, taking with it some of the heavy humidity from the air. A few sailboats were still in the water off in the distance. Gulls circled overhead. Waves lapped the shore. He took it all in, hoping for a glimpse of inspiration to get words down. Anything he could hold on to with both hands.

Damn, but he couldn't shake the emptiness inside. Even as a child, he'd had fictional characters and story ideas for company. Losing that was like solitary confinement. Isolation. He was powerless. Useless.

Lost.

Glancing to his left, he caught Faith on the other side of the beach, walking toward the water. Her arms were crossed in front of her and, just as she'd done before, she watched the ocean with still composure. Everything about her resonated serenity. If not for the loneliness and longing in her eyes, he'd swear she had no emotions. He wondered how long it took her to train herself not to desire. To want. Because Faith, for some ungodly reason, appeared satisfied with being invisible. Where others pushed and fought for more—more money, more friends, more status—Faith was content, just as she was, in her little corner of the world.

Or so it seemed to him. He knew he was right, though. He'd watched people his entire life, could read them.

She pulled a phone from her pocket and stared at the screen. After several long moments, her arms fell to her sides and she plopped her butt on the sand. Still holding the phone, she brought the heels of her palms to her eyes and rocked.

He was halfway down the beach before he realized what he was doing and stopped. She hadn't come out here for comfort or company. She'd come out to be alone. Obviously something had her in tears. Tears in general he could handle. Faith in tears? Probably not.

And he was the last person who could make someone feel better. He'd proven that over and over again.

Backtracking, although he really wanted to move forward, he made his way to the guesthouse to leave her to it.

"What can I get you to drink?"

Faith looked at the glasses of champagne Mia and Lacey held, and then up at the spa attendant. Should she ask for water? Would it be rude to refuse a drink? She never indulged in alcohol, not even wine. But as long as she didn't do it in excess, one glass wouldn't hurt.

"Whatever they have is fine. Thank you."

"So." Lacey leaned back in her pedicure chair. "Alec wants to get everyone together for a night out."

Mia wiggled her toes in the footbath. "What's he have in mind?"

"Clubbing or dinner was mentioned. What do you think?"

Faith didn't realize Lacey was talking to her until no one answered. "Oh. Sure. I can watch Ginny for you while you guys go out."

Lacey laughed. "We meant for you to join us."

Her chest swelled a little at the offer, but . . . "Oh, well . . . I'm not sure."

Alec was a bigwig author from New York, used to brushing elbows with the rich and famous. Clubbing was probably a nightly thing for him. Lacey and Cole were upper-crust elite. Martinis and caviar kind of people. Mia, though from an impoverished childhood, had settled into her new, comfortable life here. But Faith would never fit in.

"Faith's got a point. We'd have no one to watch Ginny."

Lacey mulled that over. "Would Bea do it? Ginny knows her."

Faith didn't know how long the Covingtons had employed Bea as their housekeeper, but Ginny did seem very comfortable with the young woman. She was also a hard worker and very responsible.

Mia tipped her head to the side. "Perhaps. I'd hate to ask her to stay after she's worked all day. Plus, if Cole and I are going to take that trip, I don't want to upset Ginny by leaving her with a sitter, even for just a few hours."

"I'll stay with Ginny," Faith said again, hoping they'd take her up on the offer.

"No, no." Lacey took a sip of champagne. "You have to come. We'll just have to do something Ginny can participate in."

The attendants came back and towel-dried their feet. Awkwardness caused Faith to squirm in her seat. She had never had a pedicure before. Seemed like a waste of money. But then the attendant started rubbing lotion into her feet, massaging her soles, and she had to bite back a moan. Okay, this wasn't so bad.

"We could do the pier," Mia suggested.

"Good idea. They have games and the Ferris wheel." Lacey pulled her phone out of her purse. "What's your number, Faith?"

Faith rattled it off.

Moments later a text chimed. Faith dug her cell out of her pocket, seeing that Lacey had added her to a chat with Mia, Cole, Jake, and Alec.

Lacey: How's the pier for next Friday sound? We can bring Ginny.

Jake: Works for me.

Cole: Sure. Mia? This okay?

Mia: Yes. I expect popcorn and prizes.

Jake: lol

Alec: I'm in, too. Faith, you comin'?

She knew she was wearing a stupid grin, but couldn't help it. They wanted her to join them. Were including her. Alec specifically called her out. Plus, the pier was something she could do without feeling like the oddball. She thumbed out a response.

I'll be there.

Lacey: Good. It's settled. 7? Hey, Jake. I'm getting my toenails painted a naughty shade of red.

Alec: And on that note, I'm out. Bye.

Mia laughed from the next seat. "What color are you getting, Faith?"

"I don't know." A "naughty shade of red" didn't suit her personality. Was nail polish supposed to match your personality? She glanced at the selections in the tray. There was a light iridescent blue that drew her. "This one."

"I like that color." Mia peeked at Lacey, who was still texting away. Her gaze settled back on Faith. "It took me a while to get used to all this, too," she whispered. "I grew up wondering what Ginny and I were going to eat from one day to the next. But Cole and Lacey aren't the flaunt-their-money type. They both donate to charity. And Alec and Jake came from a blue-collar family. I don't want you to feel uncomfortable around us."

These people had barely known her a week and had already accepted her into their group. Meanwhile, her parents hadn't initiated a conversation once. Faith took a sip of champagne to clear the lump in her throat. The bubbles tickled going down and caused a warmth in her belly.

"Thanks, Mia."

Her cell chimed. Seeing Alec's name on her phone shouldn't make her heart pound and her stomach flutter. Yet it did.

Alec: What color polish are you getting?

She laughed at the absurd question and typed out her response.

Blue.

Alec: Like your ocean. Catch you tomorrow.

She bit the inside of her cheek. *Her ocean.* What did he mean by that?

"Is there something going on between you and Alec?"

Faith's head whipped up to find Mia staring at her, amusement crinkling her eyes.

"With Alec? No."

"Uh-huh. That's why you're smiling?"

Was she? Oh boy. "I've been trying to help him with his writer's block. That's all."

The acrid scent of polish filled her nose as the attendant began painting her nails. The color was nearly sheer, hinting at a bluish color rather than throwing it in her face. She liked the look it gave her feet when she moved, the way it caught the light.

"You know it would be okay if something *was* going on with Alec. He's pretty sexy, if you ask me. A nice guy, too."

As if Alec Winston, a bestselling author who was too handsome for his own good, would be interested in her. Even if the sky fell and it were to happen, how could that possibly last? He'd be going back to New York in a couple months.

Faith shook her head. Why was she even thinking like this?

Lacey put her phone away and examined her feet. "Cute." She swiveled to face Faith. "You ready for that haircut?"

By the time Faith settled into bed that night with a book and a cup of steaming chamomile, she had a slightly shorter haircut with layers, toenail polish she couldn't stop admiring the look of, and five new contacts in her phone.

And plans for Friday night.

chapter
seven

Alec gave it three days, but not one syllable had been added to his book. He was going loonier than the characters he wrote about. Or used to write about. He'd held off visiting Faith so far, not wanting to delve into her being the reason why he got that one and only paragraph out in the first place.

But it *was* because of her. She'd done . . . something to get the words to click in his brain again, even if for just a short time.

And he liked her. Awkward, reserved, quiet Faith. She wasn't anything like his typical girlfriends, or anything like anyone he knew. She didn't swoon over him or demand his time. It was oddly refreshing. Perhaps that explained his interest—his curiosity mixed with the puzzle of her. The creative side of him would be drawn to someone like Faith, if for no other reason than to figure her out.

Maybe she could fix him again. He shut down his laptop and headed out into the heat, not above begging at this point.

A storm was brewing to the west, the air heavy and

ominous. Dark clouds split the sky and were heading toward the coastline fast. He'd give it another hour max before it hit.

The housekeeper let him in and ushered him to the living room, where Ginny was reading to Mia. Faith sat in a corner chair, making notes of some kind in a binder. She'd done something different with her hair. Not a drastic change. Subtle. Instead of the soft reddish-brown waves brushing her shoulders, they hovered just above, looking fuller as they framed her face.

Christ. He was noticing her hair now.

Mia glanced up. "Alec, what a great surprise. Right, Ginny?"

Ginny nodded and started jabbering about the book she was reading. Apparently she'd grown an interest in ghost stories since he'd arrived in town. He was so amused by her chatter he almost missed Faith's attempted exit.

"Where're you off to?"

She glanced at the binder in her hand. "I was going to go work in the kitchen. You know, let you guys visit."

It was like she was conditioned to be invisible. That irritated him to no end and made him want to find out why. Instead, he drew in air slowly to ebb the aggravation before speaking. "I came to see you, actually."

"Oh."

Her favorite word. *Oh*. Always surprised by any positive attention. "Writing stuff. I could use your help."

Why that made her shoulders relax, he didn't know. "Sure. Ginny and I were just about to start a batch of cookies. Would you like to join us? Is that all right, Mia?"

Mia closed the book and smiled. "Of course it's okay. You don't even have to ask."

Ginny jumped off the sofa and circled Alec. "Yeah. Help us."

He laughed. "Will I get to eat any of these said cookies?"

"*Yesss*," Ginny dragged out her answer with an eye roll for emphasis.

"Well, then. Lead the way."

Mia gave Faith a knowing look. "I'll be upstairs if you need me."

Left in the doorway alone for a second, he turned to Faith. "What was that look about?"

She shook her head. "Nothing. Come on. Let's load you up on sugar." She headed down the hallway.

"Fine, distract me with cookies, but you'll only make me more curious. You women have this ESP communication thing that could bury NASA in research for—"

She sighed and halted. "Mia thinks something's going on between us." She paused, then added, "NASA doesn't need to be informed."

Ha. Humor. He liked that. First, time to backtrack. "What does she think is going on?" Apparently he wasn't above playing coy either.

One eyebrow lifted as her lips twisted in the cutest *Oh, please* expression. "You're a writer. Figure it out."

"I'm not a romance writer."

They neared the end of the hallway. "Yet you managed to catch on, all on your own."

She had spunk buried under all that stoicism. The first stirrings of attraction started to pull in his gut. Okay, maybe not the first. "Why does this upset you?" He followed her into the kitchen.

She stuck her head in the fridge. "Because nothing *is* going on."

He should really, *really* just let this go. Somewhere in the back of his mind, he knew this. "Why does it bother you if people think there is?"

She went oddly quiet, setting two sticks of butter and a carton of eggs on the island.

"You're not going to answer me, Faith?" The tone of his voice held a challenge, but damn, his temple was starting to throb in frustration.

What was wrong with the possibility of something brewing between them? Sure, they were a bizarre mix, and it wasn't likely they'd immediately shift into romance mode. Tearing off clothes and panting . . .

And yet, stranger things had happened.

He drew in a breath. Gave himself a mental slap. He couldn't have her. Faith was more than a one-night gal, and he couldn't have anyone for longer than that.

Because he was already taken.

"I—" Faith's gaze darted to the corner and widened. "Ginny, you ready to make cookies?"

Alec hadn't seen Ginny at the table when they entered, being too engrossed in sparring with Faith. Ginny was watching them with round eyes but looked no worse for wear.

Faith pulled out a cookbook and paged through it as if the conversation never existed. "Read the ingredients and tell me what we need," she said with utmost patience to Ginny. She leveled her golden eyes on him. "You said you needed help with your writing. What can I do?"

Was he insane for thinking he'd rather find out why the thought of being with him put her in a funk?

He cleared his throat. "You did some kind of juju to help me write last time. I need you to do it again. I haven't gotten past the first paragraph."

Slowly, she nodded. Something close to disappointment filled her eyes before she blinked it away. She directed Ginny to the pantry to gather items and set a notebook in front of him. "Write down every move Ginny and I make."

The idea was as stupid as copying the contents from the brownie box, but he pulled up a stool and grabbed a pen. Outside, the storm had hit their area. Rain splattered the windows and thunder rolled in the distance. He loved the smell of rain.

As if he wasn't there, Faith patiently directed Ginny through the steps of making chocolate chip cookies. He absorbed her lilting mermaid voice, let it wash over him, until his strained muscles relaxed and his head cleared. The pen scratched the paper as he wrote their procedures, throwing in a random thought here and there to make things more interesting.

By the time they'd put the first batch in the oven, he didn't know how much time had passed or what he'd even written.

Faith leaned over the island to glance at his notebook. "Looks like you're doing just fine to me."

He focused on the paper instead of her sugary scent. There were three pages of scribbles. Scribbles that had nothing to do with Ginny or cookies or the Covington kitchen. Instead, scattered fragments of sentences penned the page.

The air seeped from his lungs. Without thinking, he stood, leaned over the island, cupped Faith's cheeks, and smacked a big one right on her mouth. He barely registered her wide eyes. Grabbing the notebook, he ran to the door.

"I owe you, Faith!"

He was off the back deck and jogging toward the dunes when her voice drifted to him. "But it's raining."

Ginny was having a difficult time concentrating on her math equations. Faith had tried redirecting her and making it fun, but it was useless. The teenager's gaze kept wandering around the kitchen. Ginny didn't have the best attention span, but it was typically better than this.

"What's wrong, Ginny?"

Ginny shrugged.

Faith took a page out of Mia's book and said, "Talk to me."

Ginny let out an exaggerated sigh. "Alec didn't like my cookies."

Faith drew in a deep breath and tried to figure out how to explain the thought process of authors when she didn't have a clue herself. Alec had run out into the rain yesterday after some kind of epiphany.

And he had kissed her.

It was gratitude, nothing more. A spur of the moment, entirely unsexual . . . kiss.

So why couldn't she quit thinking about it?

Ginny rocked in her chair, a comfort measure Faith had seen before. Poor Ginny thought her cookies tasted bad and took Alec's sudden exit as a direct hit.

"I think he was in a hurry to get home before it rained and he forgot. Would it make you feel better if we took some over to him?"

"Yeah!"

Faith patted her hand. "Okay, but we have to finish your math when we get back."

Ginny arranged some cookies on a paper plate and Faith covered it with plastic wrap. They went out the front door so they didn't drag any sand in with them upon returning and made the trek through the grove.

Nerves fluttered in Faith's belly at the thought of seeing him again. It was silly. Childish. Their conversation yesterday ran through her head, including his confusion about why she was upset over Mia's theory of something going on between them.

Faith wasn't immune to passion. She wasn't a virgin, either, but she didn't have the experience that Alec would no doubt be used to in women. Her only true familiarity with actual sex had been with a classmate in college. They'd been in the same study group and he'd asked her out during one late-night session. After a month, she'd just wanted the deed over with, and had let him do his thing. It had hurt. A lot. They'd done it a handful of times after that, but the guy had been unnerved by taking her virginity and broken up with her a few weeks later. At the time, she'd been too relieved to care. Not knowing what to do with her hands or how to turn him on had caused her brain to go into overload and prevented her from enjoying the act. She'd had a few boyfriends since, a few close calls and heavy petting. Nothing long term, and nothing that lit a fire deep within.

Nothing like what Alec Winston was beginning to make her feel. Just thinking about him made her face heat and her

stomach clench with want. He was so, so far out of her league.
If they were to cross that line as more than acquaintances,
he'd be disappointed in her lack of skill, perhaps even pity
her. Just like all the others. She'd gone her whole twenty-seven
years without a broken heart. No sense in opening herself to
one now.

Nothing would happen between them. It was dangerous
to think like this. She knew better than to even daydream.
Almost from birth she'd known her place in life. She didn't
invoke fire and passion and fantasies. She didn't even invoke
much interest as a friend. Or daughter.

Ginny knocked on Alec's door and Faith took an uneven
breath to calm down, pulling herself from her dreary thoughts.

The door swung wide to show Alec standing before her
in a fitted black tee and plaid boxer shorts. His black hair
stood up at odd angles, as if he'd fisted his hands in the
strands. Redness rimmed his eyes, indicating he hadn't slept.
Confusion marred his brow until he lifted a finger and pointed
at Faith. "You!" He grabbed her wrist and tugged her inside.
"Take a look at this."

He dragged her over to the coffee table and pressed on
her shoulder until she dropped on the couch. Gesturing to
the laptop, he said, "Eighty-five pages. That's roughly
twenty-two thousand words. All thanks to you."

He'd started writing again. Her heartbeat tripped behind
her ribs. *Congratulations* was on the tip of her tongue, but
Ginny made a noise from the doorway and distracted her.

Ginny's round eyes looked back and forth between them.
Finally, her gaze landed on Alec. "Are you mad?"

"No." His gentle voice contradicted the energy emanating
off him. "No, Ginny. I'm not mad at all. I'm just a little excited.
I'm—are those cookies?"

Ginny seemed hesitant, but passed him the plate. "You
didn't get any."

"You are my favorite person." He made a show of biting
into a cookie and moaning. "Best cookies I ever had."

Ginny beamed and clapped her hands. "Yay. Faith! Faith! He likes them."

In the span of five seconds, Alec had Faith's utmost respect and deep appreciation. Tears welled in her eyes. How a person treated the mentally handicapped, animals, and elderly said a lot about their character. Alec not only soothed Ginny, he complimented her and distracted her from why she'd grown upset. Above all, it clearly came naturally to him.

Faith bit her tongue and blinked rapidly so she didn't embarrass herself. "I told you he'd like them."

"I don't like them. I love them."

Oh boy. Time to go before she melted into a puddle at his feet. "Come on, Ginny. Back to math."

Ginny pouted and waved good-bye.

Alec's gaze followed Faith, his mouth twisting mid-chew. "Thanks, Faith. I mean it."

She nodded because she didn't think she could talk.

When they made their way back into the Covington house, Cole was leaning against the kitchen counter, reading a stack of papers and eating a cookie. "Don't tell Mia." He saluted them with the last bite and shoved it in his mouth.

Mia chose that moment to come downstairs. "Don't tell me what? That you're eating cookies again?"

Cole frowned. "But they're good."

Ginny giggled.

Faith sat at the table and waited for them to finish chatting before refocusing Ginny on her lesson. Mia had Cole on a high-protein diet, rich with fruits and vegetables, because of his injuries from when he was in the military. Cole abided by the diet, most of the time, and his leg cramps from his thigh wound were better for it. Mia also made him work out in the home gym every morning.

Faith watched them together, this mismatched family who loved each other so much. Cole was always touching Mia, smiling at Ginny. Mia put her sister above everything else, but never let a day go by without letting Cole know he was her true love, whether through words or subtle actions. They laughed and smiled and spent time together. Touched, hugged, and kissed.

Longing pulled at her chest. She wanted just a piece of that for a day. An hour, even. Some days she missed Hope so much it hurt.

Mia snatched a cookie out of Cole's hand. "Have you thought about the trip, Ginny? How do you feel about us leaving for just a little while?"

Cole and Mia were supposed to be flying out on Monday, yet the contingency plan was to take Ginny along if she still appeared uncertain.

Ginny shrugged, her posture relaxed. "Okay."

"Really, pretty girl? Are you sure?"

"Yeah."

Mia patted her chest and sighed. She pulled Ginny in for a hug. "I'm so proud of you. You'll have so much fun while we're gone, you won't even miss us."

"Can I have a party?"

Cole laughed and covered it with a cough. "A party, huh? What kind of party?"

"A slumber party." Ginny nodded emphatically. "With Lacey and Faith. Can I?"

Mia grinned. "Great idea. How about you and I make supersecret invitations this afternoon?"

chapter
eight

Alec parked the car next to Cole's in the pier's lot and turned to Faith. "You're going to love this. Jake and I used to come down here as kids. Ready?"

"Yes." Her stomach twisted and coiled, from excitement or nerves, she wasn't sure.

Ginny bounced in the backseat. "I'm ready."

Faith laughed. "Come on, then. Just stay close, sweetie. It looks like it's pretty crowded."

They exited the car and several scents accosted her at once. The salt from the ocean. Popcorn. Grilling meat. Roasted corn. Rain-drenched grass.

Ginny came up beside her and stared. "It's so cool!"

It was pretty awesome. Against the fading sun, three massive piers jutted out over the ocean. The one on the left held a twenty-story-tall Ferris wheel. Food vendors lined both sides of the one in the center, and the one to the right had carnival games inside small tents. The beach in front of the piers was crowded with people sitting in the sand or at picnic tables. A DJ played music from a stage behind the dunes.

She looked at Alec only to find him staring at her feet. A muscle ticked in his jaw.

"What's wrong?" she asked.

"Forgot you said you painted your toenails. It's a turn-on."

She looked down at her toes peeking out of her flip-flops, polished the pretty iridescent blue. A turn-on? Alec couldn't possibly be flirting with her, could he? He really knew how to shut a girl up. Or knock her over. He drew his gaze away from her feet and out over the piers, while she fought to control her breathing.

"It's busy," Alec remarked when the others came up beside them.

Cole grunted. "Tourist season."

Mia gave Cole a worried look that Faith pretended not to notice. After his injury, he didn't go out in public often, and when he did, he hid the scars on his shoulder and neck. Tonight he'd worn a polo shirt, which covered most of the scars. Cole smiled and winked at Mia, letting her know he was fine. Faith pretended not to notice that, too. She'd never had that kind of unspoken bond with anyone, not even Hope.

She trailed behind the others as they made their way across the grass and to the beach. Alec fell in step beside her, watching her from the corner of his eye.

"If I buy you popcorn, will you eat it?"

Why wouldn't her stomach calm down? "You don't have to buy me popcorn."

"I don't have to do anything besides breathe and pay taxes. I want to do it."

She fought a smile. "Yes, I'll eat popcorn if you buy some. Thank you."

"You're welcome."

Ginny wanted games first, so they headed in that direction. Jake found a tent that had a ball toss, and they stopped so he could attempt to win a stuffed animal for Lacey. On his third attempt to knock down the pyramid of bottles, Faith sought a nearby bench and sat, figuring he'd be at it a while. Lacey clung to Jake's arm, doing everything in her power to distract him. Ginny clapped and cheered him on, while Mia and Cole were involved in their own conversation.

Faith found herself laughing when Jake finally earned enough tickets to get a small stuffed animal. A dolphin, it looked like. It may as well have been roses the way Lacey responded, pulling him in for a kiss.

"Looks like you're a people-watcher, too." Alec sat next to her and handed over a bag of popcorn. "I can sit for hours, observing, imagining."

"Imagining what?" She took a bite of popcorn, letting the salt and oil melt onto her tongue. If she had a weakness, popcorn was it. Usually she just air-popped some for herself at home. This was divine by comparison. She had to bite back a moan.

The others moved one tent over so Ginny could shoot water through a pine-board cutout of a clown's mouth.

"I imagine everything. What encompasses their lives, who they go home to, their fears, desires. I get the best ideas watching people. Sometimes I just make up stuff and go with it."

"What kinds of things do you make up? Like stories?"

She tore her gaze away from Ginny and looked at Alec. Big mistake. His black hair ruffled in the breeze, sending a scent of something purely male in her direction. One corner of his mouth tilted up in a half smile, making her pulse trip. His gray-blue eyes steadily took in her face, lingering on her mouth, before he sucked in a breath and looked away.

He cleared his throat. "Take those two over there." He nudged his chin in the direction of a couple holding hands outside of a tent. "Her hairstyle is seriously outdated and so are her clothes. So she's either stuck in 1985, or . . ."

Faith took his bait and settled her gaze back on him. "Or what?"

"Or she was abducted by an invasive alien life-form and just now returned to earth. Her husband missed her terribly and is happy to have her back, thus he doesn't mention her archaic fashion sense. He was a fan of the eighties anyway. He knows the words to every Cyndi Lauper song released."

"Very interesting." A smile tugged at her mouth as she tilted her head. She couldn't, for the life of her, figure him out. Sometimes he looked lost and desperate. Then at other times, like now, he was charming and funny. It threw her off balance.

"You try."

"Me?" she squeaked.

"Yes, you." His voice dipped into a teasing timbre that sent shivers down her spine and caused her face to heat. "Give those two a try."

She glanced in the direction he was indicating. A young teenager stood beside her father eating an ice-cream cone a few feet away. "He's recently widowed or divorced. She's a sullen teenager who wants to be close to him but it's not cool, so she pushes him away."

When Alec didn't respond, she dared a glance his way.

He closed his mouth. "Okay, not to point this out, but you missed the humor mark." He glanced at the father and daughter, who were now walking away. "What gave you that idea about them?"

Alec appeared more intrigued than irritated, so she shrugged. "The father had an indentation on the ring finger of his left hand, like he'd recently removed a wedding band. It also looked like it hurt him to smile. The daughter caught herself laughing a few times at something he said, but she quickly looked around afterward to see if anyone saw her."

His eyes narrowed and his mouth quirked into a smile. "You're like that *Monk* detective on TV. Or *Psych*. I'm not afraid to admit I fear what you see when you look at me."

Before she could respond, Ginny ran over. "Can we go on the Ferris wheel now?"

The others were waiting for them at the end of the pier. Shoot. Faith hadn't meant to hold them up. She'd been so wrapped up in Alec and his little game that she'd paid no attention to the group. Jumping to her feet, she wrapped an arm around Ginny in a brief apology before making her way to the beach.

"Slow down, Faith," Alec said. "They're not going to ostracize you for talking to me."

"I shouldn't have made them wait," she called over her shoulder, not reducing her brisk pace until she hit the end of the pier.

"Hold up." Alec grabbed her wrist. "We'll meet you by the Ferris wheel," he said to Jake. "Save us a place in line." Over her shoulder, he watched until they were gone and then focused his attention on her. "Why do you do that? Half the time you attempt to be invisible and the other half is spent trying to measure up. They're not looking for perfection, Faith. Just friendship. Just you, as you are."

She stilled. It was too much. *He* was too much.

Just as you are.

Didn't he know how hard those . . . nice things were to hear?

She couldn't draw in air. The edges of her vision grayed as her heart rate accelerated. The *thump, thump* against her temple droned out the noise of the pier. She swayed, the sand beneath her unstable.

"Christ, breathe." Alec cupped her cheeks and forced her to look at him. "Breathe, Faith. You're freaking me out."

The panicked edge in his eyes brought her back, combined with his warm palms against her cheeks, his scent of soap with a trace of . . . sandalwood? Somehow the brink of black nothingness eased away and it was just her and him. The center of her chest ached as she gasped in air.

He dropped his hands and took a step back.

People were staring.

"I'm . . . I'm sorry. Let's just go."

His gaze was penetrating. It stripped her bare and left her embarrassingly wanting. He missed nothing, not a single aspect of her face.

After a moment, his jaw clenched. "Were you abused? Did someone hurt you before?" The last words were spoken in a growl that raised the hair on her arm.

"No."

She wanted to say more, to explain how new this all was, but her mouth wouldn't work. He'd see her differently. They all would. She'd be no one again. They'd only known each other a couple of weeks, but already she was more secure with herself, branching out and taking chances.

But they didn't know her, these people. She kept the scars hidden for a reason. Really, who wanted to be friends with someone who'd never had any?

How foolish to think anything would be different just because she'd changed locations.

Because he was still staring at her with that silent, invasive expression, she sucked in a breath and straightened. "They're waiting for us."

"I really want to shake you right now." He took a step closer. "I don't mean that as a threat. I'm just stating fact. I really want to shake some sense into you. There's something not clicking between here—" he lifted his hand and traced a line with his finger from her heart up to her temple "—to here," he finished.

It wasn't the first time someone had called her cold and detached, but somehow, coming from Alec, it hurt so much more.

"I do have feelings, you know," she whispered, needing him to understand at least that much. Tears burned her eyes.

She turned to head toward the Ferris wheel, but really she just wanted to go home and crawl into bed.

"I never said you didn't have feelings. I'm saying you're afraid of the good stuff."

Afraid of good stuff and not recognizing it were two

separate things. This conversation was done. She wasn't going to goad him by revealing her pathetic attempt at starting to live.

They walked the rest of the way in tense silence, meeting up with the others near the front of the line.

Ginny clapped. "Look, Faith. It's so big."

Faith looked up at the towering, spinning wheel, lit against the night sky. Her mouth dried out. She had a sinking suspicion she was afraid of heights. "Yeah. Maybe I'll stay down here, keep the numbers even."

Cole laughed. "Nice try. I'm afraid of heights, too. Mia's going up with Ginny."

Alec said nothing but she could feel his gaze on her.

Before she could think too hard or protest, it was their turn. Someone who smelled like cigars pulled a bar down over her lap after she sat in the bucket-like seat. Alec's thigh brushed hers in the intimate space. Then the ride moved.

She pinched her eyes closed. "Oh boy."

Alec laughed. "Relax. You're safe."

At the top—*the top*—the ride halted. "Why are we stopped?"

"They're letting more people on and off. It'll start again soon." He covered her hand with his over the safety bar. "Look at the view, Faith. Open your eyes."

Blowing out a ragged breath, she slowly did as instructed. And stopped breathing again. Miles and miles of black ocean spanned the horizon. The waves were lit by moonlight, the stars a picture-perfect backdrop. It was amazing.

"You know a great way to calm down when you're nervous?"

She turned her head and gasped.

Their faces were so close that his hot, shallow breath fanned her cheek. His gaze darted between her mouth and her eyes. The gray blue of his irises was almost swallowed by his dilated pupils, his lids at half-mast in the most lazy, seductive trance.

Heat filled her core. Spread. The solid muscle of his shoulder and bicep pressed against her arm, and even through their shirts, the touch was intense. She followed his cue and looked at his mouth. Firm, full lips with more of a reddish hue than most men. She wanted him to close the distance so bad she nearly begged.

When was the last time she'd been kissed?

Forget that. He had asked her something. A way not to be nervous? "How . . ."

"Distraction is the key."

He growled, low in his throat. Closer he inched, until his lips caressed hers. A barely there meeting of mouths that sparked an inferno inside her. Slowly, his gaze still pinned to hers, he brushed his lips over hers, side to side, as if trying to get a feel for her.

"You're an old soul, aren't you, Faith?" he asked against her mouth.

She shivered. Her mind was a muddled mess. She wasn't even sure she'd heard him right, or what being an old soul had to do with kissing her. And he needed to. Kiss her. Strange yet not unpleasant sensations took over her body. Her hands trembled, he stomach fluttered, her face heated, and her skin prickled in anticipation of what he'd do next.

Then the ride moved and she yelped. The feeling of falling abruptly cleared her head.

He pulled away until nothing but their thighs touched once more. Surprise was etched into his eyes, in the way his mouth hung slightly open. A second later, regret moved over his features.

A kiss, or an almost kiss, shouldn't make him feel regret. Unless . . .

Unless he was embarrassed by her.

He swiped a hand down his face and turned straight ahead, the wind whipping his hair into chaos. "Let's just stick with the view."

*   *   *

Alec hovered between loathing and self-contempt on the walk back to their vehicles. Attraction was one thing, acting on it was another. After Laura, he'd had his share of partners. But Faith wasn't some one-nighter or random hookup like those he'd gotten lost in back in New York. A woman like her played by a different set of rules. Like the forever kind. For the past nine years, he'd avoided her type.

He had no business making a play for her. No matter how soothing her voice was to his soul or how adorable he found her freckles or how amazing those honey-brown eyes looked when she stared at him. She smelled so damn good, too. Vanilla and sugar. It made him want to see if she tasted just as decadent.

Christ, he'd kissed her. Pretty much had until he remembered who he was and reined it back.

What the fuck was up with this strange urge to protect her, too? He couldn't even protect himself. Yet, like a puppet on a string, she pulled him into her orbit. Between her odd reactions to basic situations and her sweet temperament, he had this uncanny desire to know her. And not on the aloof level he kept most people. Okay, all people . . . except Jake.

Something was definitely off about Faith. At first, he had chalked it up to timidity or a discomfort with attention. But she didn't just hate attention—she flat out didn't know what to do with it. After tonight, he knew this went way beyond a simple explanation and straight into he-should-mind-his-own-business territory.

Everything about her warranted this barbaric need to defend. Or save. He didn't do that, either. He wasn't the hero in his books. He was the villain.

The chatter from the rest of the group came to a swift halt as they neared the parking lot. One look in the direction they were staring told him why.

At least twenty reporters hovered on the edge of the grounds.

Well, shit. So much for a little R & R.

"Are they here for you or me?" Cole asked him, sounding just about as elated as Alec felt. The media followed Cole, too—between his memoir hitting the bestseller list and growing up in a rich, political family, he had his share of notoriety.

Judging by the Goth clothing of a few of the people standing near the press and the fact that Alec recognized one of the reporters from New York, he guessed it was him they were after. "Me. Can you fit everyone in your car?"

Cole nodded. "Sure."

"Give me a few minutes. I'll circle around from the other direction and draw them away. You can get out without being noticed."

"What do they want?" Faith asked, her gaze trained on the reporters.

"What don't they want?" He turned to leave, but she stopped him.

"You don't want someone to go with you?"

Rotating back to face her, he almost laughed. Right about now, any other female he'd associated himself with would be checking her hair or fixing her complexion in a compact before supergluing herself to his side for her five seconds of fame. Not Faith. She was ready to stand next to him in silent support of a man she'd known all of two weeks. Because that was the kind of person she was. A fixer. Nice.

The press would eat her alive. They'd be drawn to her quicker than the pop star he'd dated last year for all of three days. Not because she was glamorous or gorgeous. Because she was ordinary. They'd sense something different about her and sink their teeth in.

"I'm fine. Head back to the house with Cole."

Wasting no time, he circled the dunes and made a show

of pulling out his keys when he emerged from the grass. The media honed in like a swarm, as expected. Alec made sure Cole's car got out of the lot before he signed a couple T-shirts, and drove home.

He decided to have a talk with Faith tonight. Set things straight between them before anyone got involved or feelings got hurt. But the lights in the Covington guesthouse were off when he drove past, and damn if disappointment didn't fill his chest at not getting a chance to see her again. He wondered who he was pacifying with this plan.

He checked his rearview mirror to make sure he wasn't followed before driving through the security gate and was satisfied no one was there. When he parked at Lacey's guest-house, Jake was sitting on the porch stairs waiting, shoulders hunched and head bowed.

A punch of worry hit Alec in the gut as he climbed out of the car. "What's wrong?"

Jake shrugged, the hapless gesture belying his expression. "Nothing. Just wanted to talk."

Alec walked up to the base of the steps and leaned a hip on the rail. "About what?"

"This thing with Faith. How serious is it?" Jake swiped the back of his neck.

Crickets and cicadas chirped in the distance as Alec studied his brother's face, wondering where the interest came from. A hundred different women had been pictured with him in magazines and literary blogs. Jake had never asked about any of them. "I've known her a couple weeks. It's not serious and nothing's going on."

"Lacey and I were behind you on that Ferris wheel. I saw you together. There was something. We've never lied to each other."

Alec shoved his hands in his pockets. Guilt tore at his gut. "Fine. Something's going on, but it's all on my end. I don't plan on acting on it. Again. Why, Jake? You trying to warn me off her?"

A rare flash of anger flared in his brother's eyes before he dialed it back. "She'd be good for you. Maybe you should see where it leads."

Alec snorted. "But?"

Jake took his time standing. "Does she know about Laura?"

His molars gnashed. "You know she doesn't." No one except the immediate family knew. They kept it that way for a reason. Jake understood the rationale behind the decision as well as he did. Nearly ten years and Jake had never brought up Laura's name. Why the hell was he doing it now? "Is there a point to this, little brother? If not, I'm tired."

"How long are you going to blame yourself? Don't you think it's time to move on? Faith isn't like the others. She's not a distraction."

"Which is exactly why I won't be getting involved." Alec climbed the porch steps.

"Alec . . ."

"Good night, Jake." He kicked the door shut behind him.

chapter
nine

Alec sighed and stared down at his cell. He'd managed to avoid Faith for two days, but Cole's text would make that difficult to keep up.

> About to board the plane to Cozumel. Mia is a mess. Can you keep an eye on Ginny and Faith while Jake is working? Just pop in once in a while. Thanks, man.

Jake's text followed two minutes later.

> Mom asked about you again. Go visit.

He scrubbed his hands over his face and rested the back of his head on the chair. He'd written nothing new for his book, guilt clawed at his stomach for how he'd handled Jake the other night, and he wanted to see Faith more than he wanted his next cup of coffee. He'd rationalized this desire with her ability to get him to write, but yeah . . .

He wanted to finish that kiss. He wanted to follow Jake's advice and see where things led. He wanted his head back in the book. But none of those things were happening, so he got dressed and headed to his parents' cozy ranch house in a suburb near the county line.

His memories of the house weren't unpleasant. Their yard was still the most beautiful, manicured one on the street. Even though Dad was retired, the landscaper in him still sought perfection. Holly berry bushes lined the front walk from the driveway to the front stoop. Lilies and dahlias mingled in a couple flower beds. Geraniums and marigolds in potted baskets hung from the fascia. There wasn't a dandelion in sight. Even the white aluminum siding was pristine.

His mother never had that kind of precision, except in the kitchen. If it involved baked goodness, she was an expert. But she was too even-tempered to be anything but pleasant. When Dad harped on Alec for staring off into space, making up a poorly fabricated story to get out of trouble, or failing math, it had been Mom who came to his rescue.

He'd come back home at Christmas. Before that, it had been a little more than a year since he'd seen them. Plenty of time for his dad to come up with some new teasing quips about his chosen profession. Millions of fans worldwide, and he couldn't get his own dad to read one of his books.

The screen door slammed shut with a clap, and he looked up to find his mom's warm smile. Her blond hair was cut in a shorter bob since he'd seen her last and she'd rounded out some.

"You're home." She opened her arms, wiggling her fingers when he didn't step forward right away.

He closed the distance and accepted her embrace, bending nearly in half to stoop to her height. She still smelled like flour. "I missed you."

"I missed you, too. Come inside. How long are you staying in Wilmington?"

"Until Jake ties the knot."

Her grin was something special and drowning in delight. "Can you believe it? I'm so excited."

"I never would've guessed."

He followed her through the foyer and toward the back of the house, breathing in the familiar scent of lemon dusting spray. He stopped short at the sight of Dad at the kitchen table, reading the newspaper. It was rare growing up to find him anywhere but the yard when he was actually home. The wrinkles on his face had deepened, but his skin was the bronze Alec remembered. Reading glasses were perched at the end of his wide nose. A new addition.

"Well, hey, son." He rose and clapped him on the back.

"Hi, Dad." With that pleasantry out of the way, he turned back to his mother, who was busy pouring sun tea.

"You're not at all concerned Jake's marrying a Covington?" Alec asked. Sure, the Covington dynamic had changed a great deal over the past year, and Alec was pretty certain Lacey loved his brother to the moon and back, but she was still a Covington and the Winstons were just the help.

The newspaper hit the table with a crack, but there was no anger in the gesture. "Why? He's not being forced into it. Not everyone weds because they're stupid enough to knock a girl up. Right, son?" He barked out a laugh at his own joke.

Direct hit. Score one for Dad.

Alec waved his hand, even though the barb hurt. They all did, not that his dad noticed. He might stroke out if his father ever thought about what he said before it spewed from his mouth. No filter, his dad. He'd never had one. Alec didn't have enough fingers and toes to count the number of times his father had embarrassed him growing up.

Alec sat across from his father and studied the ancient yellow linoleum. The counters and cabinets dated back to the year the house was built. He was pretty sure the appliances did, too.

"Lacey's a sweetheart," Mom chirped. "We're so happy for them. Aren't we, Gregory?"

Dad nodded. "Jake could do worse for himself."

Alec tried for neutral ground so he wouldn't set his dad off on any new tangents. "The yard looks nice."

Pride filled his father's smile. "Hard work pays off—not that you'd know about that, with your apartment penthouse in the city. Probably hire maids to clean for you, too."

Alec pinched the bridge of his nose. "I *do* work, you know. Books don't write themselves."

"True, true."

Mom cleared her throat. "Are you hungry, honey?"

"No," they both answered in unison.

She sliced some banana bread anyway.

Dad went back to his newspaper as if Alec wasn't there, sipping the tea Mom had set out for him. Even as a child, his father had never seemed to know what to say to him, so this was nothing new.

Home sweet home.

His mom finished slicing the bread and reached into a drawer. She set the entire loaf in foil and handed it to Alec. "To eat while you're writing. I'm so proud of you."

That made one of them.

She went on and on for the next twenty minutes about how the local libraries had his books in stock, the weather, the neighbors, and by the time he tuned her out, she was on a kick about knitting.

When she paused to come up for air, he cut in. "I have to go soon. I'm on a deadline."

The disappointment in her eyes cut. "I wish we could see you more often. It was good you stopped by."

"I'll be around this summer. I'll visit."

Alec wrapped her in a hug, squeezing until she squeaked. "I love you."

"Love you, too."

"Make him take you out to dinner tonight." He jerked his chin toward his dad.

Confusion sparked in her blue eyes. "For what occasion?"

Alec shrugged. "Who says you need one? Do it just because."

The newspaper came down again. "Waste of money when we have food right here. Unless you're buying, Mr. Fancy Writer."

"Take your wife out on a date," Alec ground through clenched teeth. Try as he may to remember his father meant well and was harmless, his patience was wearing thin.

Dad wasn't done, though. "Good one, son. What would you know about taking care of a wife?" He snorted out a full belly laugh before he finally realized no one else was laughing.

Except his dad was so fucking right. Even though they'd never actually gotten to tie the knot, Alec hadn't taken care of Laura, and look how she'd wound up. A vegetable, being fed through a tube, with machines doing her breathing for her.

Nausea rolled in his gut. He closed his eyes and sucked in a breath. Shook his head.

When he finally could speak his voice sounded like sandpaper. "I gotta go. Love you guys."

His father stood and wrapped his arms around Alec, the scent of cut grass surrounding him as he squeezed the air from his lungs. "Love you, too, son."

The blunt knock on the kitchen door caused Faith to jump. She'd been staring off into space again, thinking about Alec and why he'd kissed her, instead of listening to Ginny read like she was supposed to be doing. Thinking how darn good it felt when he'd cupped her cheek and brushed his lips over hers. Going so long without another's touch had obviously muddled her brain.

And Alec hadn't come by since.

Wow. She'd never been one for daydreaming before. This place was either growing on her or changing her. Maybe both. She didn't know how to feel about that. Daydreaming led to false hope and unrealistic versions of the truth. She'd set goals in her life, sure, but they were attainable ones.

Alec wasn't attainable.

When she opened the door, he stood on the other side, looking like a gentle breeze could knock him over. Dark circles were forming under his eyes and his hair stood at odd angles. Yet he still looked so good. Too handsome and rough around the edges for her to ignore the punch.

"Are you okay?" He didn't look right. She resisted the urge to smooth her hands over his thick black hair and across his shadowed jaw.

"No." If his face was any indication, he was just as surprised by the admission. "Am I interrupting?"

She looked over her shoulder at the table. "Ginny was just reading to me. Come in."

Ginny bounced in her seat. "Hi, Alec!"

He stepped inside and surveyed the room, not seeming to take anything in. "Hey, Ginny. Whatcha reading?"

Faith waited for Ginny to finish answering, the worry eating at her stomach lining. "Ginny, why don't you head into the living room for a break? You can have an hour of TV, okay?"

"Yeah!"

The second Ginny was out of earshot, Faith turned to Alec. "Is it Lacey or Jake? Did something happen?"

"No, no." He waved his hand. "I'm sorry. It's me. I . . ."

Drawing in a calming breath, she sat at the table and waited him out. He leaned against the island and crossed his ankles, his palms clutching the counter behind him. The position made the blue tee he wore stretch over the taut muscles of his chest and arms. He was a magnificently built man. Part of his charisma was his confidence, which he seemed to be lacking at the moment. The urge to ask him what the problem was grew fierce, but he'd come here for a reason, so she let him work it out on his own.

He sighed and swiped a hand down his face. Rubbed his jaw. "I feel like shit for what happened the other night. I shouldn't have kissed you."

This, exactly this, was why she didn't daydream. Because envisioning someone like him wanting her was dangerous to her heart. She knew better. Her family and previous encounters had taught her well.

She forced her tone to be even, not wanting him to feel guilty, while lead sat heavy in her stomach. "It was spur of the moment. Nothing to beat yourself up over."

Slowly, his gaze lifted to hers. Held. "It wasn't spur of the moment. I've wanted to kiss you since I first saw you on the beach." He straightened suddenly, those black eyebrows drawing together. Anger flared in his eyes. "Don't do that. Don't look at me like that."

"Like what?" Like the floor had just dropped out from under her? Like the room was spinning? Like every molecule in her body was exploding? Because it was. Her heart wouldn't stop pounding.

"You look like no one's ever said they wanted to kiss you before. The simplest things put this . . . this light in your eyes. I'm not capable of keeping that light there. I'm not in a position where I can offer more."

He got all this from one kiss? He was more a dreamer than she was, then. She'd never been in a long-term relationship. This was uncharted territory for her. Not that anything resembling a relationship *was* happening between them. Even if it were, he'd just slammed on the brakes.

"It was just a kiss." She didn't know if she said that for him or herself.

He shook his head. "I don't know what to make of you."

Suddenly, it hit her. This seemed like classic projection. He was deflecting. She wasn't the type of woman who got men sexually frustrated, so something else was triggering this argument and making him feel guilty. "Did something else happen today?"

"That is exactly what I'm talking about!" He paced the length of the kitchen and back, finally settling on the other side of the island as if needing a barrier. "You and your clever little mind and pretty eyes that see everything. You know things without me having to say a word." He blew out a gust of air and slapped his hands on the counter, leaning into them.

Dang it. He said the nicest things sometimes, contradicting them with a voice that was wholly pissed off. *He* didn't know what to make of *her*?

"You think my eyes are pretty?" She hadn't really meant to say that aloud, but that's what her mind chose to fixate on—the compliment. Her face heated to blazing.

He pinned her with a *duh* look. His shoulder muscles bunched with tension and the little tick in his jaw was back. He needed a stiff drink. So did she.

She had to redirect this conversation.

"Well, that settles it. You like my eyes, you don't understand me, and you kiss me with deep regret. We must get married at once." Lord, what had gotten into her?

He stilled a split second before he laughed. Long and deep and jagged.

Wow. She could listen to that all day. He obviously didn't do it nearly enough because the sound was rusty in the quiet kitchen.

She waited a few beats for her pulse to level out. "Now that you're feeling better, what really had you knocking on the door?" She rested her elbow on the table and her chin in her palm

It was as slow as the sunrise, but it eventually came: heat replaced the humor previously in his eyes. "You make me want to kiss you again. Really kiss you, not like the half-assed one the other night. A knock-you-off-your-feet kind of kiss."

Only a writer . . .

God, fire roared through her veins just thinking about it, though. No one had ever spoken to her like that before.

"Since you didn't enjoy it the first time—"

"I didn't say I didn't enjoy it." He ran a hand through his hair. Shook his head. "I went to see my folks today. My dad has a special talent for making me feel like shit, even though he doesn't mean to. That's what's bothering me."

Parental issues. To this she could relate. "That's too bad. It's probably his own insecurity showing."

"If it's one thing my dad isn't, it's insecure. He just doesn't think before he speaks. He lacks the tact gene."

Faith decided to change the subject. "Are you still doing well on the book? You had gotten pretty far—"

"No. I stalled."

And there it was. The real reason he was here. It had nothing to do with kissing her or the visit with his parents. Those things were temporary, irritating distractions to someone like him. Alec saw her as some kind of fix for his writer's block. It was the only thing of real interest he saw in her. She should've known better.

She nodded and rose. "Wait here. I'll be right back."

Faith printed off a form in Cole's office and collected Ginny from the living room. She sat both Ginny and Alec at the kitchen table and handed Alec a pencil. She slid the book Ginny had just finished toward the waiting teenager.

"Ginny, Alec's going to help you do your book report. Take all the time you need." To Alec, she said, "Don't take off if you get an idea. Let me know you're leaving first."

Faith didn't look at Alec again when she left the room, because she was pretty sure the tears welling would spill if she did. Instead, she walked up the stairs to collect Ginny's math book for later and allow a minute to collect herself.

ten

"I thought maybe we could go over some wedding ideas."
Lacey's eyes were rounded in excitement, and she clutched
several bridal magazines to her chest.

Ginny bounced on her feet. "Can we? Can we?"

"Sure." Faith let Lacey inside the front door and followed
them into the living room.

She'd gone the whole of her life never being asked her
opinion or advice, and now it seemed everyone wanted a
piece of her. Part of her was grateful to be included. The
other part warned how temporary this place and these people
were. Eventually Ginny wouldn't need a tutor and Faith
would have to move on. The rest of them would remain close,
as friends or family, but Faith was just a momentary person.

"I tagged some bridesmaid dresses. You can tell me what
color you like, Ginny."

"I'll leave you guys alone for a bit."

"No, stay. I want your opinion, too. Please," Lacey urged
when Faith hesitated.

"Shouldn't you be doing this with Mia? Maybe you should wait until she gets back." After all, they were sisters-in-law and friends. What did Faith know about this stuff?

"Oh, there's plenty to do. But August will be here soon, and the dresses take the longest to order."

"Okay," she sighed, sitting on the couch next to her. Ginny flanked her other side.

For the next two hours, they went over colors and styles. Lacey decided to let Ginny and Mia pick out their own instead of going with matching dresses. Faith liked that idea, allowing them their own individuality.

Lacey wasn't who Faith had expected. With the money and power the Covingtons had, Faith had anticipated a royal snob who ordered her minions around, like her former students and their families at St. Ambrose. Lacey wasn't like that at all. She was warm and kind and funny in a subdued sort of way. She seemed to just be coming out of her shell after being under her mother's thumb all those years, and just starting to figure out who she was as a person. Faith could relate to her random insecurities. In a way, they had a lot in common.

After going over tuxedo options—and Faith imagining how good Alec would look in one—Faith stood. Bea was off this week with Mia and Cole out of town, so she needed to get lunch started.

"Would you like to stay for lunch?"

"Oh, I can't. I have to meet with the caterer while Jake takes his lunch break. Maybe some other time. We can go shopping?"

"Sure. I'd like that," Faith said, surprised she meant it.

Lacey turned to Ginny with a smile. "I'll see you for our sleepover party tomorrow night."

"Yeah!"

When Lacey left, Faith made some quick sandwiches and a salad for her and Ginny, but after lunch the girl was restless and bursting with energy. Faith was just about crawling out of her skin, too. She couldn't pinpoint just what was wrong, except that Alec hadn't been over in two days. The book report must've helped.

She smiled, pride welling inside that she'd been able to help him work through it. The lack of productivity had obviously bothered him.

Rubbing her forehead, she watched Ginny squirm in her seat and doing anything but her math problems. Math wasn't Faith's favorite, either.

"You know what, Ginny girl? Let's quit for today."

"Yeah!"

Faith grinned and closed the workbook with a snap. "Come on. Let's go work the ants out." She laughed at Ginny's confusion. "Figure of speech. It'll be fun. I promise."

They headed into the living room where they went through the CD collection by the stereo. Ginny picked out a dance mix, which Faith set in the tray. A booming pop song mixed with a retro beat filled the room. Not her first choice, but Ginny loved it.

"Now what?" Ginny said.

"Now we dance."

Since no one else was around to hear them, Faith turned the music to blasting and grabbed the girl's hands. Ginny laughed and threw her head back, spinning and swaying. Faith picked up Ginny's crazy rhythm and followed along.

Alec hadn't slept more than four hours in two days, but hell if he'd ever felt better in his life. The words flowed. Chapter after chapter. Through the night, bleeding into the day. He was back. Sanity maintained.

Leaning back in his chair, he grinned and scrubbed his hands over his face. He should keep going, in case he lost this tangible thread, but his stomach rumbled and he was pretty sure he smelled.

He threw a frozen pizza into the oven and went to shower

while it baked. Thoughts scrambled for purchase in his head as he stood under the spray. Plots morphed and characters screamed. Grabbing a bar of soap, the manuscript played out in his head until the end while he lathered.

The book was not coming out exactly how he'd first charted it in his timeline. Instead, the female lead was quickly becoming the heroine. The Nightmare demon had kidnapped her, and her brother searched in vain, losing a bit of his own self along the way. But it was the girl who broke free and escaped, using her own hidden strength and wit. Alec was about halfway through the manuscript, about to reach the peak where everything crumbled to shit and Nightmare grew fierce with fury. This part of writing a book was always a rush like no other. The exact moment when he knew conflict collided with action and the reader would be glued to the page, hanging on to every word.

Stepping out of the shower, he dried off, dressed, and headed to the kitchen, head still in the story. He'd have to rework books two and three to accommodate this change. If he kept the childhood tie between the three female victims, he could keep the motive behind Nightmare's desire for them. Instead of the brother saving them, though, Faith would do it.

Alec's head reared back and the slice of pizza fell from his fingertips to the counter. Christ, he hadn't even realized he'd been eating. Half the pepperoni pie was devoured.

Faith.

She'd wormed her way into his head, under his skin. He'd based his female lead off her physically and emotionally. Wavy brown hair and quizzically sad eyes. Quiet strength, brilliant mind. Because of her, he'd been writing again. And holy shit, it was the best book he'd ever punched out. Even not having finished yet, he knew. This story was different. Girl power. Danger. A little romance. Fear unlike anything in his previous series.

All due to Faith.

Jake was right. She was different than the others. Not a distraction, but a destination. Part of him wanted to grasp that shred of hope for a future, for something permanent and real. Try his hand at normal again. But that wasn't possible and never would be.

Still . . . she stayed there, trapped in his mind as a maybe. As potential. Alec shook his head and tossed the leftover pizza in the fridge.

He absolutely shouldn't go over there and see her. It wasn't fair to Faith to ping-pong back and forth between brooding and flirting. So far, he'd kept himself in check. But if he kept drawing himself toward the temptation of her, he'd do nothing but tear apart her life the way he'd done to Laura. Faith was kind. She was devoted to helping others, and genuinely enjoyed it.

And for the love of God, what was it about her? What was the damn draw? She wasn't a gorgeous supermodel with pouty lips. She didn't even wear makeup most of the time. Her body didn't sport curvy hips and a full chest. In fact, she was so damn wispy thin he could probably bench-press her with one arm. Half the time she didn't seem to want him around. She'd brushed off that kiss instead of trying to rope him into a marriage proposal like every other woman he'd encountered.

So, yeah. What the hell?

Still worked up into a mild irritation, he lifted his hand to knock on the front door and froze. He sighed with dramatic flair into the humid afternoon heat. Whatever. So she was on his mind and he'd unconsciously walked over. It meant nothing.

Music boomed from inside the house, all but rattling the windows. That wasn't like her. In fact, every time he'd popped by, the house had been quiet. She and Ginny were usually working on some lesson or baking something. They'd never hear the bell or a knock over this racket, though.

Testing the knob, he found the door unlocked. He strode

in and made his way toward the living room where the noise seemed to originate. What he found had his jaw dropping.

Ginny and Faith were . . . dancing. If you could call what they were doing dancing. Ginny was jumping up and down, bobbing her head to the beat. Faith had her arms up, swaying her hips. Her eyes were closed and her cheeks flushed. The blue top she wore rose up to show a patch of pale skin near her navel.

Damn it. Just when he thought he had her nailed, understood her a measurable amount, he walked in to find this.

"Hi, Alec!" Ginny called.

Faith squealed, grabbing her chest and nearly falling. She went to the stereo and killed the power, blessedly silencing the noise. Sweat trickled down her temple and dampened her hair, curling the tendrils. Her chest heaved, drawing his gaze there.

"I wasn't expecting you."

"No kidding."

"We were just getting some energy out."

He had some ideas on more pleasurable ways of doing that. "Did it work?"

Ginny giggled as if reading his mind.

"I don't suppose there's any way you can unsee that?" Faith asked, a half smile curving her lips. No, her lips weren't pouty. They were thin and naturally a dark pink, the bottom lip slightly more full than the top.

"Not a chance." In fact, a sudden vision of her sweating with flushed cheeks for an entirely different reason came to mind.

"I figured." She wiped her brow with her forearm. "Ginny, why don't you go change into your bathing suit? We'll go for a quick swim."

"Yeah!" She bounded past Alec and up the stairs.

Alec kept his attention on Faith—as if there was any other choice.

She fidgeted. "Stuck with the book again? Do you need help to get going?"

"No."

Surprise had her brows lifting and those honey eyes widening. "Oh. Why are you here?"

Christ. As if the only reason someone would pay her a visit was because they needed something. Just who in her life had given her that theory? "I don't know. To see you."

Great. Honesty. So much for keeping her at arm's length.

"Oh." Again with the *oh*.

"Go out with me tonight."

The words were out of his mouth before his brain could warn him of the stupidity. Guess he had a lot of his dad in him after all. She was the type of woman a guy had to woo. Not the kind you met in a bar and had horizontal in under twenty minutes. He wondered if he even knew how to do this anymore. It had been a long, long time.

Her mouth opened and closed several times before he decided to clarify. Otherwise she'd think he meant anything but what he really intended. "I mean on a date, since I know you were wondering."

"How do you know what I was thinking?"

"Call it a hunch," he said dryly.

Her gaze darted to the window and back. "You said the kiss was a mistake."

"Yes."

"And that it made you feel like . . ." She waved her hand vaguely, as if not able to form the curse. He realized he hadn't heard her swear before.

"Shit," he finished on her behalf. "And I said I felt like shit for doing it, not that the kiss made me feel like shit. There's a difference."

She rubbed her forehead. "Forgive me, but I'm confused."

"So am I." He crossed his arms, wondering why in the hell he was pursuing this when she'd given him an out. "I can't stop thinking about you." Like an irritating song. And so help him, if she said "oh," he'd . . .

"I can't leave Ginny alone."

There. Another out. Perfect. They'd call it off and . . . why was his phone out of his pocket and why was he texting Jake?

Can u watch Ginny tonight? Taking Faith out.

Moments later the response came.

Jake: Lacey and I will be over by 6. Stay out all night.

He sighed in . . . relief? "Jake and Lacey will stay with Ginny. I'll pick you up at six-thirty."

Ginny bounded down the stairs, a towel slung over her shoulder, as he made his way to the door.

"Wait. I didn't say yes."

God love her. He turned and grinned at her flustered face as she stood in the entryway. "You didn't say no, either. Six-thirty, Faith." He tapped the doorframe and left.

chapter

eleven

The seafood restaurant he'd found was nestled right on the tourist strip, close enough to the beach to smell the ocean. To avoid being crowded, he'd asked for a corner table out on the back deck. Faith hadn't said much on the drive over or after they were seated. Oddly enough, the lack of conversation wasn't tense. It was a comfortable silence he wasn't used to. People tended to attempt to fill the quiet, as if something were wrong with just being.

He glanced at her over the menu, but her attention was on the people in the distance. Her plain white sundress hugged her chest and hips, flaring out in a skirt that stopped at her knees. She'd put her hair up in a loose knot and applied a minimal amount of makeup. Or Lacey had applied it for her, since his future sister-in-law had been at the guesthouse when he'd arrived to pick up Faith.

Whatever the subtle difference was, it made her eyes stand out. They took up most of her face as it was. The dusk was doing something to her skin, which appeared even softer than usual. Her freckles were barely noticeable. Around her long, elegant neck was a chain, the one she never took off. The low dip of her dress allowed him to see the charm. Little silver wings. Just wings. Interesting.

When she smiled at a family with a couple of toddlers, he wondered how he'd ever thought her plain.

The waiter came and asked for a drink order.

"I haven't even looked at the menu," she said. "I'm sorry. Just water for me, please."

"Do you drink wine?" He felt blind not knowing anything about her past or if she had any limitations from her medical condition.

"I could. I don't know anything about wine, though."

Okay, this he could handle. He gave the request for a sauvignon blanc from a California vineyard he recognized and waited until the waiter left before addressing her. She hadn't wanted to talk about her past before, but they knew each other a little better now. He had the suspicion he'd need to tread carefully with Faith. Whatever led her to Wilmington didn't appear to be altogether pleasant.

He glanced at the pendant. "Why the wings?"

Her gaze dropped, and with a reflex he'd seen often, she clutched the pendant and slid it back and forth on the chain. "I saw it in a jewelry store and it reminded me of my sister."

The sister he wasn't supposed to know about because Faith never mentioned her. Yet he'd seen the photo Lacey took. Saying something might ruin Lacey's surprise painting or break Faith's trust. "I thought you were an only child."

Her small hand released the necklace as she looked away, smoothing her napkin over her lap. "She died several years ago from cancer."

Platitudes never made the grieving feel better, so he didn't offer one. "What was her name?"

"Hope."

"Faith and Hope. That's cute." Finally, her honey gaze

returned to his, and the sorrow etched in her eyes was gutting. "Was she younger or older?"

"She was older by three and a half years."

"Does this bother you? Talking about her?"

She appeared to mull that over for several moments, eventually shaking her head. The waiter arrived with their wine and they ordered their meal. Alec hoped the interruption wouldn't break their conversation. Though hesitant, she was finally answering questions.

Alone once more, he asked, "What kind of cancer did she have?"

She cleared her throat. "A rare form of leukemia called myelogenous. It affects the white blood cells in bone marrow. Survival rates aren't high with that kind of cancer. She was diagnosed at age two, but lived until she was twenty, and it was a blessing to have her that long, considering. There were periods where she didn't require treatment, and we thought . . ." Her lids lowered in a slow blink.

His hand settled over hers on the table. "I'm sorry. We can talk about something else."

"No, it's fine." Her gaze held his and she offered a weak smile. "Honestly, I don't get to talk about Hope very often."

"Why not?"

She stared down at their joined hands, where he rubbed small circles over the soft skin of her inner wrist. "My parents took her death very hard."

Were there no friends? Other family? Certainly she had other people in her life. Then again, no one had dropped by since she'd moved, nor had she left to visit anyone.

"I'm not terribly close with my parents. Around the time Hope died, I went to college nearby, but didn't live in the dorms. After I graduated, I stayed at home, thinking they needed me."

He felt a *but* in there somewhere. What kind of parents didn't want their kid around? Especially after losing another so young. No way was Faith a problem child or a black sheep. If anything, she was the over-accommodating type. "Tell me about your sister. What was she like?"

The smile that split her face was genuine and hit him right in the center of his chest.

Removing her hand from his, she rested her chin in her palm and stared over his shoulder. "Everyone loved Hope. She was the life of any get-together. She was always smiling, making friends. It was hard not to love her. Even when she was sick, she'd find the strength to ask me about school or what happened in my day." She sighed. "I miss that most. Someone asking how my day went."

A hollow pang smacked his ribs and he stilled. Did she have no one? At all? He thought back to their scattered conversations and came up blank. No mention of anyone. Her sometimes socially awkward behavior and the shock whenever someone included her was starting to make sense. Faith wasn't particularly shy or reserved or traditional. She wasn't uncomfortable with attention. She'd just never had any. She sought acceptance.

Dear Christ. What the hell was he supposed to do with her? With this knowledge?

"How was your day?" he rasped.

Slowly, her gaze slid over to his, and damn if the sentiment in her eyes didn't undo him. "It was pretty great, actually. Thank you."

He nodded. Swallowed hard.

They sat in silence until the waiter brought their food. She ordered grilled salmon and steamed vegetables over brown rice. He looked down at his crab cakes and asparagus spears drowning in sauce.

She took a bite of her fish. "What about you? You don't seem close with your parents, based on what you said the other day."

"I'm very close with my mother and Jake. Dad's just . . ."

He fumbled for the right word. "Weird, I guess. I get the feeling he's disappointed in me. Regardless, I love them to death."

The fork paused halfway to her mouth. "After all your success? I find it hard to believe he's disappointed."

He shrugged. "I made a lot of bad choices along the way. He built his landscaping business from nothing. Blue collar through and through. I don't think he knew what to do with me, being the creative type."

She pushed the food around her plate, avoiding eye contact. Once again, he was floored by her lack of inquisition. She didn't ask, though he could tell she wanted to. For the first time in . . . well, ever, he wanted to talk. To have someone know what his life entailed and share his mistakes. Someone like Faith would understand, not judge.

"I can hear your unasked questions from over here."

Her eyes smiled even though her mouth didn't. "I wasn't going to ask you anything. I was just thinking that you're human. People make bad decisions all the time."

Maybe she did get it, more than he would've guessed. "Why aren't you asking me what mistakes I made?"

Her tongue darted out to moisten her lower lip. She took a sip of wine before answering, choosing her words carefully. "A few days ago, you said you couldn't do commitment. I'm assuming that hasn't changed." Her eyes lifted to his. "I figure you'll tell me when and if you're ready."

"That's it?"

She nodded, closed her eyes, then shook her head. "What are we doing here, Alec?"

"Eating. Some of us more than others." He nodded to her plate, of which she had yet to take more than a few bites.

"Kissing me was a mistake. Your words, not mine."

He leaned forward, resting his forearms on the table and crowding her. "I make my living by words, Faith. I repeat, it wasn't a mistake. I said kissing you made me feel like shit.

Because of those choices mentioned earlier. But for the life of me, I can't seem to stay away from you. Regardless of how bad an idea this is, and regardless of why I know I can't."

She drew in a deep breath and slowly let it out. "I'm going to tell you something, but I don't want you to take it the wrong way. I don't want you to read too much into it or ask any questions."

Her pleading gaze pinned him to his seat. Right then, he would've done whatever she asked. "I promise."

"I've spent the majority of my life feeling unwanted. I made a promise to myself when I moved here that I would start over. If you can't or won't be honest with what you want, you should leave me alone. I'm out of my element as it is, Alec."

What the hell was he supposed to say to that? The air in his lungs thinned as he stared at her, making breathing difficult. A thousand questions and arguments rolled through his head, but a promise was a promise. The blatant urge to protect her, to slay her dragons and lay claim, rose again. What kind of fucking monster had made her think she wasn't wanted?

He should leave her alone, like she asked.

"Considering I'm a writer, you leave me strangely bereft of words."

The waiter came and cleared their plates. They refused dessert. Alec paid the tab and offered her a walk down the tourist strip, more for his sake than hers—he needed to clear his head. She nodded her approval. They'd been walking for twenty minutes past the independent storefronts when she finally addressed him.

"Do you find me attractive?"

He stopped and turned to face her. This had to be a trick question. Some female ploy they all knew to confound men. "Yes."

Even though it was dark, he could see the pink tingeing her cheeks. "And it's not just because I'm helping you through your writer's block?"

That was asinine. For her benefit, he thought it through. "No."

She continued the walk as if she'd never spoken. He let her go a few steps before his brain caught up.

"Hold up." Gently, he grabbed her wrist and tugged her flush against an ice-cream parlor to get out of the way of tourists. "What game are you playing?" Christ, she smelled better than the shop behind them.

"I don't play games. I needed to know if your attraction had anything to do with me or if it was based on gratitude."

He pinched the bridge of his nose. "They just don't make them like you."

"What?"

"Nothing." He opened his eyes and forced his gaze off her mouth and on her eyes. "Why did you need to know?"

She drew a breath, and the action caused her breasts to brush his chest. "I've never been in a serious relationship. I don't know if I'm even capable. You're guarded and hesitant to enter one. Let's just see where this thing goes. No pressure. No guilt."

Just when he thought she couldn't throw him any more surprises, she blindsided him with a left hook. "You don't seem the type for flings or one-night stands, Faith." And really, that's all he could offer.

"What about a summer romance? You're going back to New York. I'm staying here. The relationship has an end date. You get your out clause and I get my adventure."

"Adventure." Is that what she wanted? Could it be as easy as that? It didn't feel right. Deep in his gut, he knew Faith didn't take relationships of any kind lightly.

Still, he wanted her.

"Fine," he said with a nod. "Come on. I should get you home."

Before his car turned back into a pumpkin.

chapter
twelve

Faith rested her cheek against the cool glass of Alec's passenger window. The wine from dinner had gotten to her. Having infrequently indulged in alcohol, she hadn't really known what effect it would have. Her body was hot, her skin tingling. She wasn't sure if she should attribute that to Alec or the wine. It had also loosened her tongue. She'd been more outgoing and outspoken than ever before.

A summer fling. Lord. As if she could handle Alec Winston, even for just one summer.

Yet she wanted a life, wanted more than to just exist. What better way to start than jumping in headfirst with him? He could teach her things. She wouldn't have to worry about making her world fit with his or all the complications, because he'd be leaving. They were temporary.

It had also felt good to talk about Hope with someone. Though the loss of her sister still cut deep, she wanted others to know how wonderful and strong she was, how lucky Faith had been to have her. Not talking about Hope seemed like forgetting she was ever here. And that would be a shame.

Alec pulled the car through the front gate and veered to the left to park in front of her guesthouse. The lights in the main house were off, even though it was barely nine. Lacey and Jake said they'd crash with Ginny for the night so Faith could stay out late if she wanted.

The dome light filled the dark car when Alec opened the door. Oh boy. Would he kiss her on the doorstep? Did guys still do that? He strode around the hood and to her side before she had her seat belt off. Taking his offered hand, she got out and walked with him to the door.

Now what? She waited, her gaze glued to his chest.

"Invite me in." His voice was a hoarse rumble that made her muscles clench. It wasn't a demand, but a gentle request.

She nodded and opened the door.

He followed her inside, glancing around after she flipped on a lamp. His gaze traveled over the picture of her and Hope on the mantel before moving on to the bookshelves beside the fireplace. "I thought you said you never read my books."

Shadows cut across his body and half his face, making him look dangerously handsome. His black hair seemed darker somehow, and she wanted to run her fingertips over the slight outgrowth on his jaw. He wore a white button-down dress shirt untucked from his jeans, which fit him well enough to tease at the glorious body that lay underneath. It had been a long time, if ever, that she felt this turned on or attracted to a man. Even the way he stood, hands in his back pockets and one foot off to the side in a careless *whatever* pose, was attractive.

His gray-blue eyes leveled on her when she didn't answer.

She set her purse on the coffee table to give herself something to do. "No, I said I've never seen any of the movies based off your books."

He glanced at the shelves again. "Pretty extensive variety of fiction here. Fantasy, romance, cozy mysteries . . ."

"Horror's my favorite, or really dark suspense."

A corner of his mouth quirked and she had to swallow a moan. "Why's that?"

She shrugged. "Reading them makes the problems in the real world seem weak by comparison."

He breathed out a laugh. The muscles in his shoulders tensed, as if straining. "And why haven't you seen any of my movies?"

What was with all the questions? "They never get it right. Movies ruin books . . ."

She didn't have time to finish her thought because he jerked his hands out of his back pockets, strode the few steps separating them, and crushed his mouth over hers.

His hands grabbed her waist, pulling her flush against his hard body as he angled his head and deepened the kiss. His tongue slipped past her lips and tasted, stroked until she had an idea of what he'd be like in bed. The rhythm and pace he'd set. The talent he'd bring. God, she so didn't think she could handle him.

Regardless, he felt too good to let go. Her fingers drove into his thick, wavy hair like she'd been wanting to do since she'd first laid eyes on him. The move seemed to spark some kind of animal instinct in him because his fingers slid from her waist to her hips and dug into her flesh. He moaned, rocked against her so she could feel the long, hard strain of his erection against her belly.

Breaking the kiss, his lips traveled from her mouth to her ear. "We need to slow down."

Lack of experience be darned, she was ready to strip off her dress. "I'm not a virgin," she whispered, and immediately regretted the slip. Her face heated and embarrassment made her head heavy. She pinched her eyes closed.

Edging back, he looked down at her. "I didn't ask."

"I figured you might think . . . with the information I gave you . . ."

The pad of his thumb pressed over her lower lip and he smiled, his gaze focused there. Moving his thumb across her lip, his eyes darkened, his lids closing to half-mast. "We should still take this slow. I'm going home to cool off." He leaned in and pressed his lips to hers, gently this time. "I still owe you that knock-you-off-your-feet kiss."

"That wasn't it?"

He grinned, and she had to lock her knees to stay upright. "You're still standing, so no, that wasn't it." He closed his eyes and drew in a deep breath, brushing his nose to hers. Groaning, he pulled away. "Next time, Faith."

When the door closed behind him, she sank to the floor and patted her chest, not recognizing the crazy sensations whirling inside. She pressing a hand to her forehead and laughed like an idiot. It took her too long to realize the feeling was . . . happiness.

Faith was dusting lemon bars with powdered sugar and checking Ginny's progress on adding sprinkles to the cupcakes when Lacey strolled in the kitchen door.

"Who's ready for the best sleepover ever?"

"I am, I am," Ginny chanted.

Faith laughed. "We definitely have enough sugar to keep us up all night."

"My party, my menu," Ginny said.

Lacey kissed her cheek. "You are so right, Ginny girl." She glanced around the kitchen. "I brought margarita mix. Do they have a blender?"

"Above the fridge." Faith moved to the sink to wash her hands. "I'm a lightweight with regards to alcohol, as it turns out."

"Oh," Lacey drawled. "Did we get a little tipsy on our date last night?" She set the blender on the island and plugged it in.

"You had a date?" Ginny was awed.

Lacey filled the blender with ice. "She sure did. With guess who? Alec."

"You did?" Ginny said, clapping her hands. "Is he a good kisser?"

"Oh boy. Mia's gonna kill me."

Lacey waved her hand, dumping margarita mix into the blender with the other and switching it on. Noise clattered as the ice crushed. "Mia won't care if we talk about boys," she shouted. "That's what sleepovers are for!"

Faith wouldn't know. She'd never been to one.

Lacey poured a virgin margarita into a cup and handed it to Ginny. Then she poured a generous finger—or five—of tequila into the blender. "Think that's enough?"

Faith laughed. "Uh, yes."

Lacey added more mix and ice. She switched the blender on again and shouted over the noise. "So, is Alec a good kisser or not?"

Faith pressed her lips together, unable to hide the giddy smile. "Yes."

Lacey's brows rose, pretending not to have heard. "What?"

"Yes, he's a good—"

The blender stopped.

"—kisser." Faith rubbed her forehead. "You tricked me into screaming that. Is he right outside the door or something?"

Lacey poured two drinks. "Nope. Just us girls. And great kisses are worth shouting about." She handed Faith a cup and clacked her own cup against it. "To the best sleepover ever!"

"Yeah!"

Faith smiled at Ginny and took a sip. The drink, despite being blended with ice, burned all the way down. "Wow, Lacey."

"It is a little strong." Her pretty mouth twisted. "I've never made margaritas before. Never been to a sleepover either."

"You haven't?" Ginny asked.

"My mom was pretty snobby. Thought we were above things like that. It wasn't proper."

Faith connected with Lacey in that minute, a bond of sorts forming. "I haven't been to a sleepover either. My sister was the one with all the friends growing up. I never got invited to any parties."

"Well," Lacey said, tilting her head. "Guess it's a first for us then. It really is the best sleepover ever. Cole has a ton of movies in his collection for us to choose from. Plus, I brought my cosmetics bag. We can do makeovers."

Oh boy.

Ginny bounced and clapped. "Me first."

"You got it."

They settled on the living room floor with blankets and pillows. *High School Musical*—Ginny's choice—played on the huge flat screen while they stuffed their faces with cupcakes and lemon bars and popcorn.

Faith had never had such an overdose of sugar in her life. She was always so careful what she ate that she decided she was going to let herself go just for tonight. She was young and healthy and it was silly to be so overcautious just because her parents were. Her parents had good reasons, with Hope's illness and needing a lot from Faith to keep her treatments going, but Hope had been dead ten years now. It was probably time to let her go. It didn't mean Faith had to forget her, right? Just move on.

The movie ended at the same time Faith's margarita cup emptied. Huh. When did that happen? She was feeling a little light-headed.

Lacey pulled out a bagful of cosmetics and got to work on Ginny's makeover. While they were busy, Faith cleaned up some of the wrappers and changed movies. Deciding she'd had enough tequila, she brought out bottled water from the fridge for everyone.

"So," Lacey said, applying lipstick on Ginny. "Mia loves Cole. I love Jake. Is there romance brewing for Faith and Alec? Whatcha think, Ginny?"

"Yeah!"

Faith tucked her feet under her and sat on the couch. "It's pretty new, guys. Besides, Alec lives in New York. I think it's just going to be a summer thing."

"Are you okay with that?"

"Not much choice." She shrugged. "It is what it is. May as well enjoy it while he's here."

It had taken all her courage to reach out and ask for what she wanted from Alec. She had no idea how to go about fully living. She'd simply seized the opportunity. Later, she'd probably think it was insane, but for now, he made her heart pound and her body want. Her response to him every time he was near reminded her she was alive.

Lacey nodded. "I see your point. I don't know if I could do that, though. I get attached—at least I do when I'm interested. I think I knew I loved Jake after our first date."

"Did he kiss you?" Ginny asked.

"Yes. He's a really great kisser." She brushed her hands together. "You, my dear, are done. You look beautiful."

"I do?"

Faith nodded. Lacey hadn't done much, just a hint of blush, gloss, and shadow, like she'd done for Faith last night for her date with Alec. "You do look very pretty."

"I'm going to go see." Ginny ran off down the hall to the bathroom.

"I'm sorry about Alec. I didn't realize it wasn't serious."

Faith smiled. "It's okay. I don't mind talking about it. It's just . . . I've never had close girlfriends before. Been a long time since a guy was interested, too. I'm not sure what I'm supposed to do."

From her spot on the floor, Lacey propped her elbow on the cushion and tugged on her earlobe. "Before Mia came back to Wilmington, I didn't have anyone. I was on committees and in clubs, but no one I could talk to like this, you know?"

Faith nodded. "I know. Not the committees part, but alone I understand."

Ginny came back in the room. Lacey took some pictures on her phone and texted them to Mia. They gathered for a group selfie before getting comfy to watch *Grease*. Ginny fell asleep halfway through the movie, so Faith went to brush her teeth and made sure the alarm was set before turning off the lamps. Propping her head on a pillow, she tuned back into the movie.

Lacey brought her blanket and pillow up on the couch and lay down on the other side. "Can I ask you something?"

Faith turned down the volume. "Sure."

"When my brother Dean died in that car crash, it was so sudden. One day he was here, the next he was gone. With your sister being sick for so long, was it better to have the chance to say good-bye?"

Wow. Faith had never thought of it like that. She envisioned Hope healthy and young and suddenly being taken from her. "I suppose, in a way, it was easier. We knew the end was looming and we got to say good-bye, but watching her slowly fade, getting sicker and sicker, was awful. I can't imagine not having the opportunity to tell her one last time how much I loved her. How did you deal with losing Dean?"

Lacey blew out a breath. "I guess I didn't. Cole held me that day and stuck by my side through the funeral, but he blamed himself for Dean's accident and went on a downward spiral for ten years. Until Mia came back, anyway."

Faith had read Cole's memoir and knew much of this story already. Connecting these people with the characters in the book was strangely eye-opening.

"Faith?"

She turned her head to better see Lacey.

"Will you be one of my bridesmaids?"

Faith stilled. Lacey held her gaze in the dark. Only the

flickers of light from the movie illuminated her face. Faith didn't see any signs of teasing, but then again, she'd always been naive. "Really?"

"Really. In the few weeks you've been here, I've grown closer to you than most people I've known all my life."

A lump formed in Faith's throat and hot tears pressed behind her lids. This is what it felt like to have friends. Bittersweet and comforting and complete. How did she go on this long without them?

"I would be honored."

chapter
thirteen

A week later, a tan Mia and Cole had returned from their honeymoon, glowing and happy. Faith was glad to have them back. Not that she hadn't enjoyed her private time with Ginny, but with everything happening as of late, she hadn't had much time to herself.

Everything was all so new and a bit overwhelming. She wasn't used to friends and attention. It took some time to adjust to these changes in her life. Add in her developing relationship with Alec, and her head was reeling.

She and Lacey had spent a lot of time together the past two weeks, talking about everything from centerpieces for the wedding to childhood memories. Lacey had even dragged her and Ginny to the salon for a haircut and pampering. Unlike her parents, Lacey and Alec didn't mind her talking about Hope. In fact, Lacey often brought up her own brother Dean and her bittersweet memories of him. It was oddly comforting to have someone with whom she shared such a deep loss, someone who understood the pain.

Alec had divided his time between writing and popping by the house—usually around midday—to see what was happening with her. But he hadn't made any romantic gestures or attempted to touch her since their date. It left a hollow sensation inside her chest. They hadn't even been dating a week and it felt like he was distancing himself. Then again, Ginny was always around and there wasn't much time to be alone.

Faith sipped her chamomile tea and stared out the window. She'd been attempting to settle down and sleep for two hours to no avail. Restless energy crawled under her skin, made her twitch. She needed to shake the uncomfortable feeling, so she paced in the dim kitchen and tried to clear her mind. Closing her eyes, she breathed deep and counted to ten.

The feeling was still there. Shaking her head, she set the tea on the counter and made her way outside. She walked past the deck and the dunes just beyond it, and settled near the shore, squishing her toes in the sand. Letting the roar of the ocean surround her, she breathed in the humid saltwater scent and smiled.

This was what she needed. She was afraid to leave Ginny after the girl fell asleep, so while Mia and Cole had been away she hadn't walked down to the beach at night—a ritual she'd grown fond of since arriving in Wilmington. Faith wondered how she'd gotten by her entire life without the ocean. The tension and uncertainty drained from her body, leaving peace in its place.

Inside her pajama pants pocket, her cell vibrated. Heart pounding, she struggled to pull it out. She'd called her parents again after dinner tonight, when she knew they'd be home, but the machine kicked in. Every day she called. They'd called back a few times, but the conversations had been forced and stilted.

"Hi, it's Mom. You called?"

Relief spilled into her body. "I was just missing you. I wanted to catch up."

A lengthy silence followed until her mother cleared her throat. "The choir is working on some new hymns. We may try them out in the fall."

That wasn't exactly what Faith had had in mind, but she'd take it. "That sounds fun. I'm on the beach staring at the ocean." Faith bit her lip, wondering if she should just say what was on her mind. "I keep thinking . . ." She blew out a breath. "I think Hope would've loved it here. It's so pretty and peaceful. The pelicans come by every morning and evening. They—"

"Listen, Faith. It's late, don't you think? You should head to bed. Sleep is important."

"Right. You're right," she whispered, blinking rapidly. "Have a good night. I'll call again soon."

"Good night."

Hot tears burned behind her lids as she ended the call. She had a great job, a lovely place to live, friends, and a boyfriend even, but she would trade all that in for one real conversation with her parents. Any attempt to breach the miles and really connect. For them to show a sign that they truly missed her or wondered how she was doing. She'd wasted most of her childhood wishing for that.

Frustration and grief rose inside. She fisted the phone and stared at it. "Why won't you talk to me?" she ground out.

"Why won't who talk to you?"

She jumped and spun to face Alec. "Oh. I didn't see you there."

"Deep in thought again?" His smile fell as he walked closer, the moon illuminating his handsome face. "You've been crying."

Darn it. She swiped at the tears with the back of her hand and forced a smile. "What brings you out so late?"

"I was writing and saw you when I took a break. Don't

avoid the question. Does this person not talking to you have anything to do with why you're crying?"

She breathed out a sigh. "Maybe." Turning to face the water, she forced herself to calm down. "My mom just returned my call from earlier."

He stepped closer to stand at her side. "Is everything okay?"

"Yes. No." She rubbed her forehead, attempting to clarify. "They won't talk to me."

"Did you get in a fight?"

If only. Lord, that brought a fresh wave of tears. She swallowed hard and cleared her throat before answering. "You told me that your dad was always teasing you, that you couldn't be in the same room without butting heads. I have the opposite problem. I'd give anything to have my parents mad at me."

He shoved his hands in the pockets of his cargo shorts and rocked back on the heels of his bare feet. "That statement requires explanation."

She put the phone back in her pocket and crossed her arms, still facing the ocean. The thought of looking at him was unbearable. How does one explain that her own parents didn't want her and never had? "Your dad acts the way he does because he cares. It might not seem that way, but he wouldn't bother if he didn't love you." Might as well get it all out. She hoped saying the rest didn't make her sound pitiful. "My parents don't bother."

He stilled when she didn't say any more. After a few heartbeats, he moved to stand in front of her and dipped his head to look into her eyes. "Are you telling me your parents don't give a shit, Faith? I doubt that, very much."

The rough timbre of his voice caused her to shiver. His gray-blue eyes held her gaze and waited. She hesitated to offer more, but then decided it didn't matter. After this summer he'd go back to New York and forget all about her. What did she care if he knew? Except he might change his mind about their arrangement and walk away now. Might see just how pathetic she really was and think her too much of a head case.

"Faith?"

For courage, she glanced over his shoulder at the ocean for a few beats before looking into his eyes. "My sister was diagnosed with her illness before I was born. The type of cancer she had caused swelling and tissue damage, primarily on the left side of her body, though in some cases the right can be affected, too. It meant numerous transfusions and possibly even organ transplants down the road. My parents weren't a close enough match to Hope's blood type."

Again, Alec stilled. Realization slowly dawned in his eyes. The muscle in his jaw clenched. "You're trying to say that—"

"I was conceived for the sole purpose of being Hope's donor. Siblings are often the best match. I was her replacement parts, except I failed, and she died anyway."

His jaw dropped. He backed up two steps and stopped. "Jesus." His hand raked through his thick black hair. "Jesus," he said again. "I don't know where to start with something like that, Faith."

Not understanding his reaction, she stared at him.

He paced away and came back. "Your sister getting sick may have been what brought you into the world, but you're not anyone's replacement parts. Your parents—"

"Don't have a bond with me." Sensing where this conversation was headed, she lifted her hand to stop him. "They never have. We talk, but we never say anything. Not of substance."

His hands dropped to his sides. "That's your guilt talking. And you have nothing to feel guilty about. It wasn't up to you to save her. Christ, you were just a little girl."

This wasn't why she'd told him. She didn't need him to try and rationalize the behavior of the two people she'd lived her whole life trying to please. Somehow, in the last few months before moving to Wilmington, she'd realized something. You couldn't make someone love you, even if those people were the ones who were supposed to love you most. She'd accepted it. She didn't understand it and she hadn't gotten over it, but she accepted it.

"It's not guilt talking, Alec. It's years of observation."

He didn't know the silence of the Armstrong house after Hope died. Even before that, there had been few visitors in Faith's hospital room when they'd prepped her for Hope's procedures. All the focus was on her sister, and that's how it should've been. Of course her parents were there, got her settled and situated, moved from room to room when need be, but Hope was the sick one.

She closed her eyes briefly and drew in a lungful of air before opening them again. Alec had stopped pacing and was glaring at her with his arms crossed, feet evenly spaced apart as if bracing for an epic battle. "You're angry."

His head reared back and confusion marred his brow. "I guess I am."

Of all the reactions she'd been expecting, anger wasn't it. Revulsion. Pity. Shock, perhaps. Those emotions were normal. But anger just made no sense. What did he have to be angry about?

She didn't know how to do this, to be in a relationship. Even a temporary one like theirs. She knew nothing about friendship or conversation or how to be around people. All she knew was how to connect with disabled kids and teach. This was a mistake, thinking she could be with someone like Alec.

"I can't tell what you're thinking," he said. "You have that look on your face, like you've shut down on me, and I can't tell what you're thinking."

A heavy weight settled behind her ribs as she took a step back. "I'm sorry I upset you. Good night."

His heated gaze lifted from her mouth to her eyes. "Where are you going?"

She pointed. "Back to the house. It's late."

"Late," he mumbled and pinched the bridge of his nose. He ground out a few choice expletives. "Stay out here for a few minutes, would you? Finish the conversation."

Faith *was* finished. Any more and she'd start weeping again. "Good night, Alec."

Alec hung up the phone after a lengthy discussion with his editor and grabbed a beer from the fridge. He'd told the publisher to give him two months and he'd turn in the book. He was a little more than halfway through writing the first draft. If he buckled down, he could make that deadline. All things considered, they were pretty understanding about the whole thing.

This morning, Alec had given Cole the first fifty pages of a partial to see if Cole could represent him. At this stage in his career, his agent did little more than act as a buffer for contracts, but Alec didn't want Cole to represent him out of obligation. He wanted to make sure Cole wanted to do it, not that he had to. Alec could call up any agency right now and have his pick of agents. That wasn't the point. He wanted someone he could trust, not someone who was in it for the money.

Alec took his beer out onto the front porch and dropped into a chair, thinking about the book launch party in New York next weekend. He'd totally forgotten about it. The last book in his series was coming out next month, and his publicist, in conjunction with the publisher, was hosting the meet and greet. It was an obligation, one he didn't want to fulfill, but he'd suffer through. After all, it was only one night.

A two-month deadline would whoosh by if he kept at this pace. After Faith's little bomb on the beach last night, he'd spent his time wearing down the floorboards instead of writing. He hadn't slept. Barely even shoved food down.

A car door slammed and Alec looked up to find Jake

returning from work. Jake walked toward the main house until he glanced over and saw Alec outside. He changed directions and headed his way.

"You want a beer?"

"Naw." Jake sat down in a chair beside Alec. "Taking a break from writing?"

"Something like that."

"Uh-oh. You were doing great yesterday. What happened?"

Alec tipped the bottle back and swallowed. "Women, that's what happened."

Jake laughed in his easy, languid style. "Already? You and Faith just started seeing each other."

Alec shouldn't have mentioned it to Jake, but he needed a sounding board, and very few people knew the whole story of Laura and where he was coming from. Alec stood and walked to lean a hip against the railing.

Alec sighed. "Faith told me . . . something serious last night. Then afterward, she said she was heading to bed. Just like that. I asked her—actually begged her—to stay and talk about it. Nope. She said good night and left me standing there. When was the last time you saw me wanting to get into a heart-to-heart with a woman? Never."

Rant over, he took a swig of beer and looked at his brother over the bottle. "What are you grinning at?"

Jake shrugged. "You're falling for her."

Maybe a little bit. Or all the way.

Hell. Screw that. "I tell you she's messing with my head and you laugh."

"Sorry." Jake looked anything but sorry with his grin still plastered in place. "Is this thing she told you something you can share?"

Alec thought that over and decided it wasn't a national secret. Jake wouldn't repeat it anyway. "She told me her parents conceived her to be a donor for her sister."

There went the grin. "Wow."

"Yeah." Alec sat back down and drained his beer. "A lot of things are starting to make sense now. She's always surprised when I come to see her as if there's an alternate motive behind my visit, and she tries like hell to be invisible." He leaned forward and scrubbed his hands over his face. "Jesus, Jake. I think her folks just fucking ignored her. What kind of people do that?"

"She told you all of that?"

"No." Alec repeated what Faith had told him to the best of his recollection.

"Sounds like you two are perfect for each other. She's as screwed up as you are, big brother."

Alec narrowed his eyes. "This thing with Faith is just temporary. There is no perfect when it comes to us. I go back to the city after your wedding, remember?"

Jake studied him with measured intensity. "Does she know that?"

"It was her idea."

Jake opened his mouth as if he wanted to say more, but shook his head instead and rose from his seat. He walked to the steps and turned. "Tell her about Laura. She deserves to know."

Alec stared out at the yard, barren and waiting to be landscaped, until night fell and the mosquitoes started biting.

chapter
fourteen

What had started out as an impromptu powwow about Lacey's wedding had evolved into drinking wine in Adirondack chairs on the beach and laughing themselves silly. Faith leaned back in her chair and sighed into the night. This was perfect. Together with two new friends, a good Chianti—not that she would know if it were a bad one—and laughter. Her stomach hurt from the hysterics, but it was a good ache.

A gentle, moist breeze blew in off the ocean, bringing the scent of salt and brine. The seagulls had grown quiet. The only sound was her friends' fading laughter and the crush of waves on the beach.

Faith's phone vibrated in her pocket as she took another sip of wine. She quickly pulled it out and stared at the screen, both excited and frustrated to see the text was from Alec. Excited because she hadn't heard from him since her admission on the beach a few nights ago, and frustrated because the message wasn't from her parents.

I want to see you tonight.

That was it. Nothing else. Was he going to make it official and end things? Without the knock-her-off-her-feet kiss he had promised?

"You look disappointed," Mia said.

Faith glanced up to find both Mia and Lacey staring at her. "Alec texted that he wants to see me tonight."

"Why is that disappointing?" Mia asked, her soft voice barely registering over the waves.

Faith wanted to talk to them, the way normal friends did with each other. Share both joy and troubles. But opening up to people was hard for her, especially after the way Alec had reacted when she'd taken a chance with him.

"I think he might break up with me." It shouldn't hurt so much. They'd barely gotten off the ground. Yet she liked him. A lot. His humor was dry and sarcastic, his mind sharp. Their conversations never lagged. And then there was the kissing . . .

"Why do you say that?" Lacey wanted to know, sitting forward in her chair to pat Faith's knee. The touch didn't create anything like the heat Alec instilled, but it was comforting.

"A few nights ago he found me on the beach. We talked for a while and I told him a few things about my family. He was pretty angry after, so I went back to the guesthouse. This is the first I've heard from him since then."

Mia and Lacey shared a look before Lacey spoke. "None of us are strangers to family issues. It couldn't have been that bad."

Faith chewed over the idea of whether to confide in them, and decided to go for broke. Maybe the girls would understand better than Alec. She gave them a version of what she'd told Alec and then took a sip of wine to cool her throat.

"The thing is," Faith said, "it never bothered me how detached my parents were until I came here. Well, it bothered me a little. Honestly, I don't think I even noticed how bad it was until I met you guys." She looked at both women, who stared at her intently. "I shouldn't have told Alec."

Mia shook her head. "I'm glad you did. Even if you guys aren't in a serious relationship, you should be honest."

"He was so angry, though."

"Of course he was," Lacey said. "I'm angry. That's a terrible thing to do to a child."

It never crossed Faith's mind that Alec's anger might be directed at her parents. She thought he was mad at her for saying too much or perhaps feeling sorry for herself. Maybe he wasn't going to end things. Was it too much to hope for that he just wanted to see her? Her heart rate accelerated at the thought.

"My mama was the same way with Ginny." Mia set her wine aside and straightened. "She just never formed a bond with her. I tried to make up for it, but I think Ginny knew."

"Ginny had you," Lacey said before returning her gaze to Faith. "Who did you have?"

Faith tried to rub away the pressure in her chest, but it didn't work. "I had Hope. Every treatment and surgery was worth it to have her as long as I did." They didn't look convinced. "I'd do it all again in a heartbeat. I just wish my parents felt something toward me, too, you know?" Ashamed to find tears in her eyes, she swiped them away angrily. "It doesn't matter. I'm here now and starting over."

"Good for you," Mia affirmed with a nod.

"And you have us." Lacey reached for her hand and squeezed. After a moment, she sat back in her chair. "I always wanted friends. Real friends."

Mia nodded. "I wanted the stability of friends. It just never happened until . . . I came home." She looked back at the house behind them and smiled.

Home. Faith always thought of home as her parents' house, but maybe home wasn't there. Maybe she had yet to find it. "What do you think I should tell Alec?"

Mia shrugged. "That depends. Do you want to see him?"

Lacey laughed. "That smile on your face says yes. Do it, Faith. Have a glorious hot affair and enjoy your summer. Who knows, maybe something will come from it."

Dangerous thinking, that. To view their relationship as anything more than two ships passing in the night would only give her a broken heart. Alec himself had said he couldn't do more. They lived in separate states, had very different lives. No, Alec wasn't long term. But she would enjoy her brief time with him.

She unlocked her phone and thumbed out a text.

The moment Faith opened the door and Alec saw her, he knew his suspicions were right on the mark. He felt differently about her than he had about anyone in a long time. More so, if he dug deep enough into his memory. She chased away the dark. And somehow, since he'd known her, his writing had grown stronger.

Yet she acted like she could take him or leave him. Faith may have seemed aloof, but he suspected that under the surface there was strength and heart. Right next to insecurity and uncertainty. In fact, she seemed like someone hell-bent on taking care of herself, but failing.

That did funny things to his chest.

She gestured him inside, but he stayed rooted to the spot, taking in the sight of her. If he'd texted any other woman and said he was coming over, they'd be wearing ten pounds of makeup, high heels, and nothing else. That wasn't arrogance on his part, just stone-cold truth. Women wanted his money, his fame, or his body. No in-betweens or exceptions.

And then there was Faith. A haphazard ponytail left wisps of brown hair around her face. The loose cotton shorts and white tee she wore shouldn't be sexy. The lamplight behind her hid most of her freckles, but he still wanted to kiss each one, strip her to see if she had more. And where.

"Hi," he forced out.

"Hello. Are you going to come inside or should we talk through the doorway?"

The last thing he wanted to do was talk. He crossed the threshold and fit his lips over hers, reaching out and tugging her flush against his chest. And damn, the spark wasn't a fluke. The same heat and need flared to life. Consumed.

Tightening his hold on her, he lifted her enough to back her away from the entry and kicked the door shut, all the while keeping his mouth fused to hers. He spun her around and pressed her back against the door, planting his palms on either side of her head. If he kept his hands off her, he could stop this before the house went up in flames. Probably.

Faith didn't get the memo. Her fingers drove into his hair and tugged. Her tongue warred with his for dominance and he was damn tempted to let her win. Just for the hell of it. To let himself be conquered for once.

When one of her legs snaked around his hips, drawing his jean-clad erection snug against the apex of her thighs, he groaned and rested his forehead against hers. Tried to breathe. "You're a sleeper," he mumbled, head still somewhere in the vicinity of that kiss.

"Sleeper?" she breathed.

God, that voice of hers got to him in ways he couldn't possibly explain. "Yeah. A sleeper. You seem all reserved and calm on the surface, lying in wait until the moment of initiation, and then you strike."

Her amber eyes lifted to his, her dilated pupils telling him she was just as affected. "That was a compliment, right?"

He laughed and dropped a kiss on her shoulder. *Smelled so good.* "Yes, that was a compliment." He'd come over here for something other than this, hadn't he? He couldn't seem to remember.

"So, you're not breaking up with me?"

He ceased his nibbling on the tendon in her neck and looked at her. Just as he suspected. Insecurity shone in her eyes, not needy attention-seeking manipulation. "Why would I do that?"

She shrugged, one of her hands still fisted in his hair. "You were mad out on the beach when I talked about . . ."

As she trailed off, he stared, wondering how to put into words the emotions she'd brought out in him with her admission a few nights back. He shouldn't care. If they were nothing more than a summer fling, he shouldn't care.

She blinked slowly. "You wanted to know about my past. I don't talk about it very often, mostly because no one's asked before, but . . ."

She was killing him. "There's no excuse for what your parents did. You should never feel bad for being put on the back burner because of someone else's faults. You hear me, Faith?"

Her head tilted, taking in his words. "Lacey was right. You're mad at my parents, not me."

She talked about him with Lacey? That was a good sign that she thought about him half as much as he did her.

Her hands dropped to his chest. "I don't . . ."

"You don't what?"

"I don't think anyone's been mad on my behalf before." Killing him dead.

He sucked in a breath and suddenly remembered why he came over. She'd never been to the beach before Mia and Cole hired her, which made it likely she hadn't traveled at all. "Come with me to New York next Saturday."

The back of her head hit the door when she startled. "What?"

He removed his palms from the door to cup her chin. "My publisher is throwing a release party I have to attend. It'll just be for one night, but I can show you around the city beforehand. Have you ever been to New York?"

"No. But why do I need to go, too?"

Alec wondered if she'd ever get out of the habit of questioning the motivation behind others wanting to be in her company. "You don't *need* to go. I *want* you to go. I'd like you there."

"Oh."

Again with the *oh*. "What do you say?"

Her gaze drifted over his shoulder as she contemplated. "Okay. As long as Mia doesn't need me in town."

"You don't work weekends." Why the hell was he trying so hard to convince her? He never brought dates to release parties.

"I'm sure it won't be a problem," she said, staring at him as if wanting to say more. She opened and closed her mouth several times before finally speaking. "If you change your mind about this thing between us, just tell me. I'd like to stay on friendly terms afterward. If you drag it out—"

"I'll tell you." A sour sensation formed in his gut, and he had to wonder why the thought of ending things made him sick. "I'm happy with the way things are, for now."

She nodded and drew in a slow breath, causing her breasts to brush temptingly against his chest. "Is that why you wanted to see me? To ask about New York?"

No. "Yes. How about a walk on the beach before you go to bed?"

Bed. Christ, he wanted her in bed, beneath him, more than he cared to analyze. Some distance was needed. After nothing more than a few kisses, Faith was in his head. Practically all he thought about. Which made no sense because he'd had sex with more women than he could count, had gotten hot and heavy with them, and none of them had him this . . . enthralled.

Maybe Faith was right. Maybe this had to do with how she'd helped him write again.

Or not.

She dropped her forehead to his chest. The move brought out something deep and protective inside him. Before he could scrutinize the sensation she smiled against his chest and straightened.

"Sure. Let's go for a walk."

They made their way outside, where the humidity had faded after sunset and the breeze was warm. Once they were past the dunes and walking in the surf, he took her hand. The action surprised even him. He wasn't a romantic by nature.

"Hi. I'm Alec and I like long walks on the beach."

That got the desired reaction because she laughed. A smooth, smoky sound that slid over his skin.

"You don't strike me as the type."

He wasn't usually, which just made his conversation with Jake all the more pressing. No matter why or when this ended, Faith deserved to know about his history. She'd shared a part of hers and needed to know what she was getting into, however brief a time they stayed together.

Except he didn't have a clue how to tell her about Laura. Before meeting Faith, women were just a string of random hookups with whom he had no intention of a repeat offense. Safer that way.

"What's on your mind?"

Alec smiled. How could he not? Faith had an uncanny ability to know things, read people. Unless it involved herself, anyway. Then she was oblivious.

He paused their walk by tugging on her hand and sat in the sand, gesturing for her to join him. When she complied, he lay back and stared at the stars. After a moment, she laid next to him, their arms and thighs touching.

"The sky looks different like this," she said, turning her head to face him. "Doesn't it? It looks bigger. Vast."

He murmured in agreement. "I take it you never did this. Laid down and watched the sky? Jake and I used to do it all the time as kids. I haven't in a long time."

"No, I haven't. There's a lot of things I haven't done, but I'm trying to make up for that." She turned her head and stared at the sky again. "I can't help but think that Hope would be disappointed in me for not living."

Not for the first time, her brutal honesty gutted him. "You

can't think that way. You missed her and followed the routine you were accustomed to living. No one can fault you for that."

"So that's not what's bothering you? My inexperience?"

What? "What?"

"You kiss me like you can't help it and then back away to cool things down. You've done it twice now. I told you I'm not a virgin—"

"Stop." He held up his hand and turned on his side to face her. "I'm trying not to rush things here."

The sound of her swallow rose over the waves as she remained focused on the stars. "Do you know anything about constellations?"

Constellations?

"No." He rolled to his back, wanting to take her abrupt change of topic as a sign. They barely knew each other. It wasn't as if there could be a future between them. Why bother getting into—

Screw it. "I was engaged once before." Still was, if only in his head. "I don't want to repeat my mistakes, Faith. That's why I don't get involved. Why I don't date a woman for more than a night. Actually dating someone, even just for the summer, is a new experience, and I'm not ashamed to admit that I don't know what I'm doing."

Plus, he cared enough about Faith to not want to hurt her. It was a special talent of his, hurting people, and it seemed she'd already had enough of that in her short lifetime. He closed his eyes and drew in a lungful of air, not realizing he'd been holding his breath.

After a few moments, she took his cold hand in her warm one and squeezed. "I understand."

His eyes flew open. "You understand?"

He sat up, but she remained inclined, her dark hair fanned around her head in the sand. Why didn't she probe him for answers? Demand to know what happened to his fiancée? Christ. She was from another fucking planet. Even a stranger would want to know the gory details. People were like that by nature. Curious.

Faith didn't follow the pattern on anything. It was as if she didn't care or lacked the genetic makeup to connect.

"Yes, I understand. I've never been close to marriage, but if I had and it ended badly, then I would be hesitant to enter into a relationship again." She moved to sit, but instead of facing him, she turned toward the water. "Commitment takes a lot of trust, and if that trust breaks, it's hard to get it back, even with someone else."

When he didn't answer because he couldn't, she turned her head his way. Weariness and acceptance looked back at him through amber eyes so soft he felt the shift all the way to his toes. For the zillionth time, she'd proven him wrong. Faith didn't feel nothing. She felt everything. An empath of sorts, able to put herself in other's shoes and feel their emotions.

No wonder she was afraid to live. He would be, too.

How had little Faith Armstrong, sheltered from the world and struggling in her own skin, manage to nail his feelings down as if she'd taken up residence in his head the past nine years? Yeah, she'd only gotten it half right, because she didn't know the whole story, but damn it.

He swallowed the boulder in his throat. Guilt he understood, and it was running rampant in his gut.

"You're angry again."

He shook his head.

"It's getting late. I should head back inside." She stood and brushed the sand off her body.

He fisted his hands. "I wasn't angry, but I am now."

Her confused gaze darted to him and away. She crossed her arms and shifted her feet, her focus on the ocean. "I'm sorry."

Anger went from simmering to boiling over. To give himself time, he stood and brushed the sand from his jeans. "Sorry," he repeated, his head about to explode. She was always walking away from him, with her mantra of *It's getting late* or *I'm sorry* or—damn the word all to hell—*Oh*.

But this time around she said nothing as she turned to leave.

"You really know how to bruise a guy's ego, Faith."

She turned. "I don't understand, Alec. You're angry. I'm leaving."

"I'm angry because you're leaving." Well, hell. That came out wrong. "Could you stop walking away from me anytime I display a semblance of emotion?"

She pressed her palms over her eyes. "What am I supposed to do? To say? I don't know how to fight."

Her hands came down and a spark of anger shone in her eyes, rocking him back on his heels. This was the first time he'd seen her even close to mad. It was hot. Damn hot.

She sighed. "And I don't know how to behave around you. Everything winds up making you upset."

Shit. Was that how she saw it? That wasn't his intention. "The only thing I want you to do or say or be is yourself, but with less leaving the second things start to get serious."

Did he just say that? He rolled the words back through his mind and . . . yeah. He had. He'd just told her to stick around. What the fuck was happening to him? Sometimes talking to her was like trying to teach a two-year-old organic chemistry.

He scrubbed a hand down his face. "Couples fight." Don't they? "And just because I'm mad doesn't mean it's targeted at you."

Besides, angry sex was hot. If they ever got to the sex part. He wanted to. Really, really badly. Yet this force she had around her—the one sucking him in willingly—should be holding him back from getting in too deep. Except it was having the opposite effect. Instead of getting hot and heavy between the sheets, they . . . talked.

She stared at him, on the precipice of running again, he could tell. To her credit, she didn't. This time, she walked closer, until her breasts flattened against his chest and they were thigh to thigh. She smelled good enough to eat. That sugary signature scent that was solely hers rose up over the breeze as she wrapped her arms around his waist.

It was the first time she'd initiated contact. He liked it, the way she'd finally surrendered, so he dropped a kiss on her forehead.

"You always smell so good." He buried his face in her hair and inhaled. "Like cupcakes and vanilla. It drives me crazy."

"It must be my lotion." Her voice quivered as he trailed his fingers down her throat. "Or body spray . . ."

Alec cut her off with a kiss, long and deep and languid. His hands drove into her hair and pulled the band out to run his fingers through the soft strands. The sweet scent intensified, as did his hard-on.

He pulled away and smiled at the drugged arousal he put in her eyes. It turned their color from amber to a deep golden brown. "I like looking at the front of you better than the rear. Not that you don't have a great backside." His hands drifted to cup her bottom to emphasize his point. "Please quit tucking tail and running. I'd rather be kissing you than thinking about doing it while I'm alone in my house."

chapter
fifteen

Faith didn't know what to make of it, but she and Alec had gotten into a comfortable routine the past week. She worked with Ginny during the day, while Alec slept back at his guesthouse. After dinner, he'd come over to her place. They'd talk or watch movies or read—like they were doing at this moment—with her reclined on the couch and her feet in his lap. After a few hours, Alec would take off for home and write most of the night while Faith slept.

They were like night and day. Oil and water. Yet this system worked. They . . . fit.

But aside from making out, Alec hadn't made a move toward the bedroom. Every time things heated up and she was sure he would finally get her naked, a switch flipped and he backed off. It was disconcerting, to say the least. She wasn't beautiful in any sense of the word—instead of sexy curves, her body had . . . edges—but she'd never considered herself unattractive. Alec had been in town a month, same as her, and he hadn't been with anyone else that she was aware of. He had needs. So why wasn't he sating them?

Faith had spent most of her life unsure of herself, and being with Alec—or not, in this case—was making her even more uncertain. She was sure he wanted her. His reactions were obvious. So, why didn't he take them there?

Sighing, she tried to refocus on the book she was reading. It was the second book in Alec's Hacked series. She'd read it twice before. The third and last book in the trilogy was the one they were attending the release party for in New York tomorrow night.

Alec peeked at her from over the book he was reading—a romance she'd picked out for him. He was loathe to comply, but did it with only minor grumbling. Faith had hoped it would spark some interest in getting frisky. So far all he'd done was caress her calf.

"You sighed," he said. "What's wrong? You don't like the book? Which part?"

She smiled. "You know you're a good author. Don't fish for compliments."

He set the book down on his lap. "It matters to me if *you* think I'm good."

She had no way to gauge how seriously that statement was to be taken, so she stared at him before speaking. The tone of his voice was hesitant, his eyes bordering on pleading. He wasn't looking for an ego boost. He was seeking her opinion, and that opinion mattered.

She tucked her feet under her legs and sat up. "I don't think you're good. I think you're one of the best horror writers to hit the market in this generation, which makes you great. I've read this book twice before."

Turning slowly to face her, he propped his arm on the back of the couch, his fingers inches from her face. "That means a lot, you saying that. Thank you." The coarse gravel of his voice indicated he'd been touched by what she'd said.

He looked around the room and patted her thigh. Like a pet. "Are you all packed for tomorrow?"

They'd only be gone one night. Packing didn't require much effort. "Yes. All except my dress for the party. Lacey's bringing one of hers for me to wear."

He was treating her like a friend, not like someone he intended to sleep with or someone he found attractive. Faith's heart fell somewhere near her stomach. She shouldn't be disappointed, yet the feeling swamped her anyway. Hurt laced her throat. For once, she'd felt wanted when he'd kissed her. Desired. Not looked over and passed by. What had changed in the last couple days?

When a knock sounded at the door, Faith was relieved by the interruption. On the other side of the doorway stood Mia and Lacey, huge grins on their faces. Some of the tension drained just from seeing her friends.

Lacey held up a garment bag on a hanger. "One sexy cocktail dress, at your disposal."

Faith didn't remember saying it had to be sexy. She'd simply asked if Lacey had one she could borrow, not wanting to go shopping for a dress she'd probably never wear again.

Mia and Lacey strode inside, but halted when they saw Alec.

Mia turned. "I'm sorry we interrupted. We didn't realize you had company."

Grinning, Alec stood. "I was just leaving anyway. Early flight tomorrow." He walked over to Faith and kissed her lightly on the mouth. Hardly a peck. "I look forward to seeing you in the quote 'sexy cocktail dress.'"

"We'll only need Faith for an hour or so," Lacey said. "You can come back. Spend the night. Continue where you left off."

Jeez. Subtle, Lacey was not. Besides, if they continued where they left off, Faith would finish reading the book and Alec would be snoring next to her.

Alec's grin widened when he looked back at Faith. "I'll

see you in the morning." He kissed her forehead this time—
her forehead—and left.

"I'm sorry," Mia said. "Did we ruin your night?"

"No, no." Faith waved her hand, surprised by the tears
blurring her vision.

"Oh, sweetie." Lacey draped an arm over her shoulders
and squeezed. "What's wrong? What did Alec do? Should
I send Jake to beat him up?"

Faith breathed out a laugh. "Thank you, but no. It's nothing." Except this nothing hurt. A lot. She'd known from day
one she wasn't the right match for Alec, but she didn't listen
to that internal voice. His actions belied his words. One minute hot, the next lukewarm. "He won't have sex with me."

Mortified, she sat on the couch and covered her face with
her hands.

"That would make me cry, too," Mia said, trying to
lighten the mood. She put her hand on Faith's knee and
squatted down in front of her. "What do you mean, he won't
have sex with you? I thought things were going well. Isn't
that the whole basis of your relationship? Just fun for the
summer?"

Faith wiped her eyes with the back of her hand and sniffed.
Leave it to her to ruin even a no-strings relationship. "I don't
know what's going on. Every time things heat up, he . . .
stops."

Lacey sat next to her and passed a tissue. "Has he said
anything?"

"Just that he wanted to take things slow."

Lacey snorted. "I'm sorry. That came out wrong." She
looked at Mia for guidance.

"I know what you're thinking," Faith said. "Alec Winston
doesn't do slow. He doesn't do commitment. Which is the
problem. If he really wanted me, he would've had me by now."
He sure acted like he wanted her.

Mia sat on the coffee table in front of Faith and leaned
forward. "Alec also doesn't spend this much time with one

person. He's been over here every night. I've seen him walking over."

"I know just what you need," Lacey said. "Come on. We're going shopping."

"Now?" Faith looked between the two of them. "It's almost eight."

"The mall closes in an hour. We need to hurry."

The next thing Faith knew, she was standing in a lingerie store having an uncomfortable stare down with a mannequin wearing a blue thong. "This is a bad idea."

"No, it's not," Lacey assured. "You're going to be spending the night in Alec's apartment in New York. Let's give him a little incentive to speed things along. Something in this store will surely make him want to jump your bones."

"It'll make you feel good, too," Mia added. "Trust me. Cole goes gaga over this one set of red satin—"

"Eww! Hello? That's my brother."

Faith sighed. It wasn't like she wore granny panties, not that Alec had even seen if she had, but lace and silk were a little out of her comfort zone. Boy shorts, thongs, bikini trim, hip-huggers . . . it was all so silly. If Alec wanted to be with her, she shouldn't need this stuff.

But as she followed Lacey and Mia through the store, a yellow bra-and-panty set caught her eye. It was completely lace and cut in an old forties style, the material soft with rounded trim for comfort. She tried to picture herself wearing it and the look on Alec's face. Wondered how the lace would feel against the sensitive areas of her skin. Her cheeks heated.

"Oh! I like that." Lacey shoulder-bumped her. "Mia, this one?"

Mia made her way over. "Yes. Elegant and hot."

"What are you going to sleep in?" Lacey asked.

"Uh . . . my pajamas?"

Mia grinned. "If the lingerie does the trick, she won't be sleeping in anything."

"You'd be able to wear this under that dress I gave you." Lacey fished through the hangers. "What size are you?"

Faith fisted the pendant around her neck and slid it back and forth on the chain. She gave Lacey her size and prayed they didn't laugh. Mia and Lacey had slender, but curvy frames, whereas Faith was lean. Her chest size was especially pathetic. Hope had gotten all the good genes in the family. Faith had gotten the leftovers.

What would Alec do if he had the chance to strip off her dress after the party? She felt shockingly inadequate already—she didn't think she could handle disapproval in his eyes. She had so little experience when it came to men. Alec had experience in spades. Could she even satisfy him? Would she even know what to do?

"You know what?" Faith croaked. "It's okay. We don't need to go to all this trouble."

But her new best friends didn't listen. Faith walked out of the store with not only the yellow lace bra-and-panty set, but a pale blue and a black one, too.

Between the flight and the taxi ride to his apartment, Alec had asked Faith a dozen times what was wrong. She didn't know how to answer. What had been a comfortable mix of conversation and silence this past week had morphed into just silence. She felt the shift in him, too. She'd caught him darting quick glances at her during the flight, only to hastily look away when she noticed. The casual way he'd touched her arm or hand while they were alone back in Wilmington hadn't followed them to New York.

Deciding to make the most of her trip despite the unsettling shift between them, she looked out the window as their taxi wove its way through traffic. New York was loud and busy, completely unlike the quiet beauty of Wilmington. Everywhere she looked there was asphalt and rushing pedestrians and flashing lights. Sirens and shouting. She wondered how Alec got any writing done here, even in his apartment. How did people breathe here?

The taxi pulled to the curb of a massive structure where doormen were waiting to be needed and concrete lion statues perched at the entrance. The building looked old and pristine among the chaos of the city.

"This is it," Alec said, as if asking approval.

Unsure of what to say, because this apartment didn't seem to suit him any more than the city, she forced a smile and made to exit the car. Alec grabbed their bags and nodded to the doormen, who addressed him by name.

Inside the lobby, which was full of white marble and brass, she followed Alec to a bank of chrome and glass elevators and waited. He had yet to make eye contact. The ride upstairs was just as tense as in the cab, and by the time they stepped off the elevator to the door of his penthouse, Faith was ready to catch a flight home.

Though she didn't know him all that well, and though they had just arrived, Alec seemed like a different person here. Tense and abrasive. Not at all like the laid-back, gentle man she knew in Wilmington. She wondered if this was how he wrote about such darkness, by living in this place and feeding off its energy. He'd written countless bestsellers, after all. Something besides his gift had to fuel the stories.

He set their bags down and unlocked the door. "Listen, I have to warn you. I made a terrible choice in interior decorators a while back."

She stepped into the foyer. "I'm sure it's not that . . . bad."

It was that bad. No, it was worse.

The walls were dark gray. The leather furniture red. And was that a . . . yes. A life-sized sculpture of a claw. Glass-top tables and horror movie posters.

"Wow," she whispered.

Alec dropped their bags by an entry table and groaned. "I warned you." He glanced around, as if trying to see it through her eyes. "It's nightmarish all right. I keep intending to have it fixed."

"*Can* it be fixed?"

He laughed. "I'll call someone after Jake's wedding."

After the wedding. When he'd be moving back.

She shook her head and forced the unpleasant thoughts away.

To her left was the kitchen. Pretty spacious, considering. Black appliances, granite counters. To the right was a short hallway with three doors.

"Come on," Alec said. "I'll give you the grand tour."

The office was clean and sensibly organized. Surprising, because she figured most authors had Post-it Notes and clutter. A plush corduroy sofa lined one wall. Several bookshelves stood against the other. Under the window and facing the door was a large L-shaped desk made out of what looked like mahogany. She didn't get a good look at any of his pictures because Alec was already moving on to the next room.

"Bathroom," he pointed out, striding past. "And this is the bedroom."

At his insistence, she stepped inside. Hardwood floors. Four-poster bed. Private bathroom. The walls were a smoky blue, darn near close to his eye color. The curtains and bedspread were a navy striped pattern. This room suited him. Masculine and easygoing.

She walked to the bay window and looked out at the view. Thirty floors below them, the city bustled and jived, but this high up they were above the noise. Part of her unease settled and released from her shoulders.

Alec came up behind her and set his hands on her hips, pulling her back flush with his chest. His lips settled over her ear, causing her to shiver.

Inhaling, he moaned. "I couldn't wait to get you alone. It's been hard keeping my hands to myself."

She curled into him like a cat. It felt like forever since

he'd touched her. The heat from his body and the scent of him caused her heart to flutter. Her breathing uneven, she made herself ask, "Why did you keep your hands to yourself?"

"I wanted to give it a little time. You're not the kind of woman I'm used to, Faith."

She couldn't tell if that was a compliment or an insult. She wondered what he saw in her at all, besides convenience. Did she have anything in common with his other affairs?

She settled on a ploy of humor. "What did the other women you were with think of your apartment? Were they a little scared of the decorating, too?"

His fingers dug into her hips. "I've never brought a woman here. You're the first."

Her heart pounded against her ribs. Turning in his arms, she looked at him. "No one?"

"No one. Trust issues." He shrugged. "You're the only woman I've met in ten years who seems to want me for me."

How . . . sad. Didn't people realize a soul-deep connection was ten times more powerful than money and fame? She'd take her new friends and contentment over all the money in New York any day.

Alec leaned in and brushed his lips over hers. "I want to make love to you in that bed. Been thinking about it nonstop since we got to the airport." Easing back, he smiled. "But I should show you around the city before the party. We'll never get out of here if we start now."

Okay. Wow. A resounding ping of happiness hit her square between the eyes. Just an hour ago she was wondering what had happened between them. But now he'd just told her what he wanted, and it was her. Alec still found her attractive.

She would rather stay here in his arms, in the bed they had yet to climb into, than head out and see the sites, but there would be time for that tonight. A little tease to get him excited about their own after-party couldn't hurt, though. Maybe saying something sexy would keep his mind on her. "Lacey helped me pick out some panties to wear under my dress. I can't wait for you to take them off."

He sucked in a breath, and with narrowed eyes trailed his gaze down the length of her as if trying to imagine the details. With a groan, he kissed her deep, pulling her against him and pressing his pelvis into her belly. "What color?" he asked, nipping her lower lip.

Locking her knees to stay upright, she looked into his gray-blue eyes, relieved to see unadulterated want in them. "You'll have to wait to find out."

Verbal foreplay didn't come naturally to her, but she found she liked it. Liked the effect it seemed to have on him. Grabbing her bottom, he squeezed and let go before taking two steps backward and shoving his hands in his pockets.

Watching her mouth, he asked, "Where would you like to go? In the city, I mean. As a tourist."

She smiled at the nervous tone of his voice, relieved he was unnerved, too. "Where would you suggest?"

He glanced at the bed and sighed. "Statue of Liberty? The Guggenheim? Empire State Building?"

"What about the 9/11 Memorial? Can we do that first?"

He rocked back on his heels. "Sure. I know a great Jewish deli not far from there for lunch." He held out his hand. "Come on."

chapter
sixteen

Alec had been surprised by Faith's request to visit the 9/11 Memorial, but he shouldn't have been. Someone like her would want to pay homage to the lives lost and pay her respects. That was just the way she was built. Sure, she'd have an interest in fine art or other attractions—she'd be interested in anything—but it said a lot about her that she wanted her first stop to be a place of such terrible loss.

They hadn't said a word while they were there. Alec had moved to New York a good five years after the attacks on the World Trade Center and hadn't visited the memorial himself. He'd watched her and the myriad of emotions that splayed across her pretty face before they moved on to walk down the street.

He'd been watching her since the airport. Something was different about her today, and he couldn't figure out what. She wasn't one to chat endlessly, but she'd been even more quiet than usual. He wondered what gears were turning in her mind.

Didn't matter. He liked looking at her. Could do it all day. She was an interesting conundrum and atypical of the female species. Alec figured the day he'd get a handle on her, he'd discover a rash of new qualities to trip him up all over again.

Faith Armstrong was something special. And she was getting to him.

Holding her hand, he walked into the deli he'd discovered his first year in the Big Apple and grinned at Zelig, who was behind the counter. He and his wife had started the business more than forty years ago. The place was still busy as hell. The scents of fresh bread, cabbage, and corned beef hit him at once. Zelig was a large, robust man, but his black hair had grown more and more gray since Alec last saw him.

"Alec!" Zelig shouted, wiping his large hands on an apron. "Long time no see. How are you?" He came around the counter and wrapped Alec in a hug.

"I'm great, thanks. This is Faith."

"Faith," he repeated, hugging her, too. "Pretty name for a pretty lady. What can I get you two? Anything you want."

Faith smiled at Alec and shrugged. "What do you suggest?"

Alec barked a laugh. "Everything." He turned to Zelig. "Give us the tabbouleh platter with the pita and chocolate babka for dessert."

"You got it!" Zelig jerked a thumb at Alec and addressed Faith. "This one here can eat me out of babka."

When Zelig went back behind the counter, Alec found a corner booth and slid into it across from Faith. "Wait until you try their food. It's an orgasm in your mouth."

Faith laughed, the skin around the corners of her eyes crinkling. "I believe you. How'd you find this place?"

After Laura's accident, he'd been wandering around the city trying to ease the guilt and stumbled into the deli late one night. Zelig fed him some chicken soup and sourdough bread, saying nothing about closing time to an obviously distraught Alec.

Alec shook his head. "Don't remember, but I'm glad I did."

Her amber eyes told him she didn't believe him, but she let it drop. "When we walked in, that was the first time I've seen you smile or laugh since we landed."

Observant, wasn't she? "I have a love/hate relationship with the city."

Before he could clarify, Zelig brought their order. "The babka's coming. You want a loaf of cinnamon to take home, too? For breakfast?"

Alec grinned. "That would be awesome."

With Zelig gone, Alec spread some of the tabbouleh onto a pita wedge and held it up to Faith's mouth.

She glanced at the tomato, roasted peppers, and herb combination before opening her mouth. She bit down and moaned. "That is good."

"Told you," Alec said. "I'd mention the corned beef was to die for, but you wouldn't eat it." Not with all the healthy consumption rules she lived under. Now that he knew part of her story, he couldn't blame her.

"In moderation is okay. Maybe we can try it next time."

Next time. There would be no next time. They were in New York for one night and then heading back to Wilmington. Where she'd stay. And he'd eventually leave. An ache formed in his gut. Heartburn, he figured.

Like she was so apt to do, Faith changed to a safer subject. "What can I expect from this party tonight?"

God, he wanted out of it. Wanted to take her back to his apartment and drive her as insane as she was making him. Repeatedly. All damn night long.

He loaded more tabbouleh onto a pita wedge for himself. "A lot of people, for one. The publicists and editors will have the press there. After some schmoozing, I'll read a passage from the book and then do a signing. It's really an excuse to make the publisher feel important. Drinking, socializing. You know, torture for a writer."

She grinned. "Should we develop a secret signal for when you want to escape? I could rub my ear and blink three times."

He laughed. "Tempting." Staring at her a moment while he chewed, he realized how uncomfortable she'd be as well. She didn't seem fond of crowds. "I should've asked you before now. Will you be okay tonight?" He didn't know how much attention he'd be able to pay her once the throng arrived. The last thing he wanted was to drag her all the way to New York only to ignore her after dumping her in among strangers.

The look she gave him was long and impossible to read. After a few moments, she blinked rapidly and took a sip of water. "I'll be fine. Thank you for asking."

What in the hell was that about? The tears. Or how close she was to tears anyway. "What's wrong, Faith?" He tried for a gentle tone but his voice just came out gruff.

"It was nice of you to ask, that's all." She cleared her throat and glanced out the window before looking back at him. "I'll be fine tonight. You do what you need to do and be the charming author. Don't worry about me."

The words were out before he could stop them. "Does anyone ever? Worry about you, I mean."

Christ. She had no connections, no family back in Charlotte. Her parents showed her little affection. She barely knew what to do with herself when anyone paid her any kind of attention. And fuck . . . he was caring too much.

As if he could stop.

Her gaze lifted to his, her expression as shocked and hesitant as he imagined his was. Those amber eyes were filled with tears, but she seemed determined to fight them back. To her credit, and his peace of mind, she did. Her teeth worked her lower lip until the urge to drag her across the table and kiss her became almost too much.

Blowing out a breath, she broke the connection and stared at her plate. "What's babka?" she asked quietly, fiddling with her napkin.

Alec had to swallow several times before speaking, and even then it hurt to force words out. "It's a coffee cake type of bread. Dessert, sort of."

She nodded slowly, still not meeting his eyes. Still looking hollow. She was too damn good for hollow.

"I worry about you." All the time. All the damn time.

Her eyes pinched closed. "Don't do that."

"Faith." He tried to take her hand across the table, but she pulled away.

"Stop it. Don't act like I matter."

Of all the damn things she'd said to him, this one took the cake. Hell, it took the whole bakery. Under the table, his fists clenched. "What does that mean? Of course you matter."

Shaking her head, her jaw clenched. Her eyes flared with hurt and anger.

And it dawned on him maybe she *didn't* matter to anyone. Before now. But he understood. Too well, he understood. Their relationship was temporary, and her mattering to him meant it would make things that much harder come summer's end.

He sat back and scrubbed his hands over his face. He never should've gone down this road. All he'd ever done in life was screw up. People. Relationships. After Laura, he should've known better. *Did* know better.

"Do we have time for the Statue of Liberty before we have to get ready for the party?"

Face still buried in his hands, Alec laughed. It bordered on hysterical before he managed to rein it in. "Sure, Faith."

Faith stared at her reflection in Alec's bathroom mirror, trying to take control over the sudden onslaught of emotions. She gripped the sink and drew in a haggard breath. It wasn't supposed to go like this. They were supposed to come to New York, have a great time, and leave. They were supposed to finally have sex, with no serious emotions involved, and enjoy themselves.

But Alec kept screwing with her head every time the conversation turned slightly personal. Kept saying sweet, endearing things as if he cared about her. He didn't, though. He'd said it himself. He'd been engaged once before and it was not an experience he'd repeat. She suspected there was far more to the end of the relationship than he let on, especially if he wasn't capable of opening himself up again, but that wasn't any of her business.

Straightening, she looked at herself. She'd pinned her hair up in a twist both for elegance and to keep it off her face. Her makeup was minimal, just enough to accentuate her assets. The small pearl drops in her ears matched the necklace. It had bothered her to take off Hope's charm, but she reminded herself she could put the chain back on right after the party.

Smoothing her hand down the dress, she nodded. Lacey had been right. The yellow strapless bra-and-panty set was perfect. It didn't show beneath the black dress, nor were the seams obvious. The dress tied round her neck, fitting snug against her chest and hips before flowing loosely to her knees. Plus, for a cocktail number, it was pretty comfortable.

She hoped Alec liked it. Enough to want to take it off later.

Shaking her head, she stepped into the low black heels Mia had lent her and forced herself to leave the bathroom.

Alec was waiting in the living room, thumbs flying over the keys of his phone as he texted someone. He looked different in a suit. More businesslike and less like himself. It fit him perfectly, accentuating his broad shoulders and narrow hips. The charcoal gray went nicely with his eyes. Under the jacket, he wore a crisp white button-down shirt, no tie.

She imagined running her hands down his chest, popping the buttons one by one until she could push the fabric from his shoulders and kiss her way lower . . .

Alec glanced up from his phone and did a double take. "Damn, Faith. You look . . . lovely."

She glanced down at herself and back to him. "So do you. Handsome, I mean. You look handsome."

Desire shone in his eyes, burning a path from her toes to her face as he looked his fill. Pocketing his phone, he stepped closer, a wicked half smile crooking his mouth. He slid his hands around her back and tugged her close. "You smell good enough to eat."

Her pulse went crazy. "Um . . . thank you?"

He amped up the wattage of his grin. "You're welcome."

Dipping his head, he kissed her. Just a brush of his lips, but her legs nearly buckled. His heat and scent enveloped her. Her breathing hitched. She needed him, more of him, tonight. It had never been like this before. She'd been attracted to other men, but nothing like this. Thinking was moot when Alec was around.

And that just served to prove she needed to follow through on their affair. At twenty-seven, she'd barely lived her life. It was time. Where she found the courage, heaven knew, but she did and she was going to enjoy it. However long it lasted. She was going to go all-out crazy and dive into a fleeting, dangerous affair with the likes of Alec Winston, and they were going to have some between-the-sheets time.

Gasping, she pulled back to look at him. She had never known this kind of yearning, this fanatical desire, and it had her rattled and reaching for logic. "You . . ."

"Yes?" he murmured, closing his mouth on the skin of her neck. "What about me?"

Her belly quivered. Heat pooled between her legs. "Um . . . I forgot."

He laughed and stepped away. "Just as well. We need to get going." His slow, steady gaze drifted down the length of her and back up, a routine habit of his, it seemed. "But later, Faith, I'll make sure you're unable to think at all."

Yes. Okay. Perfect. She could stand mindless. "Promise?"

Closing his eyes, he groaned and turned for the door. "Cross my heart."

The ride to the hotel where the event was to take place took only about twenty minutes. They didn't say much on the way. Alec appeared calm on the surface, but his hands were clenched and every few seconds he drew in a deep breath that expanded his wide chest, as if remembering to inhale. Apparently this wouldn't be much of a party for him. In his world, he had to do book signings and show the face behind the cover on occasion, but he obviously didn't like it. Faith figured he'd rather be at home with his imaginary characters than with three-dimensional ones in a crowded room. How interesting that he lived in New York, where one couldn't breathe without sharing air.

They pulled up to a beautiful old hotel where the driver stepped around to open her door. Alec had hired a car for tonight. It only illustrated the vast differences between them. She slid from the seat and stared at the building. Above a green awning, white stone and a wide, carved frieze rose to the sky. At street level, flower boxes were overflowing with color and variety.

Alec took her elbow and walked her forward, where an attendant held the door for them. "Showtime," he muttered.

The lobby spoke of old money and prestige. A high crystal chandelier rose overhead and the floors beneath them were black marble. Mahogany woodwork was polished to gleaming and expensive art decorated the walls.

Her heels clicked on the floor as Alec directed her to a ballroom to their left. Her steps faltered when she noticed how many people were there. Two hundred, at least. To the left was a bar and to the right a buffet table. The spread looked too pretty to eat. Ahead, people walked around a display of Alec's books.

So this was his world. Faith didn't belong here. She'd

never felt so out of place. Then again, she'd never felt particularly *in* place either. But this . . . this was way out of her element. She had the fancy dress and matching shoes. Her hair was up and her modest jewelry in place. Yet she wondered how quickly they'd see through her. These people with their diamonds and designer suits.

Alec took two flutes of champagne off a tray and passed her one. "Drink this fast. I'll get you another one to sip slowly after." His hand slid from her elbow to her waist and held her to his side. The move was possessive, a claim that she was with him.

She resisted the urge to rest her head on his shoulder and hide in his familiarity. "Why do I need to drink this quickly?"

He turned his head and offered the faintest of smiles. "You're nervous. It'll help." To demonstrate, he downed his glass in one swallow and set it on a tray as a waiter passed. Without missing a beat, he swiped another full glass.

Knowing he was uncomfortable as well didn't soothe her nerves much, but she did as he instructed and drank the champagne. The sweet bubbles floated down her throat and heated her stomach.

Alec took her empty flute and handed her a full one. "Just sip that one until we can get some food in you. Come on, I'll introduce you to my editor."

Over the next hour, she stood by his side, mostly quiet and feeling like arm candy, but that was fine. He was the star and she wasn't comfortable in the crowd. If Alec was uneasy, he hid it well. He laughed and discussed literature with people whose names she'd never remember. Occasionally she piped in when cued, although the company appeared uninterested in her comments.

When he was distracted, Faith slipped away from Alec's side and made her way over to the display to get some breathing room. Feigning interest in the books and posters, she eyed the items on the table and drew in a slow, deep breath.

While she was checking out some of the swag, a hand at

her lower back startled her, and she whirled, nearly sloshing her champagne onto the man in front of her.

He held up a hand and chuckled. "Sorry, miss." The man reeked of cologne and his girth was busting out of his blue pinstriped suit. A pudgy hand ran over his sleek black hair to smooth it down.

Faith slid a glance over at Alec, but he was deep in conversation and didn't see her. Her stomach flopped and twisted, but she forced a smile. "That's okay. You just startled me. Are you here for the signing later?"

He laughed without mirth. "I'm Alec's agent."

Her smile slipped a fraction at the condescending tone. She swore Alec had said that he'd fired his agent, but Faith kept that to herself. Maybe she was wrong. "Good turnout."

"Winston draws a crowd, that's for sure." His dark brown gaze raked over her chest before traveling back to her eyes. "And who are you, exactly? Your accent is southern." He made it sound like being from the south was distasteful.

The guy made her skin crawl. "I'm a friend of Alec's."

"A friend, eh?"

Before he could say any more, Alec sidled up beside her and wrapped his arm around her waist. "I see you've met Henry, my former agent."

When Alec stressed "former," Henry's eyes narrowed. "You find another agent yet, Winston? Although I suppose that would mean you'd need to actually write another book."

Alec stiffened beside her, and Faith had the overwhelming urge to defend him. Weren't agents, even former ones, supposed to be supportive?

She lifted her chin. "He's already more than halfway through the next book. He'll be finished in under two months."

Henry darted his gaze between them. "And how would you know that, miss? He doesn't let just anyone read his manuscripts."

"I never said I read it. But I have seen him working on it."

Henry's brows rose. "Have you?" He looked at Alec. "You

let your newest plaything near your material? You've never let your toys anywhere near your apartment. What gives?"

Alec growled low in his throat. "Watch yourself."

Henry took no heed of Alec's warning. In fact, he looked at Faith as if trying to dissect her and find the missing element. "Not like you to bring a date to these functions. She doesn't look like your usual."

Alec took a step forward, but Faith gripped his arm and he got himself in check.

"I told you, I'm a friend," she said.

Henry snorted. "Sure, sweetheart." He waved his hand to dismiss her. "You're all friendly until you learn he won't commit. Then you run for the next wallet. Ain't that right, Winston?"

The arm around her waist tightened further. "Enough, Henry. She's different, not that it's any of your business anymore. Leave her be."

Faith watched the interaction, her unease growing. Alec's agent was probably throwing barbs as a response to Alec letting him go. Between the books and movies, Alec had no doubt made the man a pretty penny. Losing that solid income would raise anyone's hackles. There was no sense in feeding into his bitterness.

Slowly, she ran her hand under Alec's open suit coat and rubbed a circle over the tense muscles coiling in his back. "Let's go grab a bite to eat before your reading, shall we?"

Henry didn't take the brush-off. "Different? How different can she really be with your fiancée still around? Odd threesome that would make."

Alec went so still Faith thought he would snap. Panic rose in her chest. She'd never seen him angry, not like this. Irritated, perhaps. There was no way for her to gauge how he'd respond to this latest jab, or how he typically behaved when angry. His previous engagement was already a sore spot. Why did Henry feel the need to pick at that scab?

She struggled to diffuse the situation. "I think you mean ex-fiancée, Mr . . . ?"

"Swift. The last name is Swift." His gaze narrowed before he harrumphed. "Ex? Is that the line he fed you?" He barked out a laugh. "I assure you, he'll never leave her."

The room froze. Or seemed to. Maybe it was just her.

As the words sank in, her gaze flew to Alec's. His wince was confirmation enough of the accusation. Alec stepped forward, apology in his eyes, but at the same moment his editor crossed the room to intervene. Words were exchanged.

Faith barely noticed what happened in the next few moments. Voices blended together. Air trapped in her lungs. Her temples throbbed. She took several steps backward until she bumped into a waiter.

"Sorry, ma'am. Are you all right?"

She looked at the group of men in front of her, deep in a heated discussion, and then at the champagne in her hand, only half gone.

He'll never leave her . . .

No. No, she wasn't all right.

She placed a hand on her forehead to stop the spinning. What was she doing here? With Alec? A man who had so obviously lied to her. Had lied for several weeks. He'd told her the engagement was over. Had been for several years by the sound of it. Where was this woman if they were still together? Did she not care if Alec saw other women?

Oh, God. What if they had one of those relationships? An open one where they could sleep with other people?

Faith's mouth dried to dust. Dear Lord, could she have been any more naive?

Stupid, stupid.

With a shaking hand, she set her champagne flute on the waiter's tray and made the long, long walk to the door. Only a few people stopped their conversations to stare at her obvious haste. Most continued on as if nothing had transpired, as if she hadn't just been betrayed in the worst imaginable way.

chapter
seventeen

Alec panicked and cursed when he caught Faith's retreating form out of the corner of his eye. "Mark, take care of this. I need to deal with something. I want him gone when I get back."

Trusting his editor to handle his former agent, Alec strode toward the door. He should've told Faith the whole story sooner. What must be going through her mind right now? And to hear the truth like that, in such a cold, calculating way . . .

Part of the truth.

Fuck. He was an asshole. Part of him knew he never should've brought her here, into this world that *he* didn't even want to live in sometimes. But the more time he spent with Faith, the more she pushed the darkness away. She made him want things, to be something he couldn't. Yet he'd plowed forward and hadn't even had the balls to inform her of what she was getting tangled in.

He pushed through the lobby doors and stepped outside, alarm seizing his gut when he didn't see her right away. He scanned the sidewalk, across the busy street. Sweet Faith, alone in this city. The things that could go wrong.

Wait. *There.*

She stood at the corner of the building, arms wrapped around herself and shivering as if it weren't eighty degrees. He hesitated, then walked over to her.

Her teary gaze lifted to his and away. "Go back inside, Alec."

He tried to take her arms but she wrenched away. "Faith. I'm sorry. I need to explain, I know . . ."

"Explain," she said in a hollow voice. "What more is there to say? You lied to me."

Panic morphed into desperation. "I should've told you everything sooner. I'm sorry."

She stepped away from him as if he'd slapped her. "Sorry just doesn't seem to cut it, Alec." She rubbed her forehead with a shaking hand. "I'm such an idiot."

"No," he growled, stepping closer. "I'm the idiot."

A cab pulled up to the curb and she stepped forward. No way. No way in hell was she going anywhere alone in this city. Not even in the posh Upper West Side.

"Faith, wait." He rushed over and told the doorman to have his driver pull around, then hurried back. "My car will take you back to my apartment. Here." He fumbled in his pocket for his keys and took her hand. Forcing her fingers to unclench, he slapped them into her palm. "Go back to my place and wait for me. I can't leave just yet, but I'll get out of this as soon as I can. We'll talk."

Her jaw trembled as more tears coursed down her pale cheeks, her gaze focused on the street and the passing cars. After a very tense silence, she finally nodded.

He let out a shuddering exhale, only somewhat relieved. "Please, don't leave the apartment. I'll meet you there."

His driver pulled up and walked around the hood to open the back door. Faith wasted no time sliding inside. Her gaze trained down, she twisted her fingers in her lap.

Alec closed the door himself. "Take her back to the apartment. Watch until she gets inside." He paused. "You know what?" He fished in his pocket and pulled out a hundred-dollar bill. "Walk her to the apartment door and make sure she gets in safely."

"Will do, sir."

Jaw clenched, he watched her pull away, staring at the street long after she'd disappeared from view. He was damn close to saying the hell with it and taking a cab right after her, but his publisher had given him quite a bit of leeway with the new series and he owed them. Although he loathed the crowds, it was part of his job and damn unprofessional to walk away.

Turning, he caught Henry Swift hailing a cab.

"You son of a bitch . . ."

Henry's eyes widened. He dove into the cab and slammed the door.

Alec yelled through the window. "We have a confidentiality agreement. You break it again, I'll sue you for twice the amount I made you the past ten years. You hear me?"

The cab pulled away, but not before the color drained from Henry's face and the slimy bastard nodded his understanding. He wasn't looking so smug and superior now.

Jesus. The damage was already done. Alec should've fired him years ago. Why the hell hadn't he?

Behind him, a few patrons exited the hotel, reminding him he didn't have time for brooding. The sooner he got the party over with, the sooner he could try to explain Laura to Faith.

He made his way back inside the ballroom and, upon seeing him, his editor quickly walked to the podium to make introductions. Through his brief reading, pats on the back afterward, and subsequent two-hour signing, Alec was ready to tear his hair out. By the fistful. His mind kept straying to

what Faith might be doing, thinking. Part of him feared she'd
be gone when he returned. She'd been so damn calm. She
was always calm. Why didn't she yell at him? Slap his cheek?
Hell, any significant sign of anger would've been better than
the shell shock.

As his driver guided them through the busy streets, acid
ate away at his gut. Aside from Jake, he'd never talked about
Laura with anyone. Not when it happened and not after. By
process of elimination and through the grapevine, his parents and former agent knew the details. But their prompts
to try and get Alec to discuss the accident fell on deaf ears.
What happened was off-limits.

Until now.

A thousand explanations tore through his mind, but none
of them measured up. There was no sugarcoating this story.
Once Faith knew the whole of it, she would walk away from
this relationship before it had even begun. He was sure of it.

And why did that bother him so much? It wasn't as if he
could put a ring on her finger and promise her forever. Even
if he wanted to—which, Christ, did he?—there was no
future beyond August.

He rubbed at his tired eyes, not recognizing this sensation
that had been swirling in his chest since he first saw Faith
on the beach weeks ago. It was a warning he should've
heeded. Laura had never, not once, made him feel like this.
Like he needed to see her to breathe freely, to touch her to
prove she was real. To crawl inside her mind to find all the
clever, quirky little thoughts within. The need to claim her,
have her begging and chanting his name while he drove into
her, had the blood roaring through his veins.

Falling for Faith would be selfish. Inevitable, it seemed,
but selfish nonetheless.

Alec waved off the driver when he pulled to the curb outside the apartment and started to get out to open the door for
him. He gave the man a hefty tip for his trouble and opened
the door himself.

Alec paused before exiting. "The lady, how was she when you drove her back?"

The driver turned in his seat and regarded Alec with sympathetic eyes. "She cried quietly the entire way, sir. Never said a word. I went with her up to your penthouse and made sure she went inside."

Alec nodded and thanked the man. Nausea churned in his stomach until a cold sweat broke out on his forehead and his palms grew clammy.

He'd made her cry. Faith had enough in her life to cause that—she didn't need him adding more reasons.

The lobby attendant stopped him before he hit the bank of elevators. "Mr. Winston. I have your keys, sir."

His keys. Right. He'd given them to Faith. His heart puttered behind his ribs, just wanting to get to her. "Did she leave?"

"Not that I saw, Mr. Winston. She handed them to me and said to make sure you could get back inside."

He shook his head. Damn her to heaven and back. How could she be so considerate after what he'd done? Hell, any other woman would have trashed his place and left fifty screeching voice mails on his phone. With every given right.

Alec took the keys and rode the elevator to the penthouse, hoping to God she hadn't left. Where would she go? The airport? A hotel? He'd find her, regardless.

The apartment was dark and quiet. Too quiet. His anxiety upped ten notches. He strode through the living room and to his bedroom where a bedside lamp cast a soft glow into the hall. He stopped short.

Not only had she not left, she hadn't even changed clothes. The elegant black dress still adorned her thin frame, but her heels were placed neatly by the closet door and her hair was out of the twist. Soft brown strands fell around her shoulders. She stood by the bay window with her back to him and her arms crossed.

At a loss, he just stood there.

"I hate this place." Her mermaid voice wafted over to him.

He understood. Most of the time, he hated the city, too. He wondered if he stayed to punish himself. For someone like Faith, New York would be overstimulation. Too many people, too much noise, just . . . too much everything. Strangely, he could relate.

Taking a hesitant few steps into the room, he sighed. "Faith, I'm sorry."

"Sorry for lying to me or sorry I found out?"

How very little she thought of him. Not that he could blame her. "I'm sorry I lied and I'm sorry you had to find out like that. I had every intention of telling you, but the words just never came."

She turned, and the red of her eyes had his chest tightening. "Two words, Alec. Just two words. *I'm. Engaged.*"

When she put it like that . . .

"How have you kept this a secret? I mean, you've got a woman on your arm in nearly every tabloid. There's not many people alive who don't know your name, even in passing."

He swiped a hand down his face and allowed the hurt to rise up. He had to explain to Faith in a manner she could somehow find a way to understand. He *needed* her to understand. Making his way to the corner, he sat in a chair to give her room and himself time to stall. He tossed his suit coat over the arm. Best to start at the beginning, he supposed.

"When I moved to the city, I'd just signed my first book deal and was living in this shitty apartment in the Lower East Side. Laura was a struggling artist who lived across the hall." He picked at the skin around his thumbnail with his index finger. "We struck up a friendship of sorts that quickly turned into more. Neither of us expected anything other than what it was. Sex. We were young and stupid with too many dreams and not enough money."

Faith walked over to his bed several feet away and sat on

the edge of the mattress, her steady gaze holding his. Quiet understanding emanated, urging him to go on.

Closing his eyes, he braced himself for the next bit. The pain from those days washed over him and stole his air. "A couple months later, she got pregnant. Being a southern boy, I did what I thought was right and proposed to her. She wanted to wait to get married until after the baby was born." They'd merged apartments and household items, but never their hearts. Not that Faith needed to know that part. "Things went from bad to worse. We couldn't have been any more wrong for each other. We fought constantly. My first book was a month from releasing and I was deep into edits on the second when she called me from the doctor's office to say she'd miscarried."

The baby, just a fetus, was still a fresh loss in his mind. He'd barely had time to adjust to the pregnancy, but damn. He'd loved that baby with everything he had. The hot sting of tears threatened as he looked at Faith, his control wavering.

She pressed her fingertips to her lips and looked at the ceiling, blinking rapidly. If possible, her already tense shoulders grew even more rigid. But the anger creasing her brow smoothed away when she returned her amber gaze to his.

She still had yet to say anything, and his fucked-up tale wasn't over, so he leaned back and drummed his fingers on the chair arm.

He blew out a breath. "Laura blamed me for everything. The miscarriage, not loving her, not making enough money, her art not selling. It got to the point we couldn't be in the same room without screaming at each other. One night, she yelled it was over and stormed out."

Alec could still hear her words inside his head, beating like a drum against his temples. He couldn't muster the courage to look at Faith, so he had no idea if she felt the same contempt for himself that he did.

After several minutes he cleared his raw throat. "When

she left the apartment, she got drunk with an old friend and wrapped her car around a utility pole. The friend died and Laura wound up a vegetable on life support. She's in a nursing facility here in the city."

Seconds ticked by.

Slowly, Faith rose and walked to the window. She offered him her back and nothing more. Said not a syllable. She looked so damn fragile standing there. Breakable. Then again, weren't they all?

He rubbed the back of his neck, waiting to find out what she'd do, say. Faith never seemed to react as he expected, so he held some residual strand of hope she wouldn't clock him and leave.

Nearly ten minutes passed, and nothing. Unable to stand it, he leaned forward. "Say something, Faith. Anything. Tell me you hate my guts. Tell me not to touch you again. Tell me—"

"That my heart hurts for you."

He jerked straight. "Come again?" he croaked.

She turned around, leaned against the windowsill, and crossed her arms. "You still consider yourself engaged to . . . Laura?"

Hearing Laura's name from Faith's lips did something terrible to his insides. "Yes. The accident was nine years ago and there's no hope of her recovering. The doctors say she's brain-dead." He opened his mouth again, but couldn't finish the thought. Honestly, he was still waiting for Faith to throw her shoe at his head.

"You were going to say more."

Clever, insightful Faith. "Laura's parents are very religious. They won't take her off life support even though she's not in there anymore. I hit the bestseller list several months later, which is why we were able to hide what happened from the media— the accident preceded the fame. I can afford her care at the facility. They can't."

Faith stared at him through those amber eyes. Blinked. "And out of duty, you won't leave her. Because you view this whole dreadful tragedy as your fault."

Alec didn't know whether to laugh or cry at her astute intuition. Whether to shake her or kiss her for her calm understanding. If he wanted, he could leave Laura behind and still pay for her care, but he wouldn't, because Faith was right. Guilt and remorse would forever bind him to that night nine years ago. He wouldn't or couldn't ever let it go. It was his own sick, twisted way of making amends.

Somehow, Faith got that. She's wrapped her smart, beautiful head around his intentions and didn't question the decision. Even more impressive was that she didn't try to tell him it wasn't his fault, like Jake had tried to do countless times, and she didn't offer empty condolences because they never eased the pain. If anyone knew that, Faith did.

What in the hell was he going to do with her?

The itch to touch her, to cross the few feet between them and seek comfort, was so fierce that he rose from the chair before he remembered she hadn't reacted. Her gaze was pinned to the wall over his head, lost, a million miles away.

"Give me some idea where your mind is at, Faith. Should I try to book an earlier flight home? Go sleep on the couch and give you space?"

She straightened from the windowsill and closed the distance to stand in front of him. "You should have told me sooner."

He breathed in her sweet, sugary scent. "Yeah."

"Is Laura the reason why you wouldn't make love to me?"

It didn't escape his attention that she'd used the phrase *making love* instead of sex, like they'd done previously when discussing their attraction. Laura had nothing to do with what was between him and Faith. Hell, he'd held off on crossing that line and taking her because, deep down, he knew with Faith it *would* be making love. And all he'd ever known was sex.

He shook his head and brushed his knuckles down her cheek. "You make me feel more than she ever did. That scares me because my circumstances will never change."

Her lips parted with a breath, her gaze taking in his face as if trying to reach the truth. "Alec?"

He yielded to her nearness, at her breathy sigh of a voice he couldn't get out of his head if he tried. "Yes?"

"Will you take my dress off now?"

chapter eighteen

Faith waited patiently for Alec to connect the dots, watching his face for the moment when he realized she wasn't angry at him for lying and that she didn't hate him. It was what he expected, judging by his demeanor. He hated himself enough. He shouldn't.

What happened to his Laura was a series of terrible incidents, a row of dominoes tumbling down. He was no more at fault for Laura's decisions than the road on which she crashed. All the anger they harbored for each other was just young infatuation trying to play adult in the real world. And the miscarriage . . . that had to have been the most difficult. To have what might've been ripped away by nothing more than a biology mishap and be helpless to stop it.

Alec cared about people. He may have a solitary lifestyle, and he needed his space and room to think, but no one that in tune to the nature of people could be callous. His guilt over Laura was proof enough. To lose a child he never got to hold, and to lose the hope of what that child could bring, would devastate a person like Alec. He was an all-or-nothing guy.

She wished things could be different. Wished she was a woman he could desire long term and not grow weary of. She wished he could forgive and move on, and that Laura's parents would seek peace and let their daughter go.

But none of those things would happen. So for now, she'd take this borrowed time with him and make the most of it. Part of her wanted to hold back. Think things through. But Laura hadn't been a part of his life for many years, and Alec said Laura was never coming back. If there had been no car accident, Faith figured he and Laura wouldn't still be together.

He stared at her through his gray-blue eyes with uncertainty and wonder. "Why aren't you mad at me?"

She stepped closer, until her breasts touched his chest and her hips were snug against his. "Because you weren't deliberately keeping the truth from me. You were trying to tell me all along, working your way up to it. You brought me all the way to New York so you could."

He blinked away his surprise as fast as it appeared and cupped her jaw. "You are the most fascinating creature, Faith."

She'd wanted him from the moment they'd first met and he'd startled her on the beach. Wanted him still. But she didn't have the level of experience he was used to with other women and her nerves would get the best of her if he didn't take control soon.

Swallowing hard, she looked up at him and wrapped her arms around his waist. "I don't know if I'll be any good at this."

"At what? At sex?"

"Yes."

A low chuckle rose from his throat. "Foolish woman."

He leaned in and seared her mouth with a kiss, going slow, going deep. One hand threaded in her hair and held her to him while his tongue explored and conquered. His other arm hauled her solidly against the hard wall of his chest, pinned her there with restrained strength. Delicious heat pooled between her legs. She didn't even know her feet were still on the ground until her knees buckled.

Now there was the earth-shattering kiss he'd threatened weeks ago.

"I've got you," he murmured against her lips. Reaching behind her neck, he untied the knot holding the dress. "I've been wanting to do that since you put on the dress."

"Me, too."

His grin slipped as he tugged the dress down her torso, over her hips and to her ankles. He looked up at her from where he knelt on the floor and helped her step out of the dress. Molten desire replaced the humor of the moment and had her pulse at dangerous levels. He wrapped his large hands around her calves and slowly slid them up to cup her hips.

"You look good enough to eat," he said and placed a kiss to her stomach, and another between her breasts when he rose to full height. "Smell good enough to eat, too."

Her nipples rasped against the yellow lace, begging for his mouth. Instead, he stepped away and she reeled. He opened the nightstand, removed a packet, and set it by the lamp. Then he pulled down the comforter, revealing forest-green sheets.

When he turned back, he just looked at her, as she stood there in the lingerie Lacey had insisted she buy and Faith had envisioned Alec stripping off. His gaze slid up to hers and held while he unbuttoned his shirt and shrugged out of it. A thin scattering of black hair covered his chest and trailed down to the V of his waist, disappearing. The belt was next, followed by the gray slacks and finally the black briefs. Sure, swift movements to rid the barriers between them. He stood before her in all his glory.

And he was glory.

Muscular thighs, toned abs, wide shoulders, defined biceps,

and an erection that stood at attention. The erection held her gaze. He wasn't so large that she worried he wouldn't fit, but he was close. The wide head brushed his navel, the thick shaft emerging from a light patch of black hair. He had the body of a trained runner. He had neither bulging muscles nor a thin, wiry frame—instead he was lean, toned, and tan. Her mouth watered, wanting the weight of his body pinning hers, him relieving the ache between her legs.

She swallowed hard, suddenly nervous again. When he touched her, he took her out of her head and into a dizzying passion. But he wasn't touching her now, he was looking at her as if he'd never seen a female before. She'd certainly never seen anyone like him, what with the very little practice she had.

Slowly, like a predator, he strode toward her and cupped her cheeks. This time the kiss stole her sanity. The precision with which he slid his hands down to cup her breasts through the bra, the deliberate and meticulous way his fingers grazed her nipples, bespoke of his familiarity with the female form. He knew how to touch, to taste, to drive her out of herself and back with crushing velocity.

She never knew being touched, being kissed, could be like this. Potent. Insistent.

Breaking the connection, he grazed his lips over her jaw, down her throat, and licked her collarbone. "I want you so badly I can't think."

His voice alone could make her damp and dreamy. A coarse murmur with need raking it raw. Hadn't he said something similar, before the party? Yes. "You promised you'd make me forget to think."

He groaned into her neck, a purely male sound of pleasured frustration. "Consider it done."

Grabbing the back of her thighs, he spread her legs, lifted her, and spun to deposit them both on the bed. He sprawled over her, hands everywhere, mouth everywhere.

"I knew you'd be good at this," she breathed. Or tried to breathe.

"It'll only get better, darlin'."

His voice was thick with his native southern drawl, something she only noticed when he was frustrated or confused. Or aroused, it seemed. His thick shaft pressed between the apex of her thighs, grinding into her heat, and her neurons splintered.

He unclasped her bra and tossed it over his shoulder. His tongue swept over one nipple, then the other. She arched up to meet him, tangling her fingers in his thick hair, but he was already on the move, kissing his way down her belly.

"God in heaven, Faith. You smell so damn good."

His fingers dipped into her panties. Tugged them off.

She pried her eyes open and looked down at the top of his head. Her only other lover had never engaged in oral, so she didn't know what to expect, how to react. Nerves pinged. She reached for him to draw him back up, but he pressed his mouth over the pulsing, aching heat of her core and her body bowed in bliss.

He licked, nipped, and moaned, never allowing her to fall over the edge, but pushing her so, so close. In the throes of the most spectacular frustration, praying for release, she threw her arms over her head and pressed her palms against the headboard. Surely this couldn't kill her, could it? Death by ecstasy.

"You ready to come, darlin'?"

Was he kidding? All she could do was nod.

Without warning, he climbed up her body and reached for the condom. Foil ripped. His breaths became pants and his weight settled between her thighs. Then his arms were between her and the mattress, cradling her back, lifting her to straddle his hips as he sat back.

His blue-gray eyes bore into hers, heavy with want and desperation. "I want you to come with me. I've wanted you for weeks, so we'll come together."

With hands secure on her hips, fingers digging into her flesh, he raised her enough to align himself and brought her down around his shaft.

She gasped, holding his shoulders at the full feeling of him deep inside.

Oh. Oh God, yes.

He stilled, breathing heavily into her hair a moment before claiming her mouth and kissing her with long, strong strokes of his tongue. Tension and restraint bunched the muscles under her hands, until he was quivering with need. Or was that her?

Wrapping her arms around his neck, she rolled her hips. The slide of him against her sensitive flesh made her tremble, lose whatever she'd been grasping on to.

His arms came around her back, one around her middle, the other sliding up into her hair. "Let me see your eyes."

She opened them and met his gaze, so close to the edge of control and yet achingly tender. He drew his hips back as much as the position would allow, keeping her banded in his arms, his eyes never leaving hers. After holding out long enough to make her beg, he finally drove up while urging her down, her body taking him deeper than she thought possible.

Air whooshed from her lungs. Every nerve inside her came alive. Sparked. Inflamed. The friction of him hitting her nub and the pressure of him filling her so fully had her teetering near oblivion. He pumped inside her in earnest, emitting a groan with every thrust. He chanted her name against the skin below her ear, over and over.

The surprise of her orgasm barely had time to register before it hit full force. Her inner muscles tightened, squeezing him. She arched, cried out, vibrated with the intensity of satisfaction.

He caught her before she tumbled backward, tensing against her as he sought his own release. He pumped twice more and stilled. Panted. His fevered brow burrowed deeper into the crook of her neck, his breath hot against her jaw as he relaxed. He fell back against the mattress, bringing her with him to splay over him like a contented cat.

Content wasn't even close to the term she'd use to describe what they'd just done, what she felt, but her body was too relaxed and sated to think of something more appropriate.

When they got their breathing under control, Alec lifted his head and pushed the hair away from Faith's face. Her amber eyes were more honey-colored in the dim lamplight and mischief hinted at the corners.

Would he ever stop being surprised by her? Moreover, had sex ever been like that before? That good, that satisfying, that . . . complete? Not for him, it hadn't.

A lazy smile lifted her mouth. "This might sound like a terrible cliché, and you might put me in writer jail for saying it, but that was amazing. I'd heard sex could be mind-blowing, but I figured that was just hype. My experience never brought me close to that."

She used the term *experience* in its singular form and he had to wonder if that was a slip of the tongue or if she'd only had one lover before him. "My ego says thank you."

Her smile turned into a grin. "Welcome." Sighing, she rested her chin on his chest and stared at him. Drew lazy circles in his chest hair. After a beat, the grin slipped and her back tensed beneath his hand. "Do you regret it?"

"No regret." Not in the way she was figuring. He was just starting to get a tangible thread of what was so . . . unique about the two of them together, and it made his heart pound.

"I don't believe you," she said.

"No regret," he repeated, this time more firmly.

She must've read something in his expression, because she shook her head. Shame washed over her face, so quickly he had no time to react. She scooted off the foot of the bed and covered her breasts, searching for her clothes.

Damn her. Damn him.

He pressed his palms to his eyes, hating how she could fucking see right through him. This time she had it all wrong, though, and he didn't know how to voice the feelings filling his chest. "It's not . . . Please come back to bed."

Slipping into her panties—and hell, yellow was his new favorite color—she hopped on one foot before catching her balance. If not for the hurt radiating in her eyes, he'd call her beautiful. Hair wild, skin flushed. She didn't bother with the bra, but she did fetch a pair of pajamas out of her suitcase by the closet.

He gave her a minute to dress, thinking she needed the barrier, before he got up and slid into a pair of black running shorts. "Are you hungry?"

Hungry? *Really, man*?

"No, thank you."

"No, thank you," he repeated, at a loss. He didn't know how to do this, the morning-after thing. And he had the sinking suspicion he'd not only hurt her feelings, but insulted her somehow. "Faith . . ."

"It's late. I'm gonna go sleep on the couch. I'll see you in the morning." She looked down at herself and released a sigh of resignation.

He looked at her pajamas for the first time and blinked. The top was a sheer black number and the bottoms a silk boy brief. Very hot, but not her. "I like them."

"Yeah, well . . . thank Lacey. For all the good they did."

"What does that mean?"

She turned on her heel and strode out.

He followed and gripped her arm. Soft, soft skin. *Focus, Winston.* "Answer me."

Her face turned a shade of adorable red. "Lacey took me shopping before we left." She waved her hands at herself. "This is the result."

"If you didn't like them, why did you buy them?"

She glanced at the ceiling, the wall, the floor. "I thought maybe you'd . . . notice me in them. Lacey picked them, and when she and Mia gang up, they can be pretty persuasive."

Hold the phone. "What do you mean, you thought I'd notice you?" He'd been doing nothing but noticing her since the day they met. For the life of him, he still couldn't figure out what it was about her that made her so damn special compared to the rest. Why she made him . . . want. *Feel.*

Jerking her arm out of his hand, she marched down the hall. "This is humiliating enough, Alec."

Humiliating? "Swear to God, Faith, one of these days you need to stop walking away from me or you're going to find yourself handcuffed to me." He stopped. Huh. Nice thought.

He strode after her. She'd laid down on the couch and was pulling a throw blanket over her head. He yanked it off, leaned down, and picked her up. God, she weighed nothing.

She squeaked in protest.

Depositing her on one of the bar stools by the island, he pointed a finger at her. "Stay." He rounded the corner into the kitchen and leaned his forearms on the counter across from her. "I notice you just fine. Explain."

Closing her eyes, she rubbed her forehead. "You wouldn't have sex with me. In Wilmington."

"I told you I was taking things slow . . ."

"There's slow and then there's stagnant."

He forced his open jaw shut. Faith thought he didn't want her. He almost laughed. "I'm very attracted to you, and rest assured, it was damn difficult keeping my hands to myself."

The long column of her throat worked a swallow as she stared at her hands. "I was unsatisfactory, wasn't I?"

He needed to start carrying a sign around that said, *Bang head here.* "You were so unsatisfactory that I left a bite mark on your neck trying to restrain myself and I'm still trembling from coming so hard."

Her gaze jerked to his. Held.

Christ. She was really something. When they'd first met, he'd thought her ordinary. How stupid of him. Her amber eyes could ensnare him for a decade. The scattering of light freckles on her nose added a girlish charm. That thin, pouty mouth said the damnedest things. And her voice . . . God, that voice.

"I don't know what this previous experience is that you speak of, Faith, but you rocked my world." In bed and out of it. Maybe this sudden change of mood wasn't such a bad thing. He wasn't so brainless as to assume she'd be out of his system once he'd had her—because she wasn't—but this was leading nowhere fast. He sighed and tried to steer the conversation off course. "How about an omelet? You barely ate at the party."

Still looking a bit shell-shocked, she nodded slowly.

Alec got ingredients out of the fridge that he had asked his housekeeper to stock and a skillet out of the cabinet. He chopped green pepper, tomato, mushrooms, and onions while trying to figure out what the hell to do in this situation. For the first time in years, if not ever, he wanted more. But he couldn't have that "more," so why wish it? Faith deserved better than this, so he needed to figure out a way to back out without hurting her feelings. She was not a temporary kind of woman, and the fact that he'd tried to use her as his most recent plaything tore at his gut.

"You have the what-did-I-just-do look again," Faith said, interrupting his thoughts.

Taking more care than necessary, he flipped the omelet and tried to formulate words that would make sense to her. "I don't regret the sex, Faith. I don't. I just . . ."

"Don't want to do it again."

Oh, how very, very wrong she was. "The problem is, I *do* want to do it again." Until they died from starvation from not leaving the bedroom. "So I think the best thing to do is just end it."

When she grew quiet for too long, he glanced at her. She pressed her lips together—chewing over her own thoughts, he figured. He cut the omelet in half and plated one for her and himself. He garnished the plates with a few raspberries and set them in front of her. Striding around the island, he pulled up a stool next to her and took a bite.

"Eat, Faith."

Picking up her fork, she stared at her plate. "You know how to cook."

"Enough basics to get by. Eggs aren't rocket science."

Satisfied that she'd eaten a few bites, he dug into his own omelet with vigor. Damn, but he was hungry. He'd eaten all of it before she'd even made a dent in hers.

"Take my bed tonight. I'll crash on the couch." There. He could do the right thing, after all. Except why did he feel like shit?

She didn't argue.

chapter
nineteen

"Spill it," Lacey demanded, while checking the hem of the wedding gown. "You've been mute for two days. We want to know what happened in New York."

Faith swallowed a sigh and sat in one of the chairs in the little boutique. Lacey had fallen in love with the second dress she saw, a little, satin, ivory slip style with a scoop neck and a lace back. It was sleeveless with no train, which was a good thing, considering Lacey and Jake were getting married on the beach.

Faith would plan her wedding the same way, if she ever got married, the chances of which were looking pretty slim. A simple dress, a few people, dancing by moonlight on the beach with the waves caressing her toes. Small. Simple. Perfection. Even the cake would be an uncomplicated yellow with buttercream frosting. Maybe a few pearl beads for decoration, to match the ones in her dress.

Disturbed by her thoughts, Faith rubbed her forehead. She'd never been a frivolous dreamer like other girls. She didn't spend her nights imagining the perfect wedding, right down to what color rose petals the flower girl would toss. So why did the images pop up now? Granted, Lacey and Jake's wedding was drawing closer, and they were making a lot of plans, but that didn't excuse the wayward notions in her head.

She'd spent the majority of her life unnoticed, unwanted. Hollow and secretly aching for someone to acknowledge her existence, yet too scared to prove to anyone that she was there. It was a position she'd grown used to, just a way of life. Business as usual. But then Alec came along, and for a moment, she was a somebody. Not invisible. Not a donor for parts or a nuisance to tolerate. Suddenly there was a man interested in her day and what she was thinking. The way he touched her and spoke to her made her feel alive. Free. The happiness he evoked was almost exhausting.

But a week had gone by, and besides popping over once to watch her and Ginny bake peanut butter cookies, Alec hadn't visited. For a person who'd been discarded her whole life, that hurt a lot. The pain of rejection stole her will to eat, to smile. A week ago, her heart had been soaring. Now, since he'd put a stop to their summer romance, she couldn't function past a wallow.

She kept replaying his admission over and over in her head. What happened to Laura wasn't his fault, but she understood irrational guilt better than anyone. After all, she had been conceived to save Hope and she'd failed. Deep down, Faith knew that wasn't on her shoulders, but the burden was there just the same. So yes, she understood.

Their lovemaking had been the stuff of fantasies. Specifically, hers. It was as if he knew her every desire, every need. The tender way he caressed her, tasted, and the moment his need erupted and his touch became insistent stole her breath. It was a night she'd wanted all her life. She'd come out of herself for a little while and become a woman. Not a shadow or a wallflower. A woman.

It had never been like that before, not for her. For a fleeting instant, she'd thought it had been that way for him, too.

Dang it. She was falling for him. No, she *had* fallen for him, and like everyone else, he'd walked away as if she'd never been there in the first place. Forgettable.

"Is everything okay?" Mia asked.

Faith looked up and was surprised by the haze of tears blurring her vision. She wished Hope was here. Had her sister lived, Faith would have probably been in a little boutique with her, picking out dresses and discussing flowers.

Quickly, she cleared her throat. "Sure. I'm fine. You look very beautiful in that dress," she told Lacey over Mia's shoulder. "I'm getting misty." Hopefully that explained her sudden emotion.

"Oh, sweetie." Lacey stepped down from the pedestal and patted her hand. "What happened? Didn't the lingerie work?"

At least she'd gotten two great friends out of the move to the coast. There was that. "It worked. We . . . um, you know. But it was just a onetime thing."

"Why? You guys seemed to be hitting it off." Mia sat in a chair beside Faith's and crossed her legs.

She shrugged. There was no way to explain the real reason to them without betraying Alec's trust. "Like I told Lacey, we were short term. He's got reasons why he can't commit, and I understand."

"Can't or won't commit?" Mia huffed.

"Can't," Lacey answered and pinned Faith with an understanding look. Of course, Jake would've told Lacey the story, or parts of it. "Things can always change, though."

Faith shook her head. Drawing in a deep breath, she glanced around. "Is that the magical dress? I think it's perfect."

"Me, too." Lacey beamed. "I think Jake will love it."

Mia smiled. "Jake loves the woman in it. The dress is just wrapping."

Lacey glowed. "I should hang it back up, but I don't want to. I want to wear it everywhere. It just needs an inch or two brought up from the hem, but otherwise it fits perfectly."

Lacey followed the attendant to the changing rooms, leaving Mia and Faith to browse the racks. Lacey had decided to let them pick out their own dresses, her only requirements being that they were calf-length and pastel in color.

Mia held up a pink dress with capped sleeves. "Think it's too pale for me?"

"No." Mia's tanned skin and midnight hair would look lovely in the shade. "It's pretty. I like the cut." Faith turned back to the rack. "I don't even have an idea what to look for."

"Something yellow, or maybe mint green. You'd look great in a strapless with your shoulders." Mia fished around and pulled out a strapless satin dress with a tulle overlay in a pale sunflower color. A thin, corded ribbon that ran under the breasts tied off in the back.

"I like it." She imagined herself wearing it on the beach, walking down the makeshift isle with Alec, as he was the one paired with her for the ceremony. Would Alec like it? She shook her head—she needed to stop thinking as if they were a couple. They weren't and never would be. "Shouldn't Ginny be here if we're picking out dresses?"

Mia hummed. "Cole took her out to a movie. I wanted to get an idea for our dresses before bringing her along anyway."

Cole embraced Ginny as if she was his own sister, his blood. He never grew annoyed by her inability to do things, nor did he seem irritated by having a third wheel. It made Faith's heart happy. He was a good guy, and Mia would have a great life with him. Lacey and Jake would have a great life, too. They fit well together, genuinely cared about Ginny, and were already making her part of the family.

And then there was Faith. The special needs teacher on payroll who stayed in the guesthouse. When she had taught at St. Ambrose, no one, including the staff, had paid much attention to her presence. There, Faith had known her place, her duties. Here, everything was askew and disorienting.

"What's really going on, Faith? You're upset. I can tell. I wish you'd talk to me."

Talk, like friends do. Maybe they just felt sorry for her. Perhaps that's what all this was about, them including her out of pity. How would she even go about asking?

This thing with Alec was making her question everyone and their motives. Since landing on this strip of beach, nothing in her life had fallen into its normal pattern.

She shrugged her shoulders. "I'm sorry to ruin the mood. I guess I'm just having a melancholy day."

Mia opened her mouth, but Lacey was back from the dressing room. "They'll have the dress finished by next week. Did you guys find anything?"

Mia held up both dresses.

"I love them. The yellow for Faith?"

Faith nodded. "Except yellow is Ginny's favorite color. We should let her have that one, or at least first color choice." She was family, Faith wasn't. "I'll find something else."

Lacey fingered the material. "But this cut is perfect for your frame."

Faith smiled as if her chest wasn't hurting and perused the racks. She found a mint-green dress, as Mia had suggested, and held it up for inspection. A swath of satin crisscrossed over the bodice and flowed to a whisper below the knees. It reminded her of those old movies from the forties Hope liked to watch. Dreamy and timeless.

"Would you look at that? I love it. Is it your size?" Lacey leaned over and checked the tag.

"It's a size too big, but maybe it can be altered."

Faith glanced around for the attendant and asked, pleased when they said they could take in the dress so it would fit.

As they were checking out, Mia turned to them. "With

regards to tomorrow, I've got the wine and beer, Lacey's doing sandwiches and salad. Faith, would you mind bringing fruit and your amazing brownies?"

Faith had forgotten all about the Fourth of July bonfire. The Covingtons had invited a few people for a small get-together to watch the fireworks. "Sure. I can get Ginny to help me bake. She'd like that."

"I'm nervous," Lacey said. "Jake's parents are coming."

Mia frowned. "They love you. Why are you nervous?"

Lacey lifted her hand and dropped it. "I don't know. I guess it's the first time they'll meet Dad. I'm hoping they'll behave."

Faith followed them out of the store and into the scorching heat, her own nerves going into overdrive. If the Winstons were coming, that meant she'd meet Alec's parents. Faith didn't know where she and Alec stood, though it seemed to her their summer romance was prematurely over. What would she say to them? Would they like her?

Sighing, she trailed Mia and Lacey to the car while they chattered about wedding cake. It didn't matter what Alec's parents thought. Alec didn't want more between them, so she'd just fade into the background where she belonged.

"Why are you pouting?"

Alec looked away from the Fourth of July beach party to glare at Jake. "Men don't pout."

"Fine." His brother took a long pull from his beer bottle. "Brood, then. Why are you brooding?"

"I'm not brooding."

"You are."

"Am not." Alec grinned, partly because he couldn't help it with the childish banter and partly because it would get Jake off his back.

Their family and friends were gathered around the bonfire, which was set past the dunes but clear of the water. To the left and halfway up the beach, Faith was standing with Ginny, rearranging the table of food for the fifth time.

Maybe he *was* brooding.

"You keep staring at her and people will notice."

Alec rolled his head to stretch his neck. It did nothing for his tension. "Ask me if I care."

"Don't need to. I know you care." When Alec said nothing, his brother plowed on. "You care about her, too. Why aren't you over there with Faith instead of brooding?"

Alec had spent a week holed up in the guesthouse, doing zilch on the writing front, going crazy with thinking about nothing but Faith Armstrong. What would it hurt to talk to Jake? Besides pride. "We broke it off."

Jake remained silent. A first.

"No witty comeback? I'm disappointed."

"So am I." Gone was the laid-back pose and affable grin. "I thought . . ." He shook his head. "I thought you were finally coming around. Letting go. What happened in New York?"

Alec was tempted to avoid the question, but hell. He was miserable and Jake was his lifeline most days. "I told her everything."

Jake's glance landed on Faith before returning to him. "And she freaked out? Left you?"

"Quite the opposite." Alec rubbed his hand down his face, remembering the petallike softness of her skin, the humming in her throat when she came. "We made love, then I called it off."

Sort of. That part wasn't exactly clear. Faith had gone into his bedroom and slept for the remainder of the night, while he laid on the couch in his creepy living room, desperate to touch her again. And again. Neither had actually said the phrase *It's over.*

"'Made love,'" Jake repeated dully. "Interesting phrase from you."

"What are you? Freud?"

"Doesn't take a shrink to point out you said *made love*

instead of *had sex*. Because something tells me it wasn't just sex. You've had sex with any and every female who caught your eye since you were sixteen."

"Jake," he growled a warning. He did have standards, for fuck's sake.

"No, listen to me." His brother turned and faced him head-on, an unusual fire lighting his eyes. "In nine years, not one woman has gotten close enough to breach your wall. You told her, man. You told Faith about Laura. That right there should tell you something."

Yeah. It told him he'd let his guard down and left his heart open for slaughter. Alec was amazed there was anything left of the organ to kill. And Jake wasn't telling him anything he didn't already know. Point was, he didn't know what to do about it. He wanted Faith so bad that there wasn't a stray thought that didn't lead back to her. Staying away seemed to be the best thing for both of them.

Jake sighed. "Mom and Dad are here. Lacey's nervous about them meeting her father. I'm going to go find her." He glanced across the dunes, already searching for her. "Go find Faith. Kiss and make up."

As Jake wandered off to seek out Lacey, Alec's gaze drifted over the twenty or so guests milling about the beach. Some were clients of Jake's, others were old high school friends, and there were a few of their cousins in the mix. He'd also been introduced to a handful of Mia's coworkers from the VA hospital. Their faces were illuminated by an orange glow from the bonfire as they laughed and swapped stories. None of it interested him as it used to. People-watching had once been his favorite pastime.

What in the hell had Faith done to him? Staring out at the ocean, he wondered if she was a mermaid after all. From the moment he'd first heard her speak, that was the image that stuck. Her soothing voice, the lulling hum of calm surrounding her, plus some kind of mystical magic.

She had complete and utter power over him.

He finished his beer and tossed the bottle in the recycling, noting Ginny had wandered away from Faith and was now chatting it up with a couple of girls who were summering down the beach. Faith crossed her arms and looked around, staring at the others. Her white top and blue pants clung to her in the breeze as her hair caught and danced. He'd bet her freckles would be more pronounced against the firelight.

Fishing in her pocket, she hastily drew out her cell and stared at the screen before answering. Whoever she was talking to didn't stay on the line very long. Soon, her excitement was cast aside by disappointment and she hung up. Her shoulders slumped. Her head bowed.

Alec had seen her do this more times than he had fingers and toes to count. No doubt, it was her parents calling for their mundane weekly check-in.

The fucking shitheads. What in the hell was wrong with those people? To treat a daughter that way? Their flesh and blood. How could you look at something so beautiful, so goddamn sweet his teeth ached, that they themselves had created, and not love her?

Alec's baby had been nothing more than tissue when Laura miscarried, but he loved that little mass with all he had, and he hadn't ever gotten to meet it. Granted, he only had one side of Faith's story, and there may have been more to it, but Faith was honest to a fault. He didn't question for a second that what she told him was the truth.

Looking at her now, any residual doubt slipped away with the tide. He pulled out his cell to text her. Cowardice, for sure, but she was killing him standing there all by herself, wanting acceptance from two people who were too selfish to give it.

I miss you.

She glanced down at her phone and stilled. If not for the swish of her hair in the wind, he'd swear time had stopped.

Painful minutes ticked by.

Just as he was about to make his way over, his parents approached Faith, with Lacey and Jake in tow. Feeling like he'd been dropped in some god-awful mute version of a Shakespearean play, Alec watched from a distance.

Faith said something that made his dad laugh. Before they moved on, Faith handed them a napkin with a brownie as if she were one of the waitstaff.

He followed Faith's gaze as Lacey introduced her father to his parents. He couldn't tell from this distance, but he knew that longing, yearning look haunting Faith's face. Any family dynamic, even a dysfunctional one, had to be better than pretending total ignorance.

He'd forgotten all about the text until Faith glanced at her phone again. After a few seconds, she cast a wayward glance at the guests and crossed her arms as she wandered toward her guesthouse.

Surging into action, Alec pivoted and strode past the beach and mimosa grove to the front of the property, where he could make his way to her place without anyone seeing.

chapter twenty

It seemed she didn't belong anywhere. A party full of people and she was still so alone. Most of the guests were having a great time, which was good. Faith was hoping to drum up enough courage to go introduce herself, but then Alec's text came, throwing her off.

He missed her? She didn't know how to feel about that, or if she should believe it. If he missed her, he had a funny way of showing it.

His parents were nice people. His dad was a little too outspoken, but his mother was warm and friendly. Faith got the impression Alec's dad was just nervous. After all, he used to be the Covingtons' gardener and now he was invited to beach parties on the estate and his son was marrying the Covingtons' daughter. Hope used to talk a lot when she was nervous. Endless chatter with no filter.

She opened the back door to the guesthouse and stepped inside. Not bothering with the kitchen light, she made her way to the stove to start the kettle. While she waited for the water to heat, she glanced out the window over the sink. The bonfire created enough illumination for her to move about, but she didn't want anyone to know she'd slunk off like a coward, so she kept the lights off. The party had been too much stimulation. Most people didn't understand that, and it was too hard to explain.

She doubted anyone would notice she was gone anyway, which was fine.

The kettle whistled, shaking her away from her thoughts. She poured the water into a mug and set the tea bag to steep. After locking the kitchen door, just in case a wandering guest should approach, she decided to grab a book and read until she couldn't keep her eyes open. Perhaps then she'd get out of this pattern of interrupted sleep that had haunted her all week.

"You left the party pretty early."

Hot tea sloshed over her hand when she whirled. She shook the sting away.

The deep tone of Alec's familiar voice infiltrated the quiet serenity of the guesthouse. She'd thought she was alone. Assumed, rather. He hadn't come inside without knocking first any other time.

He leaned against the living room wall by the front door, arms folded over his impressive chest and ankles crossed. No flip-flops or sandals. The sight of his bare feet sent some kind of electrical current to her knees, causing them to weaken. Why was that so sexy? Board shorts in a blue tropical pattern covered his strong thighs and narrow hips. His tee was plain white, but stretched across the muscles in his biceps and broad chest, making her want to be that shirt.

He looked casual, until she caught the tension tightening his shoulders and the wariness in his eyes. Tufts of his black hair stood up on his head, like he'd run his hands through it a half dozen times. It was windy tonight, though. Perhaps nature was the culprit for the bedhead.

She tried to swallow and failed. What was he doing here?

He didn't want complications or romantic entanglements. He'd called things off. Didn't he realize how hard it was for her to be near him?

The sting in her hand where the tea had spilled intensified to a throb. It was turning red already. She shook her hand again and set the mug aside.

He shoved off the wall and strode into the kitchen "Did you burn yourself? Let me see."

This was silly. It was fine. "I'm . . ."

The thought died away. He brought her hand to his lips and gently blew on the burn, keeping his gray-blue eyes trained to hers. A head-to-toe shiver tore through her body. She made some kind of sound in her throat—a determined whine of surrender or a plea to stop. Either. Both.

He stilled, all but his thumb, which brushed over the rampant pulse in her wrist. "Never, never stop making that noise, Faith. It's the sexiest thing. You make the same sound when you come."

Air forced its way into her lungs. Heat pooled between her thighs. Her head got more than a little light.

With a gentle tug, he drew her against him. "I missed you."

Yeah, but . . . why?

"You said that. In your text. I'm confused." And incoherent.

"As am I." Several emotions shifted over his face in the span of a few seconds. He dipped his head and brushed his lips over hers. Moaned. He drew away and mumbled something about a mermaid before he plunged into the kiss.

She fisted her hands in his shirt and yanked him closer, even as her brain screamed at her to back away. This was maddening, the need and fervor he could evoke. And when he left at the end of summer, if she didn't die from bewilderment first, she'd succumb to a massive broken heart. But this was what she'd wanted. Experience. Passion. To live.

His arms tightened around her back when he ended the kiss and nuzzled her neck. He sighed heavily. "Mermaids and cupcakes."

She chewed on her lower lip where she could still taste him. "I wasn't joking when I said I'm confused."

He chuckled against the skin below her ear. "I'd explain, but you'd think I'm nuts."

"Already there."

He laughed again, sounding rough and sexy. The shadow of his beard scraped her cheek as he drew back to look into her eyes. He tucked a strand of hair behind her ear. "What did you say to my father to make him laugh?"

She stared over his shoulder, trying to remember the brief conversation they'd had on the beach. "He jokingly asked if the brownies were safe to eat. I said Ginny and I made them, so the sugar coma was his risk to take."

A smile lit his eyes, infused his whole face. He shook his head and cupped her cheek. "I got my sweet tooth from him. At least there's something we have in common."

They had more than that in common, but that was a conversation for a later time. "Why are you here, Alec?"

The first boom of the fireworks exploded outside, lighting her tiny kitchen in red hues.

He dropped his forehead to hers. "I can't get you out of my head."

Because she was naive and tempted to believe him, and because the end result wouldn't change no matter what he was starting to feel, she slid her hands down his arms and linked their fingers. "Come on. The fireworks are starting."

His mouth thinned with an exhale. "Fireworks."

"Yes, fireworks," she said. A good distraction.

She tugged him by the arm outside, then dropped his hand. The humidity slammed into her at once, dulled only by a soft breeze off the water. The air was scented heavily with brine and salt, a smell she'd grown quite fond of these past weeks.

Leaning against the deck railing, she watched the sky explode with color. The ocean made the sound bounce and echo, but the water reflected the display in panoramic glory.

Faith couldn't tell exactly where they were setting the fire-works off, but judging by the smoke, she figured it was one of the tiny inlet islands to the south.

Alec came up behind her, sliding his arms under hers and trapping her to the railing. The solid feel of him behind her brought sparks of her own and a strange sense of ease. He rested his cheek on the top of her head and held her close.

At the last boom of the finale, he kissed her hair. "We could go make our own fireworks." He winced and turned her around. "That was awful. You'd think a writer could come up with something better."

She smiled through a sigh. "I won't think less of you."

He widened his stance to bring her closer. "You don't think less of anyone." His brows furrowed as he studied her in the dark, with only the moon for light. "I haven't written one word all week."

Writer's block again. Or still. That's why he was here. She tried to erase the disappointment from her tone. "Do you want to tell me about it? Maybe I can help. Or do you not like to discuss a work in progress?"

His chest expanded with a breath as he glanced over her shoulder. "I never talk about my books until they're turned in to my editor, not even with my agent. I'm paranoid about leaking. Other than an approved story idea, my publisher doesn't know what I'm working on." Returning his gaze to hers, he brushed the top of her nose with the pad of his thumb. "Your freckles are adorable. My main character has them, too."

So did he or did he not want to discuss the manuscript? "What's the character's name?"

"Amy."

"A female lead?" All his books had male main characters.

He swallowed. Nodded. "Yes. She has wavy brown hair, about this long." He touched the ends of her hair, his gaze watching the movement. "Her eyes are amber, but turn honey when confronted. She's just shy of frail in frame, with a voice that sounds like a mermaid call and skin that smells like cupcakes."

Her hands settled on his forearms and may have gripped a little too tight. "Mermaids and cupcakes?"

Offering a barely perceptible nod, he smiled. "Don't forget the amber eyes. They're one of my favorite parts." He shrugged, suddenly looking shy. "What can I say? You inspire me."

She fisted her pendant and slid it back and forth on the chain. "I'm really confused. What are you doing here, Alec?" Besides breaking her heart and making her desire things she couldn't have. Why did the one person who had noticed her in twenty-seven years have to be emotionally and physically unavailable?

The smile slipped. "I told you, I missed you." His gaze ran over her face and hair. "I know I shouldn't. I should just end it like we tried to do in New York, but I can't."

Her heart pounded so loud she was shocked the partygoers on the beach didn't hear. Things were changing between them faster than the roll of the tide, but with the same force. All the complications and scenarios played out in her head until she could only draw one conclusion.

Why waste time and energy denying the pull? If Hope's death and Faith's recent move away from all she knew had taught her nothing else, it was that you only get one chance to live before it flutters away.

She cupped his cheek and smiled. "I offered you the summer. I promise when it's over and it's time for you to leave, I won't make it difficult for you. But you're the one who called things off, so you'll have to decide." She could see the moment her words sank in.

He leaned in as if to kiss her, but hovered over her lips instead, until they shared the same breath. "Faith?"

"Yes?"

"Hold on."

In a blur of motion, he picked her up, strode through the patio door, and kicked it shut with his foot. Without breaking

stride, he wove through the kitchen and down the short hall
to her room. He kicked this door shut, too, and set her on her
feet.

Then his mouth crashed over hers and her back was
pinned to the door. His hands spread over her ribs and
around to her back. The hard, lean length of him pressed
against her, so she could feel every delicious ridge beneath
her palms.

"Condom?" he breathed.

"In the nightstand." Where they'd stayed since New York.

The arms around her back shifted as he lifted her and
walked to the other side of the room, her toes dragging on
the floor. He broke contact for a millisecond to search
through her drawer and come up with a foil packet, and then
his mouth was crushing hers again. Bruising. Desperate.

Her shirt was gone. The bra, capris, and panties next.

He stared at her, hands flat against the wall on either side
of her shoulders. He looked like he wanted to say something,
but he shook his head and reached behind his neck to tug
off his tee. The shorts followed. He kept his gaze trained on
hers when he rolled a condom down his generous length.

"I'll be thorough next time."

"Okay," she breathed. Thorough didn't really matter to
her right now. Him, inside of her, did.

She reached for his hips and brought him to her. Smooth,
soft skin over hard muscle. The heat of his body melted her,
his kiss drugging. He checked her readiness with one stroke
of his finger, and moaned when he found her wet. Aching
for more, she ran her hands up his abs, over his nipples, and
drew a shudder out of him. Learning what he liked as she
went along, she slid her arms around his waist, then lower,
to cup his backside.

He inhaled sharply. Dropped his forehead to her shoulder
and nipped. Feeling a little more brazen, she worked her hand
between their bodies and palmed his erection. He let out a
half cry, half moan, and his mouth opened wide against her

sensitive skin. He licked, sucked, and elicited a tremor out of her. She closed her fingers around his shaft and thumbed the tip, urgent for him to claim her body again.

It was like a piano wire snapping. With his knees, he spread her thighs. His hands gripped her hips and lifted. His chest held her in place against the wall as his fingers threaded through hers and trapped her hands above her head. Instinct kicked in, and she wrapped her legs around his waist. He was much taller than she was, so her body was stretched taut, breasts jutting out and chest heaving in excitement.

He kept her hands pinned with one of his and aligned himself with the other. Just before he entered her, he paused and stared into her eyes. Something connected, fused, between them, something more powerful than their physical bodies. Then he slid home.

It was like coming undone. Every fiber unraveled until her brain shut down and there was only the fullness of him inside of her, the slick friction of their skin and the sound of their mingled breathing. His hands found hers once more, lacing their fingers together above her head and straining the beautiful muscles of his biceps.

"That noise, Faith. That one right there. It drives me out of my damn mind." He kissed her hard, reared back, and drove deep inside. "Yes. Do it again. Again and again."

"Alec . . ." Explosion loomed. Her muscles coiled.

He groaned into her ear. Thrust harder, more urgent. "Again. Say my name again."

Right now, probably at any given time, she'd give him whatever he wanted, any time he asked. Because no one had ever made it like this. Life, companionship, friends . . . sex. Never before. "Alec."

"Faith."

That pushed her off the edge of the cliff. Him saying her name with need through gritted teeth, barely holding on himself. She tumbled off into sweet, sweet oblivion. He tensed against her while the aftershocks trembled, rocked, and finally settled.

Alec let go of her hands and cupped her bottom to spin around and slide to the floor. He stretched his legs out and leaned against the wall. The back of his head landed with a thud.

She straddled his thighs and rested her cheek on his shoulder. They stayed like that, him stroking her back and her toying with the hair at the nape of his neck, until the air-conditioning kicked in with a whirl and she shivered.

"Alec?"

"Hmm?"

She sighed happily. "You can make your own fireworks anytime."

He laughed in that rusty, rough sound she loved and wrapped her deeper into his embrace. "You got it."

chapter
twenty-one

Alec opened his eyes and winced at the sunlight streaming through the window. The edges of sleep drained away as he ran his hand down Faith's back. Warm, supple female. Waking up and having her curled against his side, the scent of her and their lovemaking still in his nose, caused the knots in his chest to loosen.

He hadn't slept with a woman—actually slept—since Laura was still around. This was different, waking up with Faith. Though not needy by any means, Faith was more giving. Laura had never wanted to cuddle. When they were done having sex, Laura would roll to her side of the bed and Alec to his.

He and Faith were still in the middle of the bed, legs and arms entwined, their breathing the only sound. He hadn't had anything or nearly anyone to hold on to in . . . well, ever. Yet instead of panic and uncertainty, a sense of rightness settled over him.

Faith had so much passion and possibility bottled up inside, just waiting for someone to uncork it. She'd come undone in his arms. Exploded. She'd managed to uncork him, too, and he hadn't even realized he'd been shelved. He wondered why no man before him had seen her openness, her true gift of healing. By his estimation, no one had ever seen her at all.

The knowledge made him want to show her how wonderful she was. She was real. More real than the majority of the population. Faith didn't live by agenda or gain. She just, quite simply, felt. She claimed she hadn't lived, and maybe she hadn't by certain standards, but there was more to the road of life than bucket lists and accumulating friends. She saw the wonder in little things. It was the most beautiful quality about her, the biggest draw. In a society of technology and fast tracks, she accumulated moments, almost as if storing them in her fascinating head to reflect on later. Nothing escaped her notice.

He'd been wondering from day one what about Faith was different, what had him coming back to her time and time again when it had always been so easy to just walk away before. She was the first person to actually see him. Not the author or the money or the man who screwed up by breaking everything he touched. Him. What was buried beneath.

Beside him, she started to stir. He stared at the dusting of freckles on her nose against her pale skin, her sleep-flushed cheeks and pink mouth, wondering how to avoid fucking up this gorgeous creature.

She stretched her slim body before she buried her face in his chest, all without even opening her eyes. "You're still here," she murmured against his skin.

It pissed him off how she never expected attention. Or anyone to stick around. He reined in the anger because that wasn't her fault. "I am." Right here where he wanted to be—however much that scared the shit out of him.

She lifted her head and offered a sleepy smile.

His heart turned over in his chest. He cupped her jaw and kissed her. A long, deep, soul-searing kiss that had more than his dick stirring. Her fingers drove into his hair, holding him there as if anticipating he'd pull away. Yeah, that was the problem. He couldn't pull away from her. Hadn't been able to for weeks now. Hell, he'd tried.

Grabbing a condom from the nightstand, he sheathed himself and rolled her beneath him. They'd made love sitting up and against the wall, but having her under him, pliant and ready with her brown hair spread over the white sheets and looking at him through those amber eyes, was the equivalent of a maelstrom. Heady, powerful lust coursed through him, making him quake.

She cupped his jaw and brushed her thumbs across his lips. Parting her thighs, she rubbed her sweet heat against the underside of his dick. "What are you thinking about?" She put the tip of her finger between his brows, smoothing a wrinkle.

"The absence of thought, actually. Whenever you're around me, even when you're not, you seem to . . ." He broke off and looked down at her, unable to finish what he'd started. It wasn't fair to her to do this, to throw any more emotion into the already heady mix.

He kissed her until there was no air, aligned himself, and thrust inside. He stilled to give her a minute, although his body screamed at him to move. To claim. Her heat gripped him in a tight fist and all he could do was whisper her name and pinch his eyes closed.

A warm kiss pressed to one eyelid and then the other before her lips drifted across his cheek to his ear. "You're my only thought, too."

"Faith . . ."

"Not now, Alec. Just make love to me. The rest comes later."

The sentiment bothered him, ate away at his gut. So he

moved inside her because doing that brought peace. He
made love to her slow and languid, with passion he didn't
know existed. And when they collapsed on the bed, a sweaty,
tangled mass of limbs, he didn't know if they were even two
separate people anymore.

Eventually, Faith got up and padded to the bathroom. He
shoved on his shorts and went into the kitchen to start a pot
of coffee. She came in moments later, wearing a T-shirt—*his
shirt*—and nothing else. He drew in a sharp inhale that did
nothing to stop his rapid pulse.

She stilled after seeing his expression and looked down at
herself. "I'll put on something else in a minute. I didn't want
to walk around naked."

"Leave it on."

"Are you sure? I—"

"Yes. Leave it on."

He'd just had her moments ago, but he wanted her again.
In theory, the desire for her should be fading by now. That's
how it had always been. Once he'd had a woman, the craving
for a repeat was gone. But his desire for Faith only grew.

Shaking his head, he handed her a cup of tea and poured
himself some coffee. When he turned back, she was staring
at him. "What?"

"You made me tea."

So he had. Until she'd pointed it out, he hadn't really
noticed. He shrugged.

She took a sip and lifted her brows. "With one spoonful
of honey."

Where the hell was she going with this? "That's how you
drink it, right?"

"Yes." As if unable to stand any longer, she made her way
to a chair and collapsed into it. Something like shock laced
with grief spread over her face as she rubbed her temples.
Her face drained of color. "Excuse me a minute, please." She
fled from the room.

He stared at her cup abandoned on the table and then the

empty doorway. Stood there for several minutes, in fact. And then, like a smack upside the head, he understood.

He set down his cup and strode after her, finding her dressed and perched at the edge of the bed, holding her cell phone with shaking hands.

"Twenty-seven years and they can't remember I hate broccoli. Six weeks and you know how I drink my tea." She looked up at him, her eyes shimmering with tears. "What's wrong with me?"

He wanted to hold her and soothe those tears away, but he remained just inside the doorway. "Nothing's wrong with you. They're the idiots, Faith." And if he ever met her parents face-to-face, he'd say that and much more.

"Maybe today will be the day I can have a real conversation with them." Desperation radiated in her voice.

He wouldn't even bet his coffee on it. Today seemed more urgent to her, though.

"Surely they wouldn't brush me off so easily today," she whispered to herself.

A few thoughts pounded inside his skull. Today possibly being the anniversary of her sister's death was at the forefront, but he had no idea if that was what she meant or if it was even the case. He had no clue when Hope had died. And since it was Sunday, Faith didn't have to work. In case his assumption was correct, he'd just keep her busy doing other things to help her get through.

"Why don't we go out and get some breakfast?"

She looked up at him. Through him. "I'm not very hungry." She grabbed the pendant around her neck, but instead of sliding it back and forth on the chain like he'd seen her do so often, she pressed her fist to her chest. "What part of the book are you stuck on?"

"What?"

"Your book. Last night you said you were stuck. At what part?"

He sighed and pinched the bridge of his nose. He had

whiplash from the abrupt topic change. "It's a little hard to explain, since you haven't read it."

"Just give me a condensed version of the—"

"Do you want to read it?" That would keep her mind off whatever was bothering her and maybe help him in the process.

"But you don't let anyone read your manuscripts."

She wasn't just anyone.

Shit. He almost swallowed his tongue. "I'll let you."

"Why? I mean, what about leaks? That's what you said last night. Aren't you afraid I might tell someone?"

He laughed.

A look of insult marred her brow before it morphed to shame.

Figuring he'd hurt her feelings somehow, he cleared the air. "I trust you, and you've helped me so far. If not for you, the book would still be a blank document." She still seemed hesitant. "Do you have anything else pressing to do today?"

Her eyes drifted shut and her lower lip trembled.

Without knowing how or why, he'd hurt her again. If she wanted him to know, she'd tell him. And she didn't. Feeling like the lowest form of pond scum, he walked to the bed and sat next to her. But then he didn't know how to console her, so he didn't.

"I have nothing else to do today." Her voice was so quiet he almost didn't hear her.

He cleared his throat. "What would you like to do?"

She opened her mouth and then closed it again, staring at her phone. "If I read your manuscript, I'll just want to read the ending you haven't written yet. Tell me about the plot and where you're stuck."

Her careful avoidance of the question only heightened his curiosity, but he let it drop. Flopping back on the bed, he gave her a rundown of the story line. Halfway through, she laid next to him on her side and propped her head in her hand.

He draped his arm over his eyes. "So Amy escaped the Nightmare demon, but he took her brother for leverage. She's connecting with the other two souls for book two and three, but I just can't decide where to go from there. Too much closure and there's not enough for the other books, too little and the readers get pissed."

"And the idea is that the three souls need to come together, fight their own fears, to defeat Nightmare, right?"

"Yes."

She chewed on her lip. "Why is Amy so important to Nightmare? What makes her special?"

He gave her a condensed version of the backstory involving the death of her parents and that night he first visited young Amy.

"But that's what Nightmare does. Finds people at their lowest and makes even sleep hell for them. Why Amy? What's the motivation? It's almost like he . . . loves her or something. As much as a demon can, anyway."

Alec stilled. His brain fired on all cylinders and in every direction.

Christ. Faith had nailed it. The demon lacked motive. And if he went with Faith's suggestion, the readers would feel a smidgen of pity for Nightmare. Would understand how much Amy could destroy not only the physical part of him, but whatever residual part of his human side remained.

It was goddamn brilliant.

He rolled over, straddled her hips, cupped her cheeks, and smacked a kiss on her mouth. "I have to go. I need to plot this out. Go punch out more pages . . ."

He stopped when her smile grew wistful. Sad. The corners of her eyes turned down and her eyebrows furrowed, even as she maintained the curve of her lips. And he remembered that she'd been upset about something, something specific to today.

"I'll get to work on it tomorrow."

She shook her head. "Don't be silly. Go. Write the masterpiece that's in your head. You'll go nuts if you don't."

It shook him how well she understood. His fingers were itching to type. But damn, he couldn't, not with her in this state. "Come with me."

"To your place?"

"Yes. You being there will be encouragement to finish faster so I can devour you. Plus, if I get stuck again, you'll be there." He ignored the warning bells inside his head. Shoved aside that it wasn't just her body he was needing anymore.

Her gaze darted over his face. Then she grinned. "I have an idea."

chapter twenty-two

They toasted a couple of bagels for breakfast and ate them with orange juice before making the short trek across the grounds to Alec's guesthouse. Faith knew he was anxious to get going on the book, so she wasted no time getting ready. Before leaving, she'd gotten an idea in her head to make writing fun for him, but now she didn't think she could go through with it. She still wasn't sure why he'd wanted her to come.

They stepped out of the drenching humidity and into the cool interior of his house. She barely got to look at the place because he was on the move. He tugged her by the hand into his bedroom and booted up the laptop sitting on the small desk by the window.

"What's this idea of yours?"

She set her purse and book down on the bed. Her stomach rioted. "Um, well I thought . . ."

He stepped into her space and ran his hands down her arms. "Don't clam up now." He kissed her forehead.

She breathed in his now-familiar scent of soap and sandalwood as her breasts grew heavy with desire. She could do this. It was time to start going after what she wanted.

Blowing out a careful breath, she took a step back. "I thought for every page you typed I could remove an article of clothing."

His jaw dropped and his eyebrows shot up. Throwing his head back, he barked out a laugh. "Oh, Faith. I love how your mind works." He closed the distance and kissed her soundly on the mouth. "Let's hope I get a lot done. That's quite the incentive. And distraction."

Her nerves leveled out and her pulse calmed. "Get to work." She tried for a teasing note, but her voice just came out sounding breathy.

He groaned and made his way to the desk while she sat on the bed and leaned against the headboard. She waited until he had the document open and started typing before she opened her book to settle in and read.

"Page," he said a while later and turned to wink at her.

She slid off one flip-flop and dropped it on the floor.

"Oh, come on! Shoes don't count."

Heat warmed her cheeks as she laughed. He had a knack for making her let go and feel good. It seemed like so long since she had laughed. "Shoes are an article of clothing."

He huffed and turned back to his laptop. The keys clicked away.

She returned to her book until it was time to remove the other shoe. The cardigan she wore over her dress was next. To tease him, she took the band out of her hair and released her ponytail with his next page, earning a scowl.

After that, though, he really must've gotten in the zone, because he didn't call out "page" again and didn't turn around to see if she was naked. She stopped taking clothes off to let him work. He needed a good solid day of writing and she was pleased he was so focused. It had been hard on him not being able to work in a steady rhythm, to have his ability blocked. She was glad he was finding himself again and that she could help.

Around lunchtime, she tiptoed into the kitchen to see what he had in the fridge. She found a couple of leftover grilled chicken breasts and whipped up a chicken salad. After toasting some bread and adding lettuce and tomato, she dug in the cabinets to find chips to go with the sandwich. Apparently, Alec had an addiction to sugar and salt—a box of packaged chocolate cupcakes sat on the shelf, the kind that had a shelf life long enough to survive the apocalypse. For a moment, all she could do was stare. It was like an omen of sorts. With a shaking hand, she brought the box down as memories slammed into her.

The day before Hope's kidney transplant, her sister had somehow smuggled a box of cupcakes like these into the hospital. She'd covertly snuck down the hall, stuck a penlight into the top of a cupcake, and whispered, "Happy birthday, little sister."

Faith had been feeling pretty down until that moment. They hadn't been allowed to share a room, and Faith had been nervous about her own surgery to remove the kidney Hope needed. Her parents had been darting between their rooms, but she'd encouraged them to stick by Hope's side, because Hope was the sick one. The nurses were nice enough in their prepping, but it sure wasn't the way Faith had wanted to spend her birthday—alone with tubes and wires.

Hot tears filled her eyes.

This birthday wasn't such a bad one, compared to the others. Maybe twenty-eight was her magic number. She'd gotten to make love to Alec first thing in the morning, and she could do worse than spending half the day in bed reading. But still . . . her parents hadn't called. She thought for sure they'd call today, on their own. Until now, they'd returned her phone calls, but she'd been the one to initiate contact.

The sound of steadily clicking computer keys drifted down

the hall. Alec was lost in his book, as he should be, so she'd
leave him to it. She took the sandwich, wrapped it up, and set
it in the fridge. Tiptoeing into the bedroom, she grabbed her
purse and turned to leave when a thought occurred to her.

Alec was typing like mad, not even aware she was there.

She slipped out of her dress and set it on the bed, then
grabbed one of Alec's shirts from a corner chair he'd thrown
aside. She put one flip-flop in the hall and the other in the
kitchen. Finally, she put her panties by the back door. Maybe
if Alec finished early enough, he'd follow her silly bread
crumbs and they could make love tonight.

She stared at the box of cupcakes on the counter and, with
a heavy sigh, snatched one to eat later and put the box away.
Alec wouldn't mind, and if he did, she'd bake him something
to replace it. It wasn't a birthday cake, but it was something.
Something was better than nothing.

Wearing only his T-shirt, she stepped outside into the heat
and quietly shut the door. If she passed anyone on the beach
dressed like this, they'd just think it was a swim cover-up.
She was drowning in the shirt and it fell well past her knees.
Still, she was relieved to make it to her guesthouse with no
interruptions.

But what to do with the rest of her day? She could go out
and do some shopping, but there wasn't anything she needed
and she wanted to be here in case Alec took a break and did
follow her not-so-subtle hints.

She looked out the window at the ocean and made her
decision. She wished Hope was here. They'd bake a cake
and sing out of key and have a ball hanging out on the beach.
Hope may not be here, but Faith could still hit the beach and
pretend her sister was sitting in the sand beside her.

She set the cupcake on the counter and dug around in the
kitchen drawers until she found what she was looking for.
Placing a small candle in the center of the cupcake, she
nodded and went in search of her swimming suit.

* * *

Alec's gaze darted over the screen, line by line. Faster than his brain could catch up, he proofed the chapters he'd written. He'd gotten all the way past the black moment where everything went to hell, and now all he had to do was set up the second book and wrap up this one. Faith had been right. What this had lacked was . . .

Faith. Shit.

He whipped around in his chair, but she wasn't there. The little green sundress she'd been wearing, however, was draped across the foot of the bed.

Grinning, he rose and stretched, remembering her little game. He'd been so wrapped up in the story, the characters shouting in his head, that he'd lost track of time.

Speaking of . . . he looked at the clock and cursed. It was already late afternoon. How had he gotten that distracted? Not that it was the first time. Hell, sometimes he went days on autopilot. But he'd never had a willing woman behind him while he typed. A willing Faith, to be specific. Amazing he'd written anything.

He strode into the hall and nearly tripped over her flip-flop. "Faith?"

The house was eerily quiet. When there was no sign of her in the living room or kitchen, he figured she was out on the beach. He opened the fridge to grab a beer and found a ready-made sandwich for him. In the same instant, he realized if her dress was on the bed, she would be naked on the beach.

Kicking the fridge closed, he turned and stumbled over her other flip-flop. And that's when he found her black underwear, right by the back door.

He laughed and pocketed the panties. She was turning into a little minx.

Except she wasn't the kind of woman to go gallivanting around without clothes, and after stepping out onto the back deck, he didn't see her anywhere. She had to have gone home, judging by the clues she'd left behind.

The image of her naked form filled his head, of her lying under him, her pale skin flushed with desire and her pretty mouth parted. Her amber eyes turning golden and her small, perfect breasts rising and falling with her gasps. The way she responded so openly to every touch, the sounds she made when she came . . .

Fuck. He was hard. And halfway down the beach before he even knew what hit him.

He found her on an Adirondack chair on her back deck, wearing a plain yellow bikini and the start of a sunburn. She was completely zonked out. A book was facedown on her stomach, her sunglasses shoved up on her head and tangled in her brown waves. The humidity had dampened her hairline so that the dewy tendrils curled madly. Dark lashes fanned her cheeks, her breasts rising and falling in an even rhythm.

His gaze traveled down to the waistline of her suit and encountered the scar he assumed was surgical. The kidney she gave her sister. He'd noticed it while making love, but in the light of day it was more pronounced. A constant reminder of her loss.

He sighed, wondering how she'd made it through the pain of her sister's death when she'd had no other outlet or support. That took guts and strength, more than any one person should have. But she did. In spades. Had it been him losing Jake, Alec didn't think he'd have survived.

She was so damn lovely it hurt. A physical, bone-deep ache that he'd never experienced and was positive he didn't want. The urge to protect her, to slay her demons, and hold her tight was so powerful that all he could do was shake his head. Because he'd never been able to protect or hold on to anything. But Faith made him want to try.

Smiling, because she could easily bring one to his face, he gently took the book and set it aside. Then he opened the patio umbrella to protect her from the late-day sun. With her fair skin, she'd probably turn lobster in another hour. He decided to let her sleep and went into the house to see if he could scrounge up something to throw on the grill for dinner. If not, he'd order in, because he was keeping Faith all to himself tonight.

He was surprised to find a couple of steaks in the freezer, as he'd only seen her eat chicken, so he turned to put them in the sink to thaw. And stopped.

On her counter was a cupcake. With a birthday candle in it.

Faith didn't eat sweets, so he couldn't figure out if it was her birthday and she set it there for show or if it was her sister's birthday and it was a sentimental thing.

Either way, he was the biggest shithead on earth. She'd been upset earlier, even through her attempt at bravery, and what did he do? He goddamn glued himself to the laptop. Ignored her like she was nothing, like her parents had done . . .

Christ. He hoped they'd called.

He pulled out his phone and found Mia in his contacts. "Do you have an employee record on Faith? A tax document? Anything with her date of birth?"

"Uh . . . She worked with Ginny at St. Ambrose, so I didn't do an application. I do have a . . . hold on." Papers shuffled in the background. "Wait. Why?"

"I think it might be her birthday. She didn't say anything to me, but . . ." He looked at the cupcake. An inadequate celebration to say the least. One that made his chest grow heavy and clench like a vise.

"Here. Social security number, blah, blah, blah. Yes! It is today. She's twenty-eight." More papers shuffled. "Why wouldn't she tell us? We could've had a cake while everyone was here for the fireworks last night and celebrated." She sighed. "Now I feel bad."

Mia couldn't feel half as bad as he did. Or Faith. To go the whole day without any well wishes, not a one . . .

"I'm calling Lacey," Mia insisted. "She can go to that bakery that's doing the wedding cake and pick up a dessert or something. I'll head into town with Ginny and get some chicken and corn for Cole to grill. Can you keep Faith busy for a couple hours? It'll be late for a barbeque, but it's better than nothing."

Yes, it was better than nothing. And he knew just the thing to keep her occupied. He disconnected with Mia and tossed the cupcake in the garbage.

chapter
twenty-three

A featherlight touch tickled Faith's arm, pulling her from sleep. Her skin was heated and she realized it was from the sun when she breathed in the scent of salt water. The steady thrum of the ocean roared in the background. Opening her eyes, she squinted to look up at Alec's face as he sat on the edge of her chair, hip to hip.

"Hi." She glanced around. Stretched. "I fell asleep."

"Sounds like a nice way to spend the day, sleeping in the sun after a good book."

She struggled to sit, bringing them closer. "How's your manuscript? You were really going to town."

He brushed a kiss over her lips, stirring her pulse. "It's nearly done, thanks to you. And an even better story because of your insight."

Warmth flooded her chest. "I'm glad."

His smile fell a fraction. "I'm sorry I got so wrapped up." He lifted her black panties, dangling from one finger. "I got your note. I'm about to make up for lost time."

Before she could retort, he swooped her up in his arms and brought her inside. A rush of cool air hit her sun-kissed skin and she shivered.

As he carried her down the hall, his gaze raked over her body. "You've got the start of a sunburn, but I think I woke you in time."

"I'm glad you did. Where are you taking me?"

Instead of going to the bedroom like she expected, he walked into the bathroom and set her on her feet. He turned on the water in the tub and grabbed a bottle of her body wash. Inhaling, he groaned and then checked the water temperature.

"Take a bath to wash the sunscreen off, and then I'll rub some lotion . . . right here." He kissed her shoulder and slid the strap of her bathing suit down her arm. "And here." He kissed the other shoulder and removed her top with one slick flip of his wrist. He strode around to her back, trailing a finger down her spine. "And here." He kissed the small of her back and crouched to slide her bikini bottoms down her legs. "Here, too," he whispered, kissing her calves.

Air seeped from her lungs. Her heart pounded in anticipation. A sharp tremble tore through her core as the apex between her thighs throbbed. Yet she couldn't move, no matter how much she wanted him. His touch was gentle, kind, where before it had always been needy and urgent. She didn't know what to do with this side of him.

He rose and faced her. With slow, seductive movements, he tugged his shirt off and his shorts down, all the while maintaining her gaze. Heat and desire shone in his eyes, but there was something else there. Something tender she hadn't seen before.

Her breath caught. "Alec?"

Naked, he stepped to her and held her hips. "Faith." His voice was raw, a coarse groan of restraint. He nuzzled her neck, kissed her ear. "I want you."

She whimpered and grabbed his solid arms. "Yes. I want you, too."

"Get in the tub."

She didn't want to step out of his arms and break the connection, but she did as he asked and climbed in. He followed and sat behind her, his strong thighs on either side of hers and his erection pressing into her lower back. The warm water, scented with vanilla, slid over her skin, creating a delicious friction between them.

He reached for her body wash and lathered a small amount between his hands. Starting with her neck, he made his way down her shoulders and back before sliding around to her front. Every stroke was heaven and torment, all rolled into one bundle. His slick, soapy hands found her breasts and squeezed.

Her head fell back on his shoulder. She arched, seeking more.

"God, those noises, Faith. You like this?"

"Yes." Her eyes fell closed, lost in his touch.

One hand kneaded her breast, circling her nipple, while the other trailed lower beneath the water. Over her stomach and right to where she throbbed for him. Only him.

His lips hovered by the curve of her ear. "I like touching you. Watching you is the most mesmerizing thing I've ever seen. You let go of your reservations and just feel. Me. You feel me."

Each word sent her higher, closer and closer to completion, until she came apart blindly. Before her tremors subsided, he lifted her by the hips and brought her down over his shaft.

He stilled. Rubbed a slow hand up and down her back when she wanted to move. "No condom, Faith. Be careful how close you tease my restraint.

She loved how he filled her. Loved how there was no barrier between them. But the consequences of going unprotected were too great. She rose off of him, already missing him inside her body, and turned to bring them chest to chest. Splaying her hands on his shoulders, she ran them over the ridges of beautiful muscle—down, down—until she could wrap her fingers around him.

He sucked in a breath and grabbed her wrists. "This is about you, not me."

That gave her pause. Nothing had ever been just about her before. Unsure of what to say, how to feel, she cleared her throat. "Then let me touch you."

He started to shake his head, but stopped. Looked in her eyes. The gray blue of his irises turned stormy, his eyes fixed and dilated on hers.

Keeping one hand around his shaft, she brought the other up to brush his lips with her fingers. His lips parted to take a finger into his mouth, and as he did, she stroked with her other hand. He bit her finger, not hard, but then released it right away, as if worried he might hurt her. Empowered, she stroked again.

"Mother of God." His head hit the back of the tub.

She watched him closely as he came moments later, fascinated by the way his jaw clenched and his breath held and his body tensed in a pleasure-pain combination. And all because of her touch. That someone like her could satisfy a man like him had hope rising in her chest, pride swelling in her throat.

Still breathing erratically, he cupped the back of her head and drew her mouth to his, kissing her in a hot exploration that seemed like way more than a simple thank-you by the time he was finished.

Afterward, he dried her body, the soft terry-cloth towel lingering over each part of her like a caress, and then applied lotion to her skin. Slow, deliberate strokes of his hands made her heart race with the tenderness he exhibited. And when he was through, she didn't have any air left in her lungs.

Because Alec had no idea if anyone else had thought to get Faith a gift while scrambling to pull off this last-minute birthday dinner, he drove her into the touristy area of the strip and parked outside a store.

"I thought we were going to dinner?" Her wary gaze traveled over the building in front of them. A jewelry store.

"We are. After." He opened his door. "Come on."

She strode around the car and met him at the store entrance, still looking adorably confused. He took her hand and tugged her inside, wondering just what the hell he was doing. This kind of gift said you cared about someone deeply, and though he did care about Faith way more than was wise, he couldn't help but think this would be impossible to walk away from. In the end, there was no other choice but to leave. He'd made his mistakes, and he had to live with them.

Yet even with all the doubt ramming his temples, the thought of what Faith might be doing today had he not figured out it was her birthday knotted his gut and tightened his throat.

"Pick out anything you want." He gestured at the glass display cases lining the walls.

"What?" Her wide, panicked gaze met his.

"Pick out—"

"No, I heard you." She waved a flustered hand. "Alec, no. I can't."

He stepped behind her and held her waist to lean down and speak into her ear. "Yes, you can. You just walk over to one of the cases and pick out whatever piece of jewelry catches your eye."

She trembled beneath his hands. "Alec . . ."

"Had I known sooner, I would've picked something out myself. Happy birthday, Faith."

"Can I help you folks?" A salesperson walked up to them, her perfume as heavy as her makeup.

"Give us a second," he said, training his gaze back on Faith.

Not one word fell from Faith's lips, but the tension in her body spoke volumes. He could've plucked her like a guitar string. "Any day now. We have dinner plans."

She shook her head violently.

Frustrated, he stepped around to face her and found tears. A lot of them. Too many for her to will away like she'd done before.

"Faith. Please? I want to. It's your birthday and I want to give you a gift." He cupped her cheeks and wiped the tears from her cheeks with his thumbs.

Earlier, he'd had the odd thought that he'd slay a demon for her. He'd been wrong. He'd slay them all. Because the sight of her like this was killing him.

She blew out a watery breath and met his gaze. "How . . ." She cleared her throat. "How did you know it was my birthday?"

"I'm an author. Research comes with the territory."

She nodded. "Thank you, but this is a bit much."

"Then pick out something small if it makes you feel better." He studied her face for a moment. "Why didn't *you* tell me it was your birthday?"

She stared over his shoulder and shrugged. "I don't know. It seemed presumptuous."

He shook his head and laughed. Presumptuous? Faith? "Pick something out." He kissed her forehead and stepped away to address the waiting salesperson. "Whatever she wants."

The woman's eyes widened with glee. "Of course."

Alec backed off and stood by the register to give her some room. Faith hesitantly stepped to the counter with the rings, but quickly moved on. He bit back a grin and pretended to check his texts. Faith moved past the necklaces and earrings before stopping near him at the bracelets, the salesperson chatting her up the entire time.

"I used to have one like that, when I was a little girl." She pointed to the top row, where a few charm bracelets were displayed on white felt.

He turned and leaned a hip on the case. "You like those?" He never would've guessed that, but then again, it suited her.

He ignored the bigger, gaudy ones. "Can she see the one on the left?"

"Of course."

The saleswoman unlocked the case and set the bracelet on the counter, disappointment twisting her mouth. Obviously she'd been hoping a woman allowed to pick anything she wanted would go with a pricier bauble. She didn't know Faith like he did.

"We have an assortment of charms to go with it. Here's the book. Just find what you like and I can add them right away. They have tiny clips to add new charms and rearrange however you want."

Faith tentatively touched the bracelet with her fingertips. "It looks a lot like the one I used to have. Hope had given it to me. I lost it at the hospital during one of her treatments."

Well, that settled that. Alec leaned in close to Faith's ear. "Go wait in the car. I'd like at least part of this to be a surprise. I'll be out soon."

Her round gaze met his. Through her amber eyes, gratitude and awe radiated. Wonder. To Alec, it seemed like she was accumulating one of her moments, storing it away in her memory to pull out at a later date. She must've seen something when she looked at him, because her gaze softened and a trace of a smile worked her lips.

The air all but crackled between them. For the first time in years, an unnamable emotion rose up to choke him, more powerful than anything he'd ever experienced. Blinding, deafening, and not altogether unpleasant. Like a fissure sealing.

She stepped closer and he had to force himself to exhale. "Thank you."

Because his throat wouldn't work, he nodded.

When Faith was out of sight in the car, he turned to the book of charms and ignored the saleswoman's curious stare. He scanned the pages, waiting for something to jump out at him. He found a seashell and pointed to indicate he wanted that one. The ocean meant a lot to her. He'd found her walking the surf, lost in thought countless times.

"I'll get to work on this one, and you can let me know if you find more you like."

Alec nodded, grateful for the minute alone.

The attendant returned just as he'd finished his selection. He pointed to an "H" to represent her sister's name, and a little infinity symbol that had "friends" engraved on it, to represent Mia and Lacey, figuring those would mean a lot to her.

There was one last charm he was debating. "I'll take that one, but don't add it to the bracelet. I'll take it in a separate bag."

While the saleswoman clipped the charms and prepared the box, he texted Mia that they'd be there in under thirty minutes.

Package in hand, and the other charm burning a hole in his pocket, he stepped out into the fading light of day with his heart pounding. He was barely in the car when Faith pounced. She grabbed his arm and climbed halfway across the console.

"That was the nicest thing anyone's ever done for me." The gratitude in her eyes burned intense, surprising the hell out of him.

"I'm a nice guy." Or at least he was when he was around her—she'd managed to bring out that hidden quality, one he didn't know he possessed. She did all sorts of things to him. It had been years since someone looked at him like she did.

She grinned, a full watt brighter than he'd seen to date. "Thank you."

He opened his mouth to say something, but her mouth crashed over his. He cupped her jaw and kissed back, letting their tongues mesh and the heat to nearly engulf the car before pulling away.

"I really like that particular form of thank-you. We'll have to get more into detail after dinner."

She brushed her fingers over her swollen lips. "Dinner is overrated."

Tempting. The only thing he was hungry for was her. Normally, he'd agree and skip it, but their friends were waiting. Not that she knew that. "I promise you, after dinner, I'll let you thank me however you want. All night."

To keep her busy in the meantime, he passed her the jewelry box. He started the car and made his way down the strip. After a moment, he cranked the air to cool things down. It didn't help much.

And when she tore her way through the wrapping, her gasp of delight was the sweetest thing he'd ever heard.

chapter
twenty-four

She was still staring at the bracelet, twirling it around her wrist, when Alec pulled the car up to her guesthouse. It was amazing. She'd hovered between tears and giddy laughter on the drive home. The charms were thoughtful and personal. Somehow, he'd worked himself into her life and had seen her better than anyone.

He was the only one who'd tried to see.

In a few short weeks the wedding would be over and he'd go back to New York. She didn't know how she'd get through. What she felt for him and how profoundly she felt it was still a whirlwind inside her head. How could she stand on the beach and not think of how they met? Sleep in her bed without remembering their lovemaking?

"You ready?"

She lifted her gaze. "I thought we were going to dinner." Instead, he'd driven her home.

"We are."

They exited the car and walked across the crushed shell

drive toward Cole and Mia's. He took her hand and rounded the house.

"Surprise!"

Faith gasped. Cole, Mia, Ginny, Lacey, and Jake stood on the back deck, the fading light behind them and a cake on the table before them. Ginny held a bunch of balloons. A small stack of presents littered a patio table. Cole turned to flip something on the grill. Chicken. Her favorite.

Since she seemed to be frozen, Alec leaned in to whisper in her ear. "Happy birthday. If you eat fast, we can get to the thank-you portion quicker."

She pressed her hand over her face and laughed, long and loud. So long that she had moisture in her eyes by the time she was through. "You guys, this is wonderful. I've never had a surprise party before."

Jake and Alec exchanged a look, one she couldn't decipher, but held an enormity of meaning. Eventually, Jake nodded slowly and draped an arm over her shoulder. "Happy birthday."

"Thank you."

Ginny bounded over, bouncing on her toes, and clumsily passed her the balloon strings. "I picked them out. I got one in every color because I don't know your favorite color so that way you aren't upset. It's a rainbow!"

Faith smiled. Shook her head. "I don't have a favorite color, so your rainbow is perfect. Very thoughtful, Ginny."

Everyone started talking a mile a minute until her head spun and Cole shouted, "Food's done."

It wasn't just the best birthday—it was the best day she'd ever had. Good friends to hang out with, a nice guy who wanted to take her to bed later, presents picked just for her, and the ocean playing its own sort of melody in the background. Never in her wildest imagination had she thought life could be so sweet. So perfect. Her heart flipped in her chest. Swelled.

Jake and Lacey had gotten her a gift certificate for a spa,

and Cole and Mia a stationery set and candles scented like a sea breeze. Ginny had colored her a pretty, yet simple picture of them together on the beach, collecting shells. Faith promised to put it up on her fridge as soon as she got home.

They sat until long after sundown, cooled slightly by the breeze, chatting about the wedding and other miscellaneous topics. Easy conversation with easygoing people. Friends. It was great finally having them.

"Oh, my God, Lacey. This cake is so good." Mia wiped her mouth with a napkin and waved off the margarita Jake held out. "I can't wait for the wedding cake. Same bakery, right?"

"Yep." Lacey sipped from her own glass. "Jake makes way better margaritas than me."

Faith grinned and leaned back on the bench seat in the corner of the deck. "We won't get nearly as drunk."

Alec took the spot next to her and slipped his arm around her waist, encouraging her to lean against him. "And when, exactly, did Lacey get you drunk?"

"Yeah." Jake's gaze swung between them. "Why wasn't I called?"

Faith laughed. "At Ginny's slumber party. One sip and we were toast."

"Yeah, but it was fun."

"That it was. We'll have to do it again, since Mia was gone the first time."

"I'll pass on Lacey's margaritas, though." Mia smiled and snuggled into Cole's side while he kissed the top of her head. She looked at each of them expectantly. "I'm pregnant."

A pause filled the space between them.

Lacey screeched and flew out of her chair, wrapping Mia in a fierce hug. "I'm going to be an auntie?"

"Yes, ma'am. And Ginny, too. Right, pretty girl?"

"Yeah! I get to read her stories and play with her. But not change diapers."

They laughed.

"Remember we talked about this, Ginny." Cole smiled at the teenager over Mia's head. "It may not be a girl. It could be a boy. And no diapers if you don't want to."

Jake lifted his glass. "Right there with you on that one, Ginny girl. Congrats, you two. Very cool."

"I'm already planning a shower." Lacey hugged Mia again. "With little booties and clothes and stuffed bears. I'm so happy for you!"

"It's still early. We're not announcing yet." Mia looked at the others. "Just our good friends and family."

Faith stayed where she was, unsure if it was appropriate to hug Mia, too. "That is wonderful news. Congratulations!"

Alec lifted his glass. "Ditto. Here's to the end of quiet nights."

Cole laughed. "Got that right. Worth it, though." He looked down at Mia's face with such love that Faith's heart thumped wistfully in jealousy.

They chatted another hour, the time flying discussing babies and names. Faith sighed happily, staring at her new friends. This night was so perfect, she wished it could last. But Ginny's eyes were drooping and Cole yawned.

"Can I help you clean up, Mia?" Faith offered.

"No, no. It's your birthday. Besides, there's not much."

They'd gotten most of it already, so she nodded. "Thank you again, guys. This was unexpected. I had the best time."

Mia waved her over and took the initiative, wrapping Faith in a hug. "I hope you had a great day."

Her throat grew tight. "I did. Thank you. And congratulations again. I'm so happy for you." Mia and Cole had had a rough go trying to claim their happy ending. She was so, so pleased for them to start a new family. "You ever need a babysitter, you know where to find me."

Mia grinned. "Thank you. I may make you regret those words."

Faith laughed. "Doubtful."

Alec took her hand, and they made their way to the beach. He was being unusually quiet, even for him, and Faith started to worry that something was wrong. He guided her toward the house, but she tilted her chin toward the water.

"Let's walk for a bit."

Nodding, he followed and stood by her side in the surf, staring pensively out to sea. A muscle bunched in his jaw. His shoulders were tense.

She wondered if she'd done something wrong or if he regretted giving her the bracelet. Maybe their relationship was hitting too hard and too close to home after getting together with friends. It was hard to tell with him when he got like this, lost in his own head. For all she knew, he was plotting a book.

"Do you want to call it a night and head back to your house? You seem like you need to be alone."

Slowly, he turned his head and pinned her with those gray-blue eyes. Even in the dark their color was intense. The wind captured his black hair, making him look like a pirate.

His gaze dropped to her mouth before sliding back up to her eyes. "I should say yes. But no, I don't want to be alone. I want you." He looked back out at the ocean, a war waging over his face.

At a loss, she stood next to him as worry ate her stomach raw. "Are you okay?"

He nodded absently, then shook his head. "All this talk of babies. Just . . . I don't know. I wasn't ready for it, I guess." He grew silent for a moment. "I should get used to the idea. Lacey and Jake will want kids someday soon."

Laura's miscarriage and the pain in his voice when he'd told her what happened kept her silent, fishing for the right words. She only had more questions. "Do you want kids? Of your own someday?" That would mean letting go of Laura and moving on, something she didn't think he'd be willing to do. Or able.

"I did, once."

Her heart hurt for him. Guilt was a terrible thing to live with, even if misplaced. But he wasn't ready to hear that, so she sighed and offered what little she could. "Let's head inside. I still have a lot of thanking to do."

He breathed a laugh and looked at her. His smile never reached his eyes. Leaning in, he whispered a kiss to her lips. "I wouldn't say no to that."

They walked over the dunes and into the house, neither saying anything as they made their way to her bedroom. Quietly, she closed the door.

The sound seemed to kick him into gear, because instantly his hands were at her waist, tugging her shirt up and over her head. His mouth sought hers, hungry and desperate. He fought to take his own shirt off, tossing it across the room. She did the same with her shorts. Panties. His pants. Briefs.

He sat at the edge of the mattress and pulled her to him, his large hands holding her hips and their bare skin connecting. His fingers dug into her flesh as his gaze skimmed over her breasts, her belly. Lower. He sucked in air through his nose, as if trying to center himself. But whatever had him distracted wasn't easing. Moment by moment his eyes grew lost, until he almost wasn't in the same room.

When he dropped his forehead between her breasts and whispered her name, she made a vow to do everything she could to help him through his grief. Laura's accident and the loss of his baby may have been years ago, but he was just dealing with it now. It was entirely possible he was starting to develop stronger feelings for her in their still-new relationship, but didn't know to handle them, which only compounded his guilt.

She slid her fingers into his hair with one hand and drew her other arm around his back, holding him to her chest. His arms instantly came around her body and squeezed. Held. She stroked his shoulders, his back. Slow, methodical circles to ease his tension until he was ready to face her again.

A minute or two passed before the wetness of his tears dripped onto her skin, hot and heavy. Silent tears. She said nothing, not wanting to hurt his pride or make him ashamed to cry. He needed to let go. She was just glad she was here when he did. When Hope died, there had been no one to hold her and help her understand. No one to lean on to absorb the endless pain. Her parents were too torn up in their own grief to see anything else. At least, for Alec, she could be that crutch.

He didn't sob or shake, but his body started to sag against hers and it was becoming harder to hold him. Without a word, she gently encouraged him to scoot back so he was no longer at the edge of the mattress and straddled his lap. She held his head on her shoulder, his face buried in her neck, as his arms banded around her back. He'd stopped crying, but his breathing was shallow as he worked out the rest.

"Christ. I'm sorry, Faith." He nuzzled her neck and let out an uneven breath.

"You've been sorry long enough."

His head lifted. Brows furrowed, he stared at her.

"So have I. Maybe we should both stop."

He cupped her cheek and drew in a breath. "I wish I could."

She did, too, but hopefully that would come in time. "You're tired. It's late. Lay down with me?"

"In a minute." He pressed a kiss between her breasts. There was nothing sexual in the move, just tenderness. His finger traced her scar, low on her belly. "Is this from your surgery?"

"Yes."

"How old were you? I'll bet you weren't scared for a second."

The problem was, she'd never stopped being afraid.

She climbed in bed and lay back, opening her arms for him to join her. He followed and pulled the sheet over them before tucking her in the crook of his arm. They lay there in the dark as he ran his thumb over her shoulder. Her lids were heavy, her body exhausted, but she wanted to answer him.

"I was thirteen and I was scared. Terrified, actually." She tilted her head up to look at him. "I'd given her bone marrow and several blood transfusions, but they were going to put me to sleep for surgery. All I could think about was who would help Hope if I didn't wake up."

"What did your parents say?"

She rested her cheek on his chest. "They didn't know. They kept moving between my room and Hope's, trying to be with us both. I put on a brave front so they could stay with Hope. She needed them more than I did."

"That's bullshit." He turned on his side and faced her, propping his head in his hand. "I'm sorry to say it like that, but it's true. You may have been conceived to save your sister, but she wasn't their only child."

"You're angry again." Just as before, she reeled at the frustration rolling off of him. She'd gone from being invisible to mattering so much in such a short period of time. "They did their best by both of us. They died a little when she did. Don't be angry for me. It's done. In the past."

He stared down at her, his lips thin and his eyes fierce. "It's not done. You're still donating. Day after day, you're waiting for them to love you like they did her. That's their hang-up, not yours."

"Alec—"

"No. Listen to me. You are not the sum of all your parts, Faith." His gaze darted over her face, her hair. He tucked a strand behind her ear and sighed, his gaze softening. "You're so much more than that."

His words pierced her heart and made her realize that was exactly what she'd been doing. She'd been giving her parents pieces of herself in the hope that they'd love her a smidgen of how much they loved Hope. But if they didn't by now, they never would. Still, it hurt. So, so bad it hurt.

When would she ever be good enough? She'd let Hope down. She'd let her parents down. Mostly, she was letting herself down. And Alec? He'd leave her behind soon, too. Because it seemed that's all she was ever good for. A short blip of time until her services were complete.

He flopped to his back and drew her to his side. "I was supposed to be making love to you. Some finish to your birthday this turned out to be."

The pensive, solemn mood had passed, and the stirrings of need started to swirl within her. Not greed or blind lust, but the need to soothe. To touch and be touched.

She draped her leg over his hips and slid over him. The thickness of his erection grew between their bodies as she stared down at him. He tried to flip her over and take control back, but she didn't let him. Tonight wasn't about the climax. It was about the path there.

He dropped his hands to her thighs and stroked. She kissed every inch of skin, touched him with all the emotion trapped inside. And when she took him inside her, they both gasped.

She kissed him softly, on his forehead, his cheeks, his mouth. "I wouldn't change one minute of this day, Alec. Not one minute."

He looked in her eyes and swallowed. "Neither would I."

When they'd both been satisfied, he kissed her hair and tucked her against his side. In time, his breathing evened out, his chest rising and falling in sleep.

But her eyes didn't close until near sunrise.

chapter
twenty-five

Because things had been going so well between him and
Faith, Alec figured he'd fuck it all up and accept his mother's
dinner invitation. She'd wanted to have Lacey and Jake over
before the wedding, and when she found out from Jake that
Alec was seeing Faith, she'd jumped all over it until he
relented. Faith being Faith, she was thrilled by the idea and
surprised to be included. He hoped that happy little bubble
of hers wasn't popped by his father's lack of tact.

Things had . . . evolved since the night of her birthday a
few weeks ago. They'd slipped into a comfortable routine.
Domestic, even. She worked with Ginny during the day, and
he dragged himself out of bed before noon to work on the
manuscript. They had dinner at his place, walked the surf,
and slept at her house. Sometimes, she cooked. Other times,
he'd grill something. On the weekends, they hung out with
Cole and Mia, and Lacey and Jake, either on the back deck
or on the beach. Drinks. Good conversation.

He and Faith made love nightly. Talked endlessly. He

couldn't wait for her to get off work to tell her what he'd written that day, and he enjoyed when she'd relay some cute thing she and Ginny had done together.

Christ. They'd turned into a sappy movie of the week. And he liked it.

He didn't know how he was going to leave town in one piece. He was starting to realize it wasn't just the wide open expanse of Wilmington, of home, that finally gave him peace—it was her. Here, and with Faith, he could breathe. There was fresh air and sun. New York had been his own form of torture. The city had beauty and qualities he loved, but the air was recycled, the buildings a trap. There was no room, no one who gave a damn about him. He hadn't known he'd been holding his breath for almost ten years. No wonder his writing had stalled.

He glanced at Faith in the passenger seat next to him, her brown waves caught in the wind as his convertible hugged the highway. She had her face tilted toward the sun and a smile wide enough to encompass the state.

Turning back to the road, he gripped the wheel with more force than necessary. He didn't know if he could write without her. The book had been turned in to his editor, and Cole had agreed to represent him as his agent, so things were back on track.

Except, what happened if he returned to his apartment and the words were gone? She wouldn't be there every night to work out the plot. No muse. No fix.

Hell. That was only half the problem. The rest was Faith herself. Ten years and no woman had made him question the guilt, the decision to live with what he'd done. Ten minutes and Faith had him wanting to move past it as if none of it mattered, as if it hadn't happened.

It did matter. It had happened. Laura's life was gone. And all because he couldn't take care of what was his, couldn't love what was in front of him enough.

"It's a pretty house."

Faith's voice snapped him out of his head. He looked at his parents' cozy ranch and wondered how they'd gotten there. Jake's car was in the driveway in front of his and the smell of barbeque wafted in the humid air.

His gut turned to ice. "No matter what crazy-ass thing my father says, just remember you like me and I'm good in bed."

She laughed, the sound filling the holes in his chest. "Come on."

The next hour went by in a blur. Faith fit right in with his family as if born into it. She helped his mom make a pasta salad, set the picnic table with Lacey and Jake, quipped with his dad about baseball. It was all so ordinary. So normal. Even Dad was unusually well behaved. Not a stupid, tactless thing spilled from his lips.

By the time the food was gone and the sun was setting, his parents had tortured Lacey and Faith with countless stories of their youth. All he could think was, did Faith's parents have any stories like these? Had they looked at her, noticed her enough to see the true gem?

His dad got up to head inside and grab another beer from the fridge.

Alec leaned back in his lawn chair and stretched his legs out. At least his knee had stopped bouncing. He hadn't realized how nervous he was bringing Faith here until the muscles in his shoulders unknotted. Taking each other to meet the parents was something serious couples did. And they were serious. That much was certain. Except serious didn't equal permanent.

"I'm going to run to the ladies' room real quick." Faith patted his hand.

He nodded. Watched her go.

"I really like her."

He turned his head to look at his mom. "I'm not surprised."

"She's so sweet," Lacey said. "It's hard not to like her. She's got a big heart. You should see her with Ginny."

Jake smiled nauseatingly at Lacey. "Ginny's got a thing for Alec, too. Eats up everything he says."

Alec took a sip of beer. "It's the writer thing. She's into spooky stories right now."

"Are you getting serious with Faith?" His mom's pleading eyes met his. "You haven't brought anyone home since . . ."

"Laura. Since Laura, you mean. You can say her name. I won't go up in flames." Alec drew in a breath. Released it. His mom wasn't to blame. "And Faith and I can't be anything more than this. I'm going back to the city after the wedding."

"Oh. I figured, you know, since . . ." Mom shook her head. "Never mind."

Jake leaned forward and rested his elbows on his knees. Anger seethed in his eyes. "Nice, man."

He shrugged. Let his brother stew. No way would he lie to Mom. That kind of hurt was worse than the pity in her eyes.

Christ. He wanted out of here. This too-cozy little shin-dig was grinding his very raw nerves to dust, only reminding him of what couldn't be.

He dug his toes in the grass. In the silence that hung, it dawned on him how long Faith and his father had been gone. Alone in the house. With God knows the kinds of things his father would say . . .

"I'll be right back."

He tossed his bottle in the trash and walked through the kitchen to the living room, where their voices rose over the sounds of the Braves game. Worry pinched his gut until Faith laughed. He stopped in the doorway, unseen as of yet.

"What book are you on now?"

"Just finished the last one. Nightmares, I tell you. This is why I stick to baseball memoirs or true crime." Dad barked out a laugh. "But, hey, my son wrote it."

The air left his lungs in one fell swoop. The edges of his vision grayed. He pressed a palm to the wall to stay upright.

His dad had read his books? His dad, who joked every chance he got that his son got paid to daydream?

"You must be so proud of them both. Jake's done an amazing job with Lacey's property. It's magical. The wedding will be lovely."

Dad nodded. "Jake was the easy one. Always getting dirty, digging a hole. Typical boy mischief. He shares my eye for landscaping. Alec was always off in his own head. Couldn't hear a thing you said or follow a rule to save his life."

Faith grinned. "I hear the creative types are hard to raise. But you know, he probably got that from you. Gardening is an art, too, just a different form."

Dad laughed. "Miss Armstrong, are you saying I gave myself this headache?"

"Afraid so."

Alec had heard enough. He turned and strode through the kitchen, pushed through the back door with shaking hands. He glared at his parents' postage-stamp yard. The trim grass, strategically placed flowers in varying heights and colors, the mature birches. But the pounding in his head wouldn't abate.

Jake stood. "Alec?"

He looked at his mom. "He read my books?"

Mom pressed a hand to her chest, her eyes panicked and wary at his tone. "I—"

"Twenty-five bestsellers and all I ever got was laughed at. Don't you think you could've told me? Given me some measure of peace that I wasn't a total joke to him?"

Faith and his father stepped around the house, coming into the yard from the front.

"What's this about, son?"

The pounding in his skull amplified, until he couldn't see through the haze. He never doubted his father's love. His respect, maybe, but never his love. But over time, the thoughtless things his dad said, over and over, had grated at his patience until fury boiled. "It's about you telling my girlfriend how goddamn proud you are, when all you've ever done is make fun of me."

Jake stepped forward, his hand extended. "Alec, calm down."

Calm down. *Calm down?*

"What the hell for?" He rounded on Jake. "That's what I do, right? Get irrational and go off the deep end? Except I'm not the one who went off the deep end that night. Laura did." A sharp jab pierced his chest. His voice rose, until the shouting in his head matched his tone. "Maybe I should've tried to stop her, but I didn't. How could I have known what would happen? Huh? *She* got in that car drunk and *she* crashed it. *Her*, not me. And I'm the one paying for it. I'm the one living with it. *It wasn't my fault!*"

His voice raked, until it was like roaring through broken glass. A pulsing, violent vibration ripped through him. Perhaps he was losing his tact gene, too. Like father, like son.

And then he realized what he said.

He froze. Stumbled back into the screen door. Agony clawed his chest. His breath heaved in and out. His hands fisted. Shook. His insides felt torn to shreds.

Who knew? He was alive after all.

"It wasn't my fault," he said again, a whisper for his ears only, as if trying the words on for size.

"That's right, Alec. It wasn't."

Her mermaid voice washed over him, filled him with a measure of warmth. The sweet scent of her soft skin teased his nose. He looked up into amber eyes. Kind, understanding eyes. Too kind for him.

The images of Laura drifted away. Her broken body. A shell hooked up to tubes and wires. The antiseptic smell he'd always associate with her. With that night.

"I have to get out of here."

Faith reached out for him, but he brushed her off. He couldn't have her touch him right now, couldn't stand it. He'd fucking shatter.

The others stood in the yard, jaws slack and eyes round. Frozen. No one moved. No one spoke.

He shoved off the door and strode away on legs that barely held him upright.

Jake walked up to the base of the deck stairs and rammed his hands in his pockets.

Alec blinked and turned his attention back to the ocean. Stars littered the sky. The water was a black ribbon in the distance, the waves rhythmic against the shore. Only the slight breeze made the humidity bearable after a brief thundershower had swept through an hour before. He'd sat through the downpour and was still soaked through.

"I drove Faith home, in case you were wondering."

Alec closed his eyes and sighed. Shit. "Thank you." He didn't recognize the sound of his own voice. His throat was still raw from screaming. "Is she upset?"

Jake turned and sat next to him on the step. "She took it in stride. You should go check on her yourself."

He planned to, but he needed to get his head on straight first. Running to her every time he had a problem had to stop. In a couple of weeks, they'd be over. He couldn't keep depending on her.

"You scared the shit out of me," Jake said. "And Mom. Dad went into the house and never came back out."

Alec had scared the shit out of himself, too. "I'm sorry."

"Me, too. I think I pushed you too hard."

"You didn't. It's just . . ." He ran his hand through his hair. "I can't do the right thing for both of them, Jake. I can't leave Laura in the state she's in, and I can't give Faith the hope that I will." Most of all, he couldn't forgive himself and move forward. His knee bounced, the nervous energy starting anew. "Let's take a walk."

Instead of turning left, Alec veered them right, away from the houses and to the abandoned area on the other strip of the shore. There was a half mile between the Covingtons' private beach and the foreclosed house he'd driven by earlier in the summer. The sand was dotted with broken shells and seaweed. Eventually, the dunes gave way to rocky bluffs, a dark wall lit by the half-moon.

Alec stopped at the rotted, broken steps of the empty house. Two stories up, the mini-mansion stood dark. He could write a book about the look of the place alone.

"You could buy it."

He looked at Jake. "I could ride a purple unicorn over the ocean, too."

Jake crossed his arms. "You have the money. You could hire a team of carpenters to fix the place. Or level it to the ground and start over. The point is, you could."

Alec rubbed the back of his neck. He'd never tear the house down. It had character, and in this day and age of cookie cutters, that said something. The roof had an A frame–like slant, the exterior a log cabin feel. There was an upper and lower deck for each story, and the entire eastern face was windows. He remembered from when his dad did the landscaping that it had four bedrooms and two baths. The living room was a wide-open floor plan with ceiling beams and a redbrick fireplace. There was a small office of sorts, off the den. The kitchen had needed help, even back then, but it was roomy. Let in a lot of light.

What the hell did it matter? This was just Jake, getting ideas in his head again.

He did an about-face and started walking back the way they came. A topic shift was in order or his brother would be relentless. "Your wedding is two weeks away. Are you getting nervous?"

"Not even a little bit."

Alec studied his brother as they walked. "You really love her. Good. I'm glad for you."

Jake sighed and tilted his head toward the stars. "The first time I saw her, after all those years, she stole the wind right out of me. She was just as pretty as she was back then, but she'd finally grown into her smile." He glanced down at his feet. "I didn't think she'd give me the time of day. But she and Cole were always nice to us, nothing like their mother. Dean too, rest his soul."

They stopped by the stairs of his guesthouse.

Jake glanced at the house, down the beach. "Who'd have thought it, big brother? That one day we'd be a part of their world. Now you're as rich as them."

Alec wanted to say that the money didn't matter, but Jake knew that. It was about finding his particular brand of happy. And Jake had. "Will Lacey be upset if I steal you away for a bachelor party this Friday?"

Jake grinned. "Naw. They're doing some girly thing at Mia's that night. I'll call Cole, have him meet us here."

Alec nodded and turned toward the stairs. He needed to get out of these damp clothes.

"Alec."

He turned.

"About what you said at Mom and Dad's . . ."

He gripped the railing until it hurt. "Yeah?"

Jake took a step closer. "I've been waiting almost ten years for you to say that, and I'm relieved you did. No, just hear me out," he insisted when Alec opened his mouth. "None of what went down was on you. What you did in the aftermath, it was honorable. But you need to ask yourself where you'd be if she hadn't wrecked that car." He stared at his feet before glancing up again. "Would you still be together? Would you even still be living in New York?"

Alec ran a hand down his face. Shook his head.

Jake was right. So right. But the fact remained, she *did* crash the car, after storming out on one of their fights, and he didn't stop her. In his head, he knew the blame wasn't his. He got that now. Yet his heart wouldn't read the memo. Laura couldn't tell him what she wanted anymore.

Jake's shoulders slumped. "It doesn't matter, does it? You're still going back."

Alec swallowed past the rock in his throat. "Yeah. I'm still going back."

Several minutes later, after Jake had walked away, Alec spotted Faith on the beach and did a double take. She was sitting just behind the surf with her knees drawn up to her chest and her arms around her calves. She was still wearing the sundress from the barbeque, as if waiting for him to show up.

His heart beat hard against his ribs. She was just a wisp of a thing, but she had enough compassion and heart for ten people.

Years ago, he'd vowed to never hurt another like he'd hurt Laura. And damn it, nine years wasn't a long enough stretch between heartbreaks.

Faith sensed Alec before she saw his form walking toward her in the dark. It took a lot of restraint not to launch into his arms. His long, easy gait belied the tension in his shoulders. His bare feet ate up the sand until he plopped down next to her, facing the ocean.

She'd baked, tried to read a book, and checked her phone half a trillion times since getting back, but she couldn't get her mind off of him and what state he might be in. She was worried sick. From what she'd learned, for the past however many years since the accident, Alec seemed to be dealing with the tragedy by not dealing with it. He'd done everything from pay Laura's bills to avoid his basic need of connection with others, but he hadn't truly dealt with anything.

All that had changed today. He'd exploded. There was no other word for it. He'd hit his breaking point. Part of her wanted to go to him once she'd gotten home, but in the end, she hadn't.

"I made you a pan of brownies." She closed her eyes and mentally slapped herself. "That came out wrong. I meant to say, I was worried about you and made brownies because I thought the comfort food would help when you returned. But you didn't come and I was tempted to eat the whole batch. Then I thought, I'd just have to make more because what would make you feel better when you came if there were no brownies, so I didn't eat them." She paused. Her cheeks grew hot in embarrassment. "They have powdered sugar on them."

Maybe God would have mercy and strike her now.

It wasn't like her to be this rambling, chaotic mess. But darn it . . . she was terrified. She cared about him, too much, and it felt like not enough. She'd gone through her whole life feeling like she was never, or would never be, adequate. This time around, with him, the knowledge gutted her. Because sometime between the day she'd left home and this very minute, he'd become all that mattered.

Alec mimicked her pose and drew his legs up, resting his forearms over his knees. "I'm sorry." Though he addressed her, he spoke toward the water, his voice hollow and raw. "I'm so sorry, Faith."

Her chest deflated. Her pulse evened out for the first time in hours.

She took in his profile, his clenched jaw and furrowed brow, and chose her words carefully. His self-deprecating expression made her throat clog with tears. She didn't want to lecture, but in her opinion, he had made a lot of headway by acknowledging he wasn't solely to blame for what had happened to Laura. No doubt he was confused and torn up inside right now.

Releasing a slow breath, she faced the ocean. "I know you are."

He dropped his head. Shook it. "I keep telling myself to keep my distance, to not read anything into the . . . joy you bring me." He rubbed the back of his neck. "You're inside me, though, in that place I thought dead. I can't give you the same happiness, Faith."

"You already have," she whispered, closing her eyes. She

didn't have to look at him to know what he was trying to say. Nothing had changed. She had hoped he'd want to stay after the conclusion he'd reached at his parents' house, but his guilt and honor were too great. And she wasn't exactly the kind of person who inspired unconditional love. "You already have."

He reached out and pulled her into his lap. Wrapped his arms around her like that would be enough to bind them together. "I wasn't expecting you." He kissed the top of her head. "I just . . . I didn't expect you."

For once they were in complete sync, because she never expected anything. She rested her cheek on his shoulder and buried her face in his neck. "The best things are unexpected."

He wove his fingers into her hair and urged her to look at him. Lowering his head, he brought his mouth to hers. His firm lips met her softer ones, the contrast a detonation. He explored tenderly, unhurried, without his usual walls in place. And she met him halfway, pouring what she felt but couldn't say into the kiss.

Running her hands up his shoulders, she held his jaw and skimmed her fingers over the rough stubble. "Make love to me. Here, on the beach. Please." It was dark and late. No one would see them and the dunes would provide cover.

His gaze searched hers. Their breath mingled.

Finally, he swallowed and nodded. Without taking his gaze from hers, he pulled out his wallet and set it next to them in the sand. His hands skimmed under her dress, to her panties and slid them down her legs. He unbuttoned his shorts and shoved them over his hips. Securing the condom, he lifted her so she could swing her leg around and straddle him.

To any passerby, they'd just look like a couple snuggling on the beach. Her heart flipped at his discretion, the care he took with her body and maintaining a semblance of modesty on her behalf.

With their gazes locked, she rose up and sank down over

him. He swallowed her gasp with a kiss, rocked into her, and held her tightly to him.

It felt like good-bye.

Afterward, he carried her inside and into the shower, where they washed the sand and the rest of the day's hurt away. All she could think was how healing water could be. The ocean, their lovemaking under the spray—all of it filled the emptiness inside, soothed the endless ache she'd grown to accept as normal.

And when he tucked her into bed, cocooning her in the warmth of his arms, she fell completely in love with him. She'd been teetering on the brink since they met. Perhaps she'd fallen long before now. But acknowledging it to herself was freeing somehow.

He kissed her shoulder. "After I'm gone, promise me you'll hold tight to Mia and Lacey, to the friendship you forged with them. You're not alone anymore, Faith. If you need to tell Mia about my past, then do it. But don't let them go."

"I won't let them go," she promised. And she didn't think she'd ever let him go, either. Not really. Alec would be it for her, always.

chapter
twenty-six

Alec and Cole dragged a very inebriated Jake up the stairs of his and Lacey's house. Jake serenaded them the whole way, as he had in the limo coming home.

"Man," Cole grunted. "You're heavier than you look. At least you're a happy drunk."

"Word." Alec kicked open the bedroom door. "In bed you go, lover boy."

Jake flopped face-first onto the mattress. Halfway through his second rendition of "Free Bird," he passed out cold.

Cole looked at Alec, breathing heavily and rubbing his thigh. "Lacey's going to kill us."

"Not if she's just as drunk over at your house."

They made their way downstairs to the kitchen. Cole dropped in a kitchen chair and grimaced.

"You okay, man?"

"Yeah. The leg still throbs sometimes." He accepted the beer Alec handed him. "I think we did this all wrong. Aren't we supposed to get plastered at a bachelor party? Why are we sober?"

Alec sat across from him. "I'm not much of a drinker. A beer now and then. There's still time. Have at it."

Cole laughed. "I don't remember the last time I got drunk. Before Iraq, most definitely. Jake had fun. That's what counts."

Alec nodded and sipped his beer. They'd taken Jake to a few different men's clubs, where he'd rejected every stripper and lap dance offered. Giving up, the three of them wound up on the pier with a bottle of Captain, swapping stories. It made Alec wish they'd been closer as kids. Cole was a good guy.

"What do you think about Lacey and Jake? They moved kind of fast."

Cole tilted his head. "They did. Lacey loves him, that's what's important to me. Jake treats her well. He works hard and doesn't want her for the money. I think he's had his eye on her for a long time." He shook his head. "Growing up the way we did, it was hard to know who to trust. Lacey especially had it hard after Dean died. She tried so damn hard to be perfect. Jake brought her out of her bubble. I trust him."

"Remember when he used to put bullfrogs under her porch swing when we were kids?"

Cole laughed and leaned back, settling in. "Yeah. I remember her squealing most of all. Before they started dating, Jake was here this one day, cutting the grass. Lacey and Mia stared at him through the window for a solid hour, unable to believe he was the gardener's son all grown up. I almost stomped outside to make him put a shirt on, until I realized the old Lacey wouldn't have done that before. Stared at the help, I mean."

Alec didn't have any more reservations about his brother marrying Lacey. Covington or not, she and Cole were good people. "So, you and Mia? Never thought I'd see the day. You were hung up on each other as teenagers, if memory serves."

Cole's gaze wandered off. "I was all kinds of messed up before she came back. I don't think I ever stopped thinking about her. Not for a day." He shrugged. "Just meant to be."

Meant to be. Alec rolled the phrase around in his head, dissecting the meaning. If he followed that thought train, everything from Laura's accident to meeting Faith would've been in fate's hands, making them just putty with which to play.

He set his beer down. Picked at the label. "How did you know? With Mia, I mean."

A ghost of a smile traced Cole's lips. "I always knew. And the fact that you're asking means you know, too. You could do worse than falling for Faith."

Alec drew in a breath and shoved the bottle aside. "Seeing as you're my agent now, there's some things you ought to know."

Being his agent was only part of the reason, but Alec told Cole everything. The miscarriage, the accident. Telling Cole didn't rip his heart out like it had with Faith, no doubt because the more he talked about it, the easier it got. Plus, Faith had a personal, vested interest in his past, whereas Cole was a friend. Alec's mistakes didn't affect him the way they did Faith.

When Alec was through, Cole set his hands on the table between them and leaned on his forearms. "Christ. So she's still in the care facility?"

He nodded.

"Are you her legal guardian?"

Alec took a healthy swig before answering. "No. That would be her parents. Back then we didn't think about living wills." He stared at the table. "She wouldn't have wanted to live like that."

"Have you tried contesting the guardianship?"

"Laura was an only child. She's all they have left. I can't take her from them a second time."

Cole was silent for so long that Alec was forced to look up. What he found in Cole's eyes was a near reflection of his own pain.

In a move that seemed involuntary, Cole rubbed his shoulder. "I created and toppled a series of dominoes that led to my brother's car accident. Years later, in Iraq, I was the only survivor when my unit drove over an IED. I get the guilt, I do. But their deaths weren't on my head any more than hers is on yours. It took Mia for me to see that."

Alec nodded. "I know. Somewhere in the back of my head, I know that. But I couldn't live with myself if I completely moved on." Not that he was doing a bang-up job of living with himself currently. "What kind of a man would that make me?"

"It would make you human."

Alec pressed his palms to his eyes, but the pounding in his head continued. The visions of Laura were still there. Laura, pale and shaking after the miscarriage. Laura, flailing her arms and yelling as she stormed out the door. Laura, lying in a hospital bed looking like death . . .

His gut turned to ice.

"For the record, I don't believe she's living anymore, Alec. You wouldn't be leaving her. You'd be letting her go."

Cole's argument had merit, as did Jake's. It had for a long, long time. But they didn't have to wake up every morning and look at Alec's face in the mirror.

The wedding had gone off without a hitch, as Faith had expected. The groomsmen were handsome in their khaki pants and white button-down shirts. The bridesmaids carried white lilies and offered a splash of color in their dresses. Lacey shined in her simple, elegant gown. Jake hadn't taken his eyes off her for a second.

They'd taken pictures at sunset and cut the cake as the first stars twinkled overhead. To accommodate the fifty or so guests, a tent was set up down the beach with ten round tables decorated with a floating candle and sea grass stems. Alec and Cole had given a perfect toast, and Mia helped Ginny say a few words, earning immense applause.

The heat of the day had cooled and a gentle breeze off the ocean brushed over Faith's skin where she sat at one of the tables, watching the first dance. She smoothed the skirt of her mint-green dress, glad Mia had talked her into it. It was pretty flattering on her thin frame.

"Stupid hormones." Mia fanned her face, but her eyes misted over anyway.

Faith's cheeks actually ached from smiling so much, not that she planned on stopping. "It's okay to cry at weddings. Everyone does. Besides, look at them."

Jake and Lacey danced with their foreheads together, grinning like fools in love.

"I still think it's the hormones. I hope the whole damn pregnancy isn't like this."

Cole laughed and draped his arm around her shoulders. "I love you. And I'll buy stock in tissues."

Faith sipped her champagne, throat tight with her own tears. She was so happy for her friends and so brokenhearted for herself. The onslaught of emotion was like a hurricane. Alec hadn't actually said when he'd be leaving, but she knew it would be soon. He'd been pensive all week. Contemplative and quiet—not quite broody enough to distance himself, but the shift was obvious.

Their time was almost up.

The first dance ended and everyone cheered. The band started an upbeat song, a country tune she didn't recognize, and it had Ginny bouncing on her toes.

"Can I dance now? Can I?"

Mia grinned. "You go ahead, pretty girl. We'll be right there."

"Faith, come on!"

Faith turned in her seat to look at Alec.

He nodded. A faint smile tilted his lips, but it didn't reach his eyes.

Faith followed Ginny to the makeshift dance floor, set on the beach between the tent and the bar, and laughed when Lacey threw her hands in the air. The two of them, ridiculous and carefree, encouraged her to be the same. Why not? Fun was fun.

Faith raised her hands and bounced around, bobbing her head to mimic them. It was exhausting and liberating. She laughed so hard her stomach ached. They made it through three songs before the music changed and she needed a rest.

But when she went to head over to the table, Alec and Jake were seated side by side. Alec's gaze was on the table and Jake's brows were drawn together. Jake waved his hand and dropped it midsentence. Alec shook his head.

Faith took a step back and turned away to give them a moment. Alec's father was right behind her.

"Would you care to dance?"

"Oh." She reached for her pendant, but it wasn't there. Instead was the pearl-drop necklace Lacey had given the bridesmaids. "Yes. Thank you."

He took one of her hands loosely in his and circled her waist with the other. "Nice wedding." He had a deep, rumbling voice like Alec's, but humor in his eyes like Jake.

She didn't know how to dance formally, so she followed his lead and prayed she didn't cause damage. "Everything came out perfect."

He nodded and stared over her shoulder. "I want to apologize for what happened at the house—"

"There's no need. Sometimes things just need to get hashed out."

He seemed to contemplate what she said before responding. "I'm a traditional man. I tried to raise my sons that way, too. I don't always say the right thing. In fact, most times I don't, but you didn't need to be put in the middle." They moved a few steps as he cleared his throat. "I was angry with

Alec's choices, still am, but it's his life and I love him. Sometimes, I just don't know how to express that, and I say things that make it worse."

It didn't seem like an excuse, but more an explanation. His father was embarrassed, both for himself and his son.

"The thing with anger, I've learned, is it only hurts yourself. You raised two wonderful sons. Both strong in character and heart. Be a little proud of yourself."

He misstepped and paused. But the song ended and another cued to start. He dropped his hands and nodded. "I wouldn't be upset if we saw more of you, Miss Armstrong."

"Call me Faith, and I'd like that."

As he backed away, she let out a silent exhale and was about to check on Alec when Jake took her elbow.

"Dance with the happy groom?"

Why was she so popular tonight? Any other time she'd be glad to accommodate, but she just wanted to spend some time with the man she loved before he was gone. And something told her that would be sooner than expected. But manners were manners, and this was Jake's night.

He set them in motion. "I can see why he likes you."

She blinked up at him, her stomach doing a little flop. She knew Jake was talking about Alec, but couldn't think of anything worth saying.

"You have this way of looking at people that makes them want to spill their secrets. What secrets did my dad tell? He doesn't hold his tongue very well, but we love him."

She opened her mouth and closed it again. "It wouldn't be a secret if I told you."

He laughed in way completely unlike Alec. Hearty, but just as addictive. "Touché. Dad's a man of too many words, and Alec not enough. Well, except on paper, that is. You got Alec talking and my dad to shut up. I've been trying for years to accomplish what you did in a couple months."

Tears pricked her eyes. She blinked rapidly and glanced away. Alec was standing by the bar with his father. His dad's arm was draped over Alec's shoulder and they were both grinning, involved in some story with a cluster of Alec's cousins. Her heart sighed.

"For what it's worth, Faith, I'm sorry he's going to hurt you. He doesn't mean to do it, but he knows no other way."

Darn it. More tears. Maybe Mia's hormones were contagious. "Thank you."

They finished out the song in silence, and she'd never been so grateful to be alone. Taking a glass of champagne from a passing waiter, she walked to the surf and downed it in two gulps. Her stomach heated but her nerves remained frayed. Closing her eyes, she breathed in the salty air and let the sound of the music and the waves calm her.

"I see my family has driven you to drink. In solitude, no less."

Despite the tightness in her throat, she smiled. "You have a beautiful family."

Alec studied her for a moment before glancing out to sea. Shoving his hands in his pockets, he rocked on his heels.

"You're leaving tomorrow, aren't you?"

He glanced down, nodding.

Though Faith had known it was coming, it did little to prepare her for the pain tearing through her chest. No other hurt could compare. "Then take me home. Please."

He brooked no argument, just held out his hand for her to take.

The house was quiet and dark, like her mood, so she didn't bother to turn on any lights as they made their way to her bedroom. The moon illuminated a portion of the bed and floor, creating slats of light. Not knowing what else to do, she sat on the edge of the mattress and stared at her hands.

He walked over and stood in front of her, hands in his pockets as if afraid to touch. "Would it be easier on you if I left and went back to the guesthouse?"

She shook her head. Nothing would make this easier. She

fortified what little courage she had left. "There's something I want to tell you."

He looked down at her expectantly.

It took everything she had in her to meet his gaze. "I love you."

Though he hadn't been moving, he froze. Seconds ticked by. And then his hands were out of his pockets and scrubbing his face. "Faith." He shook his head and paced away. Came back. "No, Faith."

She rose and held her ground. "I love you."

His gaze flew to the ceiling and back to her, pleading. "Christ. Don't do this. What am I supposed to do here? To say?"

Taking a steadying breath, she grabbed his hands. "There is nothing you need to do or say. Love is a gift, one I knew little about before you, and like any other gift, all you have to do is accept it. It doesn't need to be returned."

His jaw clenched, but other than that, all he did was stare through wild, vulnerable gray-blue eyes.

Finally, when she thought she couldn't take any more, he cupped the back of her neck and hauled her against him. One arm banded around her back, the other held the back of her head. His body shook as she pressed her face to his chest.

They stood for she didn't know how long, until slowly, he slid his hand into hers and set them into motion. A dance. He rested his cheek to the side of her head and sighed.

And when he spoke, his voice was rough with unfiltered emotion. "I never got to dance with you."

chapter
twenty-seven

To say he woke up the following morning wouldn't be accurate, because Alec had never fallen asleep after they'd made love. He'd lain awake all night, watching Faith sleep, stroking her arm, wishing she hadn't actually said the words he knew to be true. Almost wishing she didn't mean them. Except he wanted her to feel the same, and the utter fullness that encompassed his heart wouldn't allow him to reject the gift she'd given.

He hadn't told her he loved her back, not because he didn't, but because it wouldn't change anything. And Christ in heaven, he loved her more than he loved any one thing or person. More than his need to write, than air, than his own troubled life.

Regardless of everything they'd been through, he hadn't loved Laura. Not like this. Not to the point he'd crumble to ash without her. That's how he knew it was real with Faith. Because he hadn't actually missed Laura. He'd just harbored the guilt and sadness for what could have been. What hap-

pened to her was tragic, and he'd give up just about anything
to undo that day. But that wasn't possible.

He wasn't out the door yet, and he missed Faith.

The pink hue of dawn peeked through her window and
the squawk of seagulls told him he'd put things off long
enough. They'd said their good-byes last night. There was
no need to drag this out and make it harder on her.

Carefully, he slid from the bed and tucked her arm under
the sheet. He dressed quietly, watching her, because he
couldn't seem to stop. She was beautiful in a natural way.
Without makeup and frills. She didn't need them. He didn't
have a picture of her—and that was probably a good thing—
so he'd take this mental image with him.

He shoved his hand in his pocket and pulled out the little
charm he'd bought for her bracelet weeks ago. Even then
he'd known. In fact, he was pretty damn sure he'd loved her
the second her amber eyes met his that day on the beach.

Striding into the kitchen, he scratched one word onto a
piece of paper and headed back to put the note and the charm
on her nightstand.

Closing the front door behind him was the hardest thing
he'd ever done. A panic attack nearly made him turn around,
but somehow he put one foot in front of the other.

He walked across the drive, attempting to let the heat
and humidity soak into his bones. The effort was fruitless.
He had a feeling he'd never be warm again. When he made
it across the mimosa grove and onto the other property, Jake
was leaning against the hood of Alec's car with his arms
crossed, eyes tracking his movements.

Alec schooled his voice to resonate a calm he didn't feel.
"Aren't you supposed to be in bed, making love to your wife?"

Jake offered a lopsided grin. "Don't worry. I did. Many
times. And I have the whole honeymoon to keep doing it."
He straightened. "I wanted to see you off." He pulled Alec
into a hug that had the air whooshing from his lungs. "I love
you."

Alec gritted his teeth and closed his eyes. "Jesus, man. I love you, too."

Instead of preaching at him like Alec expected, Jake pulled back and smacked his shoulder. "Drive carefully."

Alec made no promises, and a week later, as he sat in his home office in his New York apartment, thought it was probably a good thing he hadn't. Alec had almost no memory of the drive back and only a vague recollection of what he'd done to pass time since returning. It was as if someone had vacuumed out his soul. There was nothing left. He should be appreciative for the shocking numbness, but that would take effort.

He knew he'd written the first two chapters of the next book, because they were on the computer screen, but damn if he knew how he'd managed it. It wasn't a half-bad start either. Only minor tweaking needed.

He'd eaten whatever his housekeeper put in front of him, not that he'd tasted anything. Coffee kept his brain going, because if he stopped drinking it, he'd fall into bed, where the sheets still smelled like her. Which was probably all in his head, because their trip to the city had been weeks ago, yet he hadn't allowed the housekeeper to change the sheets because . . . shit. They smelled like her.

Sighing, he threw his pen down on the desk and leaned back in his chair. He pressed his palms over his eyes. Groaned. Wanted to weep.

Fuck this. What he needed was air and to be outside of these walls. The torment of missing Faith would never cease if he kept this up. He was one step away from being loonier than his characters.

He strode into the living room and stopped. Tilting his head, he examined the creepy as hell room he'd hated since the minute the decorator finished with a flourished wave of her hand.

One by one, he took down the posters and framed covers, tossing them into a pile in the middle of the floor. The sculpture was next. Raising it over his head, he dropped it on the frames, satisfied when the glass cracked and the sculpture shattered. He shredded the cushions on the red couches with a screwdriver and sat back on his haunches, breathing heavily.

Anger was better than feeling nothing. There was production in anger.

Paint. He could change the wall color himself. Yes, he needed paint. A lot of it to cover the dark, slate-gray cavern. Something happy. So fucking happy it made his teeth ache. Like the mint green of Faith's bridesmaid dress.

Growling, he grabbed his keys and slammed the door behind him so he could go to the hardware store. To not buy mint-green paint.

He needed this. A mindless task that involved physical work. Maybe that would eradicate Faith from his head.

Except, as the taxi dropped him off and drove away, Alec stood on the sidewalk facing Laura's nursing home. A pleasant twenty-bed facility with white trim and shaded by sycamore trees that he had no intention of ever setting foot inside again.

He froze, his joints locking and his limbs nothing but deadweight.

Blackouts and missing time were the first signs of insanity. But no. He wasn't crazy. He was desperate and lonely and missing home. This was where he was supposed to be, even if his subconscious knew it before he did.

It was time. Long past time.

Nausea rolled in his gut and threatened to choke him as he made his way to the front desk to sign in. The white halls and antiseptic smell were the same, as were the simplistic pictures and the pounding of his heart behind his ribs.

Out of respect for her parents and because visiting would serve no purpose, he hadn't been here since the day she'd been admitted. He paid the bill once a month and called the nurse weekly, as a formality. Unless they read his books, no one here knew his face.

Her room at the end of the hall was the nicest money could buy, even though Laura would never be able to open her eyes and see it. Pink curtains shielded the harsh sunlight coming from the window just feet from her bed. Against the wall were beeping monitors and a pump bringing oxygen to her lungs. Cards and stuffed animals dotted every square inch of available space.

He stood just inside the doorway until he could force his feet to move to her bedside. The short, wispy strands of blond hair had grown out to shoulder-length—gone were the dyed pink tips she'd preferred. The luscious curves that had first drawn him to her were withered to an almost skeletal state. They had her dressed in a blue blouse she would've hated and a loose pair of white pants. A capped IV was in one arm and a catheter bag hung on the opposite bed rail.

Because his legs could no longer hold him, he sat on the side of the bed by her hip and lifted her cool hand. He swallowed hard, taking in the tracheotomy tube protruding from her windpipe.

"Hey, Laura. It's been a long time."

Of course, she didn't respond, but talking to her gave him an odd sort of comfort. He rubbed circles in her palm with his thumb, remembering she used to like that small touch. Her fingernails were neat and clean. Before her accident, she was always elbow deep in acrylics while working on a canvas. It was strange, seeing her hands without at least some dried paint around the cuticles.

"Jake got married. I went home for the wedding. You would've hated it. Elegant and traditional. It was really nice, though."

He sighed and gathered his wits to tell her everything. She may not be able to hear him and understand, but that didn't make the telling any easier on him.

"I met someone in Wilmington. Her name's Faith and she's really quiet. I know, a total contrast from you, but we . . . fit somehow. She has this crazy way of drawing out the best in people. Somehow, she found some good in me."

His breath hitched and his voice cracked, sending tears pouring down his face. "I tried not to fall for her. Honest, I did. But she's so damn lovable." He wiped his eyes, but more tears came anyway, so he gave up. He felt like his chest was cracked wide open, splitting his ribs and exposing all the ugliness inside. "Even my dad loves her. But, Christ. Her own damn parents don't. I know we complained about ours a lot, but hers take the cake. They made her believe she was invisible. I mean, she did nothing but love them and give them everything she had, and they just . . ."

He stilled as his voice trailed off, his gaze landing on the wall, eyes not seeing what was in front of him. Rather, the image of Faith's face at the moment she had bravely confessed her love floated in his memory. Even when she knew he'd leave. Even though she knew he might not say it back. Even though no one had ever shown her any real version of love in her own life.

"They let her go. Just like I did." Cementing her belief that she wasn't someone worthy of their love. That no one would stick because, hell, everyone in her life walked. "I'm no better than they are."

Slowly, he moved his gaze back toward the woman in the bed. Adrenaline tore through him, making his body shake. "I guess I really came to say good-bye." He sniffed and blew out an uneven breath. "I'm going to make sure you're taken care of, however long you're here. You'll get the best of everything. Always. But I can't do this anymore. You and I . . . we never would've made it. And to keep lying to myself, to keep holding the guilt inside over a mistake you made while too young and swamped in grief, wouldn't be fair to Faith. Or myself."

Though it hurt to let go of her hand and lay it gently on the bed, hope bloomed in his chest. It had been so long since he felt it that he almost didn't recognize it. He leaned down and kissed her forehead. "I wish you well, Laura."

Mia shoved another Tootsie Roll in her mouth and spoke around it. "Are you sure you don't want one? Candy therapy works wonders."

Faith leaned back on the Adirondack chair on the deck and forced a smile. She'd been doing that for a week, forcing a smile. Love wasn't supposed to be like this. It wasn't supposed to hurt so bad you couldn't eat, couldn't sleep. It was supposed to be joyous and everlasting.

Love wasn't supposed to sneak out before dawn and leave a heart-shaped charm for the bracelet it bought you with a note that said, *Always*.

She sighed. "You and baby are craving the sugar. I'm good."

Mia had been coming by to keep Faith company in the evenings, after she was finished working with Ginny. Lacey and Jake were due back from their honeymoon any minute now, but Mia had taken it upon herself to be Faith's babysitter so she wouldn't wallow too deep in misery while they were gone.

It was nice of Mia to try and make her feel better, but nothing was going to accomplish that. Alone or with friends, busy or bored, Alec was there, hurting her all over again. Hurting himself. When would this end? When would the pain stop?

"Why don't you go back to Charlotte for a couple of days?" Mia suggested. "Maybe the comfort of home will help."

"There's nothing there for me." Another realization she'd come to this week.

She closed her eyes and drew in a deep breath. Alec had wanted her to cling tight to her friendship with Mia and Lacey. He was right, too. Her friends should know more about her, other than that she had a sister who died. Opening her eyes, she looked at Mia and spilled her guts.

"So, there's no one but you guys. My parents will always be my parents, but they're not you guys. I'm better off in Wilmington."

Mia took her hand in hers and squeezed. "Then here you shall stay. You'll always have us."

Appreciative that Mia didn't barrage her with questions or sympathy, Faith looked at the ocean. Sunlight hit the waves and reflected. A few sailboats dotted the horizon. Calming as the water was, it, too, only reminded her of Alec.

"I think I need to find my own apartment." There wasn't anywhere on the estate she could go that didn't tie back to a painful memory. She'd miss waking up to this view, but she needed a change. She couldn't keep going on like this.

"I'll help you look for a place, if that's what you want."

Faith didn't know what she wanted, besides Alec. And she couldn't have him.

Mia leaned forward. "My mother was an alcoholic. I think she drank to forget about the pain, until one day she got so deep in the bottle no one could get her back out." She sighed and glanced away. "Like your parents with you, she never formed a connection to Ginny. I don't know why. Maybe because of her depression or Ginny's disability, who knows. I tried to make up for that by being everything Ginny needed. I had no support system and no backup plan." She trained her blue gaze on Faith. "And then I came back here. It wasn't easy, and there was a lot standing in our way, but Cole loved me. The rest of it didn't matter. My mother's inability to love wasn't Ginny's fault, and it's not your fault either that your parents are incapable. They're the ones with the loose wire, not you."

Faith didn't know what to say, other than Mia and Cole were perfect for each other. Ginny was darn lucky to have Mia. It took a lot of strength to not only carry on, but to carry someone else when there was nothing left. She knew Mia was right, too, but it was hard to argue the point when her parents had been perfectly capable of loving Hope.

Regret and understanding shone in Mia's eyes. "You just need one person, Faith, to make you believe in yourself. One person to make you believe you are someone. Because you are someone. Don't doubt that for a minute."

Lacey swept around the house and onto the deck, holding several shopping bags and a brown paper-wrapped package. "I'm suntanned and I'm exhausted." She plopped onto a chair. "Honeymoons are awesome."

Mia grinned. "Sounds like you had a fabulous time."

"It really was spectacular. What's wrong?" Lacey zeroed in on Faith.

Before she could answer, Mia filled in the gaps for Lacey.

"Oh, sweetie." Lacey jumped off her chair and wrapped her in a hug. "Jake didn't tell me Alec was already gone. I thought he'd wait until we got back . . . never mind. How are you holding up?"

"I tried to offer candy therapy, but she refused."

Lacey peeked into the nearly empty bag. "Craving much?"

Faith laughed, for the first time in too long. "She's been eating them day and night for the past week."

Lacey patted Faith's knee. "I have something that might make you feel better. I meant to give it to you before the wedding, but things got crazy with last-minute details." She lifted the package and handed it to her. "It's sentimental, so be prepared. I just . . . I hope you like it."

Faith accepted the package, confused. "You didn't have to get me anything. What's the occasion?"

"Consider it a late birthday present. It's not exactly store bought."

Lacey and Mia exchanged a look she didn't understand, so Faith tore into the wrapping.

The instant she recognized what she was looking at, tears blurred her vision. She slapped a hand over her mouth.

"Oh. Oh no. I made it worse." Lacey moved to sit next to her, their hips brushing. "I painted it, so I can destroy it. Don't cry."

"I . . . love it."

Through the watery haze of tears, she looked at the image of herself and Hope smiling on the canvas. Faith recognized the pose as one from a photo taken in the hospital. The one sitting on her fireplace mantel. Except in Lacey's painting, Hope had all her hair and the beach spread out behind them.

"Sweetie, stop crying," Lacey said. "Are you sure you like it? I won't be offended."

Mia came over and sat on her other side. The two people she'd grown to love as if they were her own sisters sandwiched her in a hug.

Hope would have loved them, would have loved this place.

"I love you guys. Thank you, Lacey. This is perfect."

chapter
twenty-eight

Faith sat on the edge of her bed, phone clutched in her hand and the portrait Lacey gave her a few days ago in front of her for courage. Sunlight spilled into the room through the window at her back, the warmth calming her nerves.

Alec was right. It was time to stop wasting her time and thoughts and efforts trying to make her parents love her. Time to stop offering her heart to those who would never accept it. She'd spoken to her parents twice since Alec left, and both times the conversation had been shallow and brief. She'd tried to talk about Hope, about her feelings, but they'd rushed her off the phone.

She sucked in air and connected the call. Her parents' answering machine kicked in, playing their greeting. Right about now, Dad would be picking up Mom from choir practice, so it was the perfect time to leave a message. If she waited just ten more minutes, they'd be home. Mom would make lunch and Dad would start a pitcher of unsweetened tea. They'd stand side by side in the kitchen, as they did every day, barely conscious of each other.

The beep startled her and she fisted her pendant in reflex. "Hi. It's me." She cleared her throat. "I'm sorry to leave a message like this, but when I try to talk to you, you don't let me. I just . . . I want you to know that I loved her, too." She pressed her hand over her eyes to try to combat the tears and get through the message. "I miss her, too, and I'm sorry, so sorry I couldn't save her like you wanted."

She rose and paced the floor, pausing a moment to catch her breath. "I even understand why you did what you did. But she died and I didn't. I'm still right here and all I ever wanted was for you to love me half as much . . ."

Cutting herself and that thought off, she shook her head. "None of that matters." Her gaze dropped to the bracelet on her wrist. "I fell in love. I wanted you to know. It's the best and worst feeling imaginable. And I'm going to miss Hope every day, but I'm moving on. I love you."

Her voice cracked as she disconnected the call. Hot tears trailed down her cheeks as her chest released a violent sob. She curled up on her bed and wept. Soul-jerking tears that she had subdued for too long. She pressed her face into the quilt and let go.

Afterward, as her cheeks dried and the vise in her throat eased, she vowed to shed no more tears for the past. If it took all her energy and years to accomplish, she was going to move on. She had wonderful friends, a job she loved, and the ocean to heal her when things became too overwhelming.

When she thought she could manage, she got up and padded down the hall to the kitchen to start a kettle for tea. A knock on the front door came as she took a bag out of the cabinet. She wasn't expecting anyone, especially not Jake, as she opened the door.

"Hey." He rocked on his heels. "Mia said you were on the market for a new place?"

She pressed a hand to her forehead. "Um, yes. I'm not in any hurry, but I planned on looking for an apartment next week."

He nodded and swallowed, seeming nervous. "I think I found the perfect spot. Are you up for a short drive?"

"Well . . ." She glanced over her shoulder toward the kitchen. What the heck? She needed to get out of the house anyway. "Sure. Just let me turn the burner off."

Pocketing her cell and keys, she moved the kettle and switched off the stove.

They climbed in Jake's pickup truck and made their way down the drive.

He turned the radio down. "It's not far."

"Okay."

She tilted her face toward the window and the trees whizzing by for all of thirty seconds before Jake pulled into another driveway. She lifted her brows in question.

"Told you it wasn't far."

A house came into view. It resembled something more appropriate for the mountains than the beach, and it needed a lot of help because it had obviously been left unattended for a long time, but she liked the unique architecture. The front porch wrapped around both sides. Unlike Lacey and Jake's house, or Cole and Mia's, this one was higher up on the bluff. Behind the house, the ocean gleamed in the sun for as far as her eye could see.

"Jake, I can't afford this." By like five million dollars or so.

He turned to her but didn't meet her eye. "Just trust me. Let's go take a peek."

Sighing, she followed him out of the truck and over the broken concrete driveway. Palm trees, mixed with pines and overgrown fauna, surrounded the property. The porch seemed sturdy. The exterior was in decent shape. Considering it was composed of logs, it didn't need paint.

Instead of knocking, Jake turned the knob on the front door and stepped inside. "Come on."

"Jake, we can't just walk into someone's house."

"It's been in foreclosure for years." He rolled his eyes when she still wouldn't budge. "Come on, darlin'."

She stepped inside and through a small foyer to a living room that was way bigger than it looked from the outside. A floor-to-ceiling redbrick fireplace was situated in one corner. To the right was a staircase and straight ahead the kitchen. Nearly the entire ocean side of the house was glass. There were hardwood floors throughout, although they needed to be refinished. Two small rooms with built-in shelves were off the living room, and she imagined they'd make a great office or library.

Jake hurried her along to the second floor and pointed out three bedrooms. "The master is through here."

Again, she wondered what they were doing here. Never in her wildest dreams could she afford this house. It was lovely and full of promise. It spoke to her of serenity and just enough seclusion to be comfortable. But still, it could never be hers.

She walked into the master bedroom and gasped when she saw the wall-to-wall windows. The ocean spread out before her, and a set of patio doors led out to a porch. It was so amazing her eyes misted. Oh, to have this view every day . . . Not that she could.

Jake cleared his throat from behind her. "Do you like it?"

"Yes. I love it . . ." She turned and the words died in her throat. The blood rushed through her veins with such force that the roar in her ears deafened.

Jake slipped from the room.

Alec crossed his arms and smiled. "I'm glad you like the house. Because I bought it."

Faith stood staring at him through those round amber eyes that he missed with every beat of his heart, and he knew he hadn't prepared himself enough for what seeing her again would do to him.

Ten days. Ten of the worst goddamn days of his life he'd spent away from her. It was an eternity as far as he was concerned. His hands itched to touch. His arms needed to hold. But he stayed where he was—he had to follow the plan.

"Alec?"

Her mermaid voice whispering his name was nearly his undoing. He took a step forward.

"What are you doing here?" She fisted her pendant. "Wait? You bought the house? *This* house?"

Distracted by the way the light softened her pale skin and haloed around her body, he almost didn't answer her question. He'd missed her freckles, too. Every last one of them.

He cleared his throat. "Yes. I bought *this* house. Would you like to know why?"

She nodded and ran her hand across her forehead as if not believing her own eyes.

"I pictured you opening your eyes every morning here in this room, with the view of the ocean you love so much, and you'd smile as you woke up. You would drink your tea out there on the deck, shaking your head at me for eating a donut and guzzling coffee. You do have much healthier eating habits than me. I may try to break you of some of those in the next thirty years."

Her eyes went from wide to bulging. "Alec—"

"Not done." He nudged his chin toward the hall. "The three other bedrooms are to fill with kids. Loud, energetic little monsters with my sense of adventure and your big heart."

Her gaze darted to the doorway and then back to him. "Kids?"

He shrugged. "I prefer three, but we can negotiate."

"Three kids," she mumbled, her tone indicating she wasn't fully caught up to him yet. His Faith, ever surprised.

Though he grinned—because damn, she was adorable all flustered—his heart was pounding a mile a minute. There was no guarantee she'd want the same things. The option of a future together hadn't been a possibility before, and now that it was and he was doing his spiel, he was in full freak-out mode. He had to make her see, make her understand, there was no future for him without her.

"Can you follow me downstairs? I can tell you the other reasons."

"Oh. Yes. Sure."

With her following silently at his heels, they descended the stairs and stopped in the living room. "I'd like to tear down the wall between those two rooms and make it one so I can use it as an office. On your days off, you could snuggle on an oversized armchair here and read a book while listening to me type. I know you like the sound because you get this little smile on your face when you hear me working."

The confusion in her eyes began to clear, and was replaced with hesitant optimism.

He waved his hand toward the kitchen, indicating she should precede him. After only a moment, she walked around the corner and then came to an abrupt halt.

Her gaze swept the room, taking in Cole, Mia, Lacey, Jake, Ginny, and both his parents. Slowly, she craned her head around to look at him.

Alec came up behind her and dropped his hands on her shoulders, touching her for the first time since being home. He brushed his thumbs over her soft skin and inhaled her sugary scent. The pull was still there between them, stronger than ever, even with her in shock at finding the others waiting in the kitchen.

He kissed her temple and spoke into her hair. "The house can hold our whole family. For get-togethers or holidays. Whatever. Not only the family in front of you, because make no mistake, they are your family now, but also the family we can build together. The one I want to make with you."

She emitted a choking sound—of disbelief or joy, he wasn't sure. Her hand flew over her mouth, then both hands covered her face. Her shoulders shook with a sob.

Alec darted a quick glance at Jake.

Jake shrugged, looking just as lost.

Alec blew out a breath and dug in his pocket. "Turn around, Faith. Please, look at me."

She dropped her hands and moved to face him, her teeth working her lower lip and doing everything in her power to hold off the tears. Her eyes shimmered, pleading with him.

"I said good-bye to Laura while I was in New York. I should've done it a long time ago, but I wasn't ready. I hadn't met you yet." He dropped his forehead to hers and swallowed past the lump. "I put my apartment on the market. The bank accepted the offer I put on this house. The house I want for us, because I don't ever want to be away from you again."

He edged back far enough to hold out a little black box between them. It held an antique ring with a tear-drop diamond. The beauty was in the intricate gold band, as the carvings and design were similar to her pendant's. It wasn't big, nor was it flashy. It was perfect for Faith. Delicate and unique. An old ring because she was an old soul.

Her chest stopped rising and falling. Her eyes grew huge.

"I love you, in case you hadn't figured it out. Marry me?"

Her gaze lifted from the ring to his face, exploring every inch as if searching for a lie. One day, if it was the last thing he did, she'd look at him and accept that she was worth the moon and more. In the meantime, he'd work at it for as long as it took. Forever if he had to.

I love you, he mouthed and tucked a strand of hair behind her ear.

"You're my one person." She smiled and took his face in her hands. "Mia said it only takes one person to make you believe in yourself. You're my one person. I love you, too. So, so much. Of course I'll marry you."

The air whooshed from his lungs. He wrapped his arms around her and lifted her to her toes, smacking a kiss on her lips. They had an audience behind her—an audience who was cheering like fools—so he'd do a proper kiss later. In private. All damn night long.

"I love you, Faith." He cupped the back of her head and kissed her again, wishing like hell the others would just go away for a while. Two weeks. A year, tops.

Jake laughed. "You had us worried there for a minute, Faith."

"Yay." Lacey clapped. "A baby shower *and* a wedding to plan. I can't wait to get started."

Faith laughed, but her gaze never left Alec's. "I can't wait to get started, either."

Congratulations went around many times over as he slid the ring on Faith's finger. Cole warned them to be careful of how much leeway they gave Lacey in planning, and Mia waved her hand, dismissing his concerns. His parents chimed in, chatting about venues and ideas for the house.

But in Alec's opinion, Ginny said it best.

"Welcome to the family."

Keep reading for a preview of

Kelly Moran's Covington Cove Novel

return to me

Available now from Berkley Sensation!

Midsummer: Thirteen Years Before

Cole stood by his bedroom window, looking down at Mia while she sat reading in the grove. He'd been doing a lot of that lately. Watching Mia. These feelings for her had been stirring in his gut since the first time he saw her. He'd already received the warning glare and talk from his mother. Covingtons were set to higher standards than where Mia came from. Meaning, the trash should be kept out, where it belonged.

According to Mother.

He hadn't touched Mia. Not since the night of the bonfire last year when he'd almost kissed her. But damn, he wanted to. She was only sixteen. He was eighteen. Bound for Harvard and great things. In so many ways, she was just a kid. A kid he had no business dreaming about.

The winters in Charlotte were long, this last winter the

longest. He'd thought about her often and wondered what she was doing. Who she was with.

Their long summer talks remained in his head. Her voice, so soft and innocent. It didn't matter what crap his mother threw at him, Mia could calm him down. Make him forget. He'd spent less and less time with his friends and more time with her. She didn't care what car he drove or what school he went to. There was no competition with her. He could be himself.

Mia had more class and dignity than the whole of Father's country club. Yet, to his parents, she'd always be the help's daughter. A person to acknowledge only in private, to be polite. He'd done that for three years.

Dean was being groomed for the family business now that he'd passed the bar. Cole had already gotten the career lecture from Father. He had no interest in finance law. He didn't know what he wanted to do. And what in the hell was wrong with that? What eighteen-year-old knew what he wanted to do with his life?

That was completely unacceptable for a Covington. Cole was sick to death of being a Covington. What major would Mia think he should study? She knew him so well. She was the only one who knew him. Their time together, their world, felt like a cherished secret between just them.

He pressed a hand to the glass, wishing it was her skin. But that couldn't happen. If his mother got bent out of shape over a few glances, imagine her rage if she found out he did more than look.

Still, a guy could dream.

At the knock on his door, he turned. "What's up, Sis?"

Lacey walked across the room and followed his gaze out the window to the grove. A knowing smile crossed her face. "Why don't you tell her how you feel?"

Cole barked a laugh. "As if. Imagine what people would say."

Lacey shook her head in disappointment.

He didn't have the heart to burst her bubble.

"You're a snob."

He wasn't. He just pretended to be for the sake of family reputation. One day—one day he'd say to hell with that and go after what he wanted.

"Hey, kid," Dean said from the doorway.

Both he and Lacey turned, but Cole knew his brother was talking to him. "Hey. Thought you weren't coming in till next week."

"I'll catch you two later." Lacey gave Dean a quick hug.

Dean closed the door. Cole raised his brows in question. He crossed his arms and leaned against the windowsill.

"Mother wants me to have a chat with you."

Cole tipped his head back, thunking it against the window. "What now?"

Dean laughed. "She comin' down hard on you, is she?"

Cole straightened. "Just lay it on me."

Dean sat on the edge of the bed. "Where to start? Your grades? She thinks you're distracted." Dean cleared his throat. "By the maid's daughter."

"Jesus, Dean. Not you, too."

Dean lifted his hand, his face saying this wasn't coming from him. "Look, Mia's a great girl."

"But?"

Dean shrugged. "No but. She's a great girl. My advice to you is to make sure you know what you want before she realizes you've been watching."

Unsure how to interpret this, Cole stared at his brother. "You don't care if I chase the help's daughter? Mother does."

Dean sighed. "Here's the thing with Mother. She's an unhappy woman, which means she's only happy making everyone else around her miserable, too." Dean stood. "You know why she's so hard on you, more than Lace and me?"

Cole shrugged in nonchalance, but inside he was dying to hear Dean's thought.

"Because you stand up to her. You don't fit her perfect mold.

Lacey and I do what we can to keep her off our backs." Dean's eyes lost their spark, leaving an almost dejected absence in its place. "Don't lose that edge, Cole. It's what makes you so passionate, so unique."

Cole didn't know whether to hug him or laugh at him. The perfect son, in a roundabout way, had just told the black sheep he envied him.

Cole turned and looked out the window again, but Mia wasn't sitting in the grove anymore. She and Lacey were walking toward the beach, laughing at some joke. Damn, she was beautiful when she laughed. Made his chest ache in a sweet, painful way.

He sighed. Better to watch from a distance.

When Cole looked back to ask Dean if he wanted a swim, too, Dean was gone.

Present

"Rose!" Another crash hit the floor. "*Rose!*"

Two days and Cole still hadn't come down. Two days of yelling for Rose. Two days with no human contact, no food.

Mia waited him out downstairs, hoping to hear his door crash open. Hoping this plan of hers wouldn't make her fall flat on her face. She'd moved her things into the bedroom next door to his. She didn't think he noticed. One of the nights was a loud one, but she didn't step one foot inside his room.

She was waiting for him to come out, to acknowledge he needed help. Then she'd do what she could if he let her.

After a few more crashes, Cole quieted down again. She closed her eyes and sighed. He needed to eat. Hopefully that basic human need would be enough to drive him out.

She finished the last of her sweet tea and rose to rinse out the glass. She stared out the window at the darkening sky and tried to remember when she last saw the sunset over the ocean. The answer came immediately. Ten years ago, since she hadn't had the heart to return to the coast after what happened.

She glanced up at the ceiling. He was quiet now. She could slip out for ten minutes. Sliding into her flip-flops, she closed the kitchen door behind her.

The smell hit her first. The distinct scent of salt water and seaweed. The cry of gulls above could barely be heard over the crash of the tide. She closed her eyes as a breeze hit her face, humid and soothing. She'd forgotten how peaceful this place could be. How healing.

Opening her eyes, she stepped off the porch and onto the sand. As she edged toward the water, the red and purple sky melted into the green blue of the water until a thin black line separated the heavens from earth. Their last day together had been like this.

Warm. Beautiful.

Her cell buzzed. She pulled it out and answered, hoping everything was okay with Ginny.

"It's Lacey. I just . . . wanted to see how things were going."

Mia kicked off her flip-flops and sat on the beach. Cole's house was in a private area of Wilmington Beach. Not a soul was around to hear her.

"It's going. He's on a hunger strike currently." Mia elaborated for Lacey's benefit.

"That's brilliant. He hasn't kicked you out yet?"

"Oh, he has. Several times, in fact."

Lacey laughed, a sound from deep in her belly, one that Mia hadn't heard in too many years. They'd been friends once. Mia didn't realize how much she missed that, having been too ravaged by the hurt to see past it. Cole wasn't the only thing taken away from her back then.

Mia didn't have any friends. She'd never really had friends. There were a few women from college she talked to once in a while, but over the past couple years that had dwindled down to Christmas cards. She had no one. The truth hurt. There was only Ginny.

"How are you holding up?" Lacey asked at length.

"Oh, you know. Slumming it like this is hard."

Lacey didn't laugh this time, but Mia heard the smile through her words. "It is beautiful there, isn't it? I miss it so much sometimes." She paused. "Oh, Mia. You deserved so much more than you got in life."

Mia wasn't expecting that, nor the swift wave of tears clogging her throat. Lacey didn't say what she did out of pity, and Mia knew that. Lacey, Dean, and Cole weren't like the other Covingtons. She pressed her lips together until she could speak. "That's nice of you to say, Lace."

At hearing her long-ago nickname, Lacey must've been feeling sentimental also. Lacey sniffed. "I have to go. I'll check back in with you soon."

He was freaking starving and she was strolling on the damn beach. She made quite the vision, though, standing there against the sunset. He'd pictured that in his head about a thousand times, too.

He still couldn't believe she was here. Like a crazy hallucination. Part of him was so damn relieved he wanted to weep. Maybe he'd get to say all the things he didn't before. Amend the past and let her know how very sorry he was that he couldn't be stronger for her. The other part of him just wanted her gone. Back in his memory, where he couldn't hurt her again. Either way, he wasn't so numb anymore. Bits of emotion seeped their way through the cracks.

Seeing her out there made his chest splinter wide open.

He kept waiting for her to disappear. Dissolve into nothing, making him realize this was all a cosmic joke at his expense. He blinked his eyes, looked again. She was still there.

And the nimble little minx wasn't going to feed him. He'd have to go downstairs. He hadn't tried stairs in months. He needed to go down now while she was out, so she couldn't see how weak he'd become.

He rose and stood in place for several seconds to get his bearings. Once he felt ready, he bore weight on the left leg and quickly transferred to the right. This concentrated form of walking was how he got to and from the bathroom. Stairs were an entirely different matter. He made it out of the bedroom and stared down the curving staircase, which was too wide to grasp each railing with both hands.

He scooted to his right to hold the railing with his strong side. He hopped down the first step, landing only on his right leg. When that seemed to work, he repeated the motion until he reached the bottom step, sweating and completely out of breath. After waiting a good minute, he hobbled into the kitchen doorway just as Mia came back in from the beach.

Her eyes widened. "You're out of your room."

"And you're still here. Where's Rose?"

She walked to the sink to wash her hands. "I gave her the rest of the week off."

"*You gave her* . . . You had no authority to do that!"

Drying her hands on a towel, she shrugged. "She's getting up there in years, Cole. You can't keep her on those hours. I'm here."

Yeah, she was. Why? He should be pissed. She'd barged in here after ten years, pushing her way back into his life and throwing his world into chaos. Looking at her, at everything he wanted and couldn't have, he just couldn't hold on to the anger.

Through the years, he'd come to idolize the memory of her. Put her up on a pedestal. What they had was so long ago and they were so young. It still got to him, either because of how it ended or because of the thought of what could have been. He hadn't had anyone in his life since she walked out that he could trust as openly as he did her. No one he connected with on such a deep level.

"What's for dinner?"

"BLTs."

He made a noncommittal sound.

She fisted her hands on her hips. "I thought you'd hold out at least another day. I wasn't planning on something special."

He didn't need special. He just needed sustenance. "It smells good."

"I haven't started cooking yet."

Right. He hobbled to the table and plopped down in a chair as she pulled a package of bacon out of the fridge. After she laid the strips in a pan, she turned to face him. "I was wondering if it would be okay with you if Rose moved into the guesthouse? She's staying with her daughter and could use the privacy. Plus, it would save her from driving."

"Aren't you staying there? Where would you sleep?"

A crooked smile creased her mouth. "Not kicking me out today?" He didn't respond, so she shrugged. "I've been in the bedroom next to yours the past two nights."

The bedroom right next to his. A whisper away.

"Is it okay?"

He couldn't concentrate with her around. "Fine, fine."

"She needs normal hours, too. Nine to five."

"Fine." He should've done that long ago, but he'd grown too dependent on Rose.

Mia poured a glass of orange juice and set it in front of him. He drank it as she sliced tomatoes. The smell of apple-wood bacon filled the kitchen and he damned near leapt for the pan. She finished compiling two sandwiches and set them in front of him. He had just enough manners left to wait for her to join him. They ate in uncomfortable silence until she pushed away the second half of her BLT.

"You still eat like a bird," he mumbled.

"And you still eat like a famine is coming."

She glanced at his empty plate, then up at him, and a smile traced the corners of her mouth. He almost choked. The smile eventually made it to her eyes. He couldn't look away from all that blue. Somewhere in the space between them the past collided with the present.

"Your eyes are still blue." He hadn't realized he'd said it aloud until her smile fell and her eyes rounded in painful memory.

Long ago, when either was having a bad day, he would tell her, *Your eyes are still blue*. And she'd retort by saying . . .

"And you're still rich."

His gaze dropped to her mouth. Back to her eyes. "Yeah."

Abruptly, she stood and cleared their plates, pulling him from the past. A dull ache throbbed behind his eyes. She loaded the plates into the dishwasher and then sliced some strawberries into a small dish. After adding whipping cream, she set them in front of him.

"Dessert."

This wasn't his idea of dessert, but he took a bite and chewed.

"Now that you're done brooding upstairs, I'm making some changes around here."

He dropped his fork and stared at her. "Like what?"

"Tomorrow, you shower and shave. You look like a vagrant. Afterward, I'll cut your hair. And we're burning that robe."

He looked at himself, unable to argue. He'd let himself go to hell. He hadn't even cared. Strange thing, he kinda cared now. If the last memory she had of him wasn't bad enough, this one would trump it. He needed to start complying with her demand to help him, show her he could be a good guy again. Then at least when she left this time around, it would be under better circumstances and with a better image of him.

"I'm implementing a diet high in calcium, vitamin C, and protein. You're also doing one hour a day in the gym with me three times a week. The days we're not in the gym, we'll take a walk. I'm off on Sundays, so you are, too."

He'd barely made it down the stairs tonight. "And if I refuse?"

Her grin was wicked.

He sighed. The sooner he complied with this, the sooner she'd be gone. Though that thought broke a chunk of his heart away, he knew she had to go. They were all wrong for each other as kids and nothing on that front had changed. The longer she stayed, the blurrier the line became. In *his* mind anyway. She still hated him.

He sucked in a sharp breath when his leg suddenly throbbed, not in the usual spot, but lower in the calf. It intensified until he cried out.

She knelt by his feet. "What's wrong?"

"Hurts," he ground out.

"Where?"

He pointed.

"Does it usually hurt there?"

He shook his head.

"Does it feel hot or more like a cramp?"

"Cramp."

She stood. "It's a charley horse. Bring your toes up and flex your foot."

He did as she said and the pain lessened. He blew out a breath.

Mia walked to the fridge and pulled out a Gatorade. "You're dehydrated. Drink this tonight. If the pain returns, just flex your foot. With your injuries, you have to watch for blood clots. If it ever feels hot, sharp, and stabbing, you call the doctor right away."

He nodded, bringing his foot down. The leg still cramped, but not as harshly as before. She knelt by his feet again, this time with a bottle of hand lotion from the sink. "What are you doing?"

"Rubbing the calf to loosen the muscle." She squirted a quarter-sized amount of lotion into her palm.

"No."

"But, Cole . . ."

She could *not* touch him. He'd lose it. "I said no!"

The roaring tone of his voice careened her backward. He felt like an absolute shit but couldn't bring himself to apologize.

Several seconds ticked by before she straightened. She rubbed the lotion into her hands. The silence continued. "I'm going upstairs to straighten your room. The next time you have a flashback or an episode, I'll be there. We'll see if we can get you through it."

She was still too damn nice for her own good.

As she walked past, he grabbed her arm. "Why are you doing this?"

She didn't look at him. "Closure."

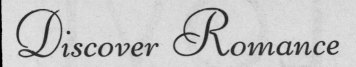

Discover Romance

berkleyjoveauthors.com

See what's coming up next from your favorite romance authors and explore all the latest Berkley, Jove, and Sensation selections.

See what's new

~

Find author appearances

~

Win fantastic prizes

~

Get reading recommendations

~

Chat with authors and other fans

~

Read interviews with authors you love

berkleyjoveauthors.com

M1G0610

LOVE
ROMANCE
NOVELS?

For news on all your favorite romance authors,
sneak peeks into the newest releases, book
giveaways, and much more—

"Like" Love Always on Facebook!

f LoveAlwaysBooks

M1063G0212